Cutting the Fringe

by

Carl R. Smith

authorHOUSE

1663 Liberty Drive, Suite 200
Bloomington, Indiana 47403
(800) 839-8640
www.authorhouse.com

This book is a work of fiction. Places, events, and situations in this story are purely fictional and any resemblance to actual persons, living or dead, is coincidental.

© 2004 Carl R. Smith
All Rights Reserved.

No part of this book may be reproduced, stored in a retrieval system, or transmitted by any means without the written permission of the author.

First published by AuthorHouse 05/04/04

ISBN: 1-4184-3385-3 (sc)
ISBN: 1-4184-3384-5 (dj)

Library of Congress Control Number: 2004093054

Printed in the United States of America
Bloomington, Indiana

This book is printed on acid-free paper.

Introduction

In his poem "The Battle field" William Cullen Bryant said "Truth crushed to earth will rise again." In this second novel in Carl Smith's "Fringe" series, it is evil that rises again after being crushed. At the end of book one "Fringe Patriots", it appears that the Ten Little Indians, who threaten America's security and economy, have been defeated. In book two "Cutting the Fringe", a new leader emerges, and without a thought or hesitation Clay and his comrades go into battle once again with the remaining members of the Ten Little Indians.

General Matthews, the newly elected chief orders the gruesome death of yet another one of Clay's dearest friends. Now, Clay is more determined than ever to extract his own brand of vengeance. With the senator's blessing, and the aid of his rag-tag team he begins the arduous task of demolishing the blood-thirsty Indians once and for all.

Carl Smith has overcome incredible odds and a troubled childhood to serve his country in the military, and now to write a fictional account of those perilous times. I am pleased to have been one of his high school teachers and now one of his friends.

Dr. Paul Kelley

April 2004

Prologue

The second book of my father's "Fringe Patriots" series continues the saga of true friendship and love. It was the writing on the back of a matchbook cover that grabbed my father's attention so very long ago. "A friend is that person who walks in when everyone else walks out." It sounds simple, elementary really; and yet true friends, those willing to lay down the very life they possess, seem to be one of the greatest blessings this life on earth has to offer.

In the prologue of book one, my father spoke of his abject childhood, one coveted by none and pitied by all. I have seen my father's pain, but I have also seen my father's hope, a hope that has inspired him to pour his heart into a book that may provide solace to another in despair. My father's book is a marvelous accomplishment, but it is, by far, not the greatest one. He has given his children a lifelong example of faith, hope, and love. He has been the person who walks in when everyone else walks out. He is a father; but, more than that, he is a dad.

My dad's greatest desire for this series is to provide encouragement. No one is destined to repeat the mistakes of their past. Whatever your beginning may have been in this life, the ending is entirely up to you and you alone. Seek Truth, and you shall find it. Give love, and you shall receive it. Life could become much more than you have ever known.

"Greater love has no one than this, that he lay down his life for his friends."

Written by: Danielle N. Smith, my only daughter.

Thanks to Melodye and Elaine for all your help

Characters

Henry Clay Smith

Clay is a young man in his early twenties, with chiseled features and a broken nose, giving him a somewhat rugged look to his otherwise childlike appearance. He is six foot tall with blond hair and greenish-brown eyes. After being abandoned by his mother and forsaken by his siblings, Clay was raised at The John Tarleton Home for Children in Knoxville, Tennessee. He is extremely talented in the martial arts, and is blessed with a photographic memory.

Entering the military at the tender age of sixteen, Clay was certain he had found a substitute father in his Commanding Officer. However, after being framed for murder, he and his three dearest friends survive the initial onslaught from the Ten Little Indians, or Fringe Patriots, as he chooses to call them.

Dr. John Wayne Murphy

Johnny is in his mid-twenties, six feet-two, with light-brown skin and dark brown eyes. He and Clay have been the best of friends since childhood. When Clay's father used to beat him and would leave him tied to a huge tree in the yard overnight, Johnny would sneak out of his house, some two doors away, and sit with his friend throughout the night, sneaking back before dawn so the two would not be punished further. The two were separated when Clay was eight years old and reunited in the military some ten years later. Johnny is a brilliant young naval surgeon whose association with the Ten Little Indians is also no picnic. Once reunited, they swear never to allow anyone to ever separate them again. He is incredibly loyal, and totally selfless; ready, at "the drop of a hat" to do anything for his friend.

Senator Robert M. Lazar

Senator Lazar is from Minnesota. He is handsome and distinguished, standing more than six feet tall with thinning, salt and pepper hair, and dark eyes. Married for the second time to a beautiful woman named Patricia who is more than fifteen years younger than him. They have two children from his former marriage.

The senator has some presidential aspirations. He is a republican, and he is well respected by everyone on Capitol Hill.

Susan

She is a physical therapist and a dear friend to Clay. They met at Walter Reed Army Hospital, while they were each serving their country. Susan is almost six feet tall in her stocking feet, with short blond hair and huge blue eyes. Clay calls her, Marilyn Monroe, in an extra tall. She is strikingly beautiful. Although she prefers the attention of other women, she adores Clay, and delights in their times of intimacy.

Gidget

Gidget is just as short as Susan is tall; standing barely five feet high. Gidget has dark black hair, big brown eyes, and olive complexion. In her own right, she is just as beautiful as Susan. She and Clay also met at Walter Reed Army Hospital; however, she is the daughter of an air force general. She has an insatiable appetite for men, and Clay most of all.

Sergeant Shackelford

Shack was Clay's trainer for quite some time. They developed a friendship based on mutual respect. Shack is the typical G I, he stands about five feet nine with brown hair, in a crew-cut, and hazel green eyes. The sergeant could have been the model for the G I Joe Dolls. He is a soldier, first and foremost. Sergeant Shackelford loves his country, and he has an affinity for battle.

Tim Siler

Tim is a reporter for the Washington Post. He was introduced to Clay by the senator. Tim is short and frumpy, with brown hair and eyes. His clothes are seldom pressed, and his glasses are normally dirty. However, he is brilliant, and he lives vicariously through the exploits of Clay and Johnny.

Tim knows everyone who is someone, and his connections reach far and wide.

Jolene

Jolene is the senator's nanny and housekeeper. She is from Scotland. She stands five feet nine or better, very slim, with red hair and bright green eyes; just enough freckles to make her even cuter. Her accent is endearing to most everyone. At first she doesn't seem to care for Clay, but things change rapidly when danger rears its ugly head.

Chapter 1

The snow was coming down so hard Clay could barely see the road in front of him. *This better be a great meal*, he thought. It had been snowing most of the day and it was really beginning to accumulate. By the time he arrived at the senator's residence the snow must have been a foot deep and the roads were almost impassable.

He pulled into the circular driveway and stopped in front of what he hoped was the sidewalk leading to the front door. When he opened the car door it barely cleared the mounting snow. Carefully he made his way to the front door a little unsteadily; however, safe and sound, all parts still vertical.

Clay couldn't help remembering the last time he was here. It was of course, the night of the senator's supposed suicide. He could still see the fear in the eyes of the senator's wife, and he could almost feel the touch of her cold hands. A faint smile crossed his face as he remembered Sergeant

Shackelford, and how the sergeant kept ribbing them about the way in which to kill a man, a man already dead for two days.

Suddenly he realized it was his thoughts and not the snowy evening that were causing him to shiver. He shook his head as if to dislodge the thoughts and clear his mind before ringing the bell.

The door opened and the senator greeted him warmly, smiling brightly enough to increase the luminance of the already well-lit foyer.

The senator extended his hand. "How the hell are you, Clay? My wife said you wouldn't make it in this blizzard, but I told her you'd be here. It sure is good of you to come."

Clay shuffled the bottle of wine he was carrying to his left hand and grasped the senator's hand firmly.

"No problem, I'm always ready for a free meal. I hope this wine is appropriate. I wasn't sure what we were having."

"It's perfect," the senator replied, taking Clay's coat and proceeding to hang it on the coat rack next to the stairwell. "Clay, would you like a drink? That should warm you. I'm afraid the wife and I are about two drinks up on you. Scotch and soda, right?"

"Yes Sir, that'd be great, thanks."

The senator returned with Clay's drink in hand. "Look, Clay, if you don't mind we'll discuss business after dinner, there's no need upsetting the missus."

"Sure, Senator, I'm in no hurry to get back out in that snowstorm. The roads are a mess."

Cutting the Fringe

"I hope you're hungry. My wife's a great cook, and she's been at it all afternoon, just hoping you'd make it. Do you like prime rib?"

Clay smiled, remembering his last prime rib dinner with Johnny at the Jolly Ox. "Yes, Sir, I love it. Remind me to tell you sometime about the last time I had prime rib. I think you might enjoy the story, it involves Dr. Murphy."

The senator motioned for Clay to follow him. "Tell me after dinner. I think my wife is ready for us."

Just as the two of them entered the hallway headed for the dining room, Ms. Lazar came into view. She was even more attractive than Clay had remembered.

"Gosh, Mr. Smith, I'm so glad you made it. Bob said you would. Dinner is on the table, and I hope you're hungry."

"Yes, Ma'am, I sure am."

As they entered the dining room Ms. Lazar took Clay's arm. "Mr. Smith, you sit here across from me. Jolene will be serving from the end closest to the kitchen."

The senator walked around the table and held a chair for his wife. After she was seated Clay took his place across from her. "You sure do set a beautiful table, Ms. Lazar. I love flowers; they give a room such warmth."

"Thanks, but I can't take credit for the table it was all Jolene; however, you're right she does a marvelous job. But the cooking was all me."

The senator began opening the wine Clay had brought. "Clay, you have excellent taste in wine. This is just what the doctor ordered."

Clay laughed, "Actually, you're right, it's one of the many brought back from France by Dr. Murphy. I do; however, know the difference, and price doesn't seem to mean very much."

Jolene served the soup. It was a beer cheese variety, and very tasty. The salad came next, and with that Clay nibbled. He wasn't much of a salad lover. He wanted to save room for the main course.

They ate and talked for more than an hour and a half. By the time dessert came he was about to pop. They talked about a myriad of subjects. All in all it was a very pleasant evening.

Clay was taken with Jolene's accent. Jolene, with fiery red hair and big green eyes, was from Scotland. She was maybe five feet ten, and very slender. Her rosy cheeks had just enough freckles to make her cute, and the apron she was wearing was longer than her skirt. She had pretty legs, and she wasn't afraid to show them to the world. Clay noticed that the senator couldn't seem to take his eyes off her, and she was acutely aware of that fact as well. The senator's wife didn't seem to mind; in fact, she actually appeared to enjoy watching.

When dinner was over Clay and the Senator retired to the den for cognac and cigars. He noticed immediately that the drapes had been replaced since his last visit and the senator's desk chair was also new.

The senator poured them a huge drink and offered Clay a cigar. The senator snipped the end off both cigars and offered him a light, which he graciously accepted.

Leaning back in his chair, the senator began to speak. "Clay, I'm sure you've been following the general's trial. He will be sentenced next week, and they're probably going to put him away for the next twenty or thirty years. Unfortunately a new man has taken the reins and he may be even more ruthless, if that's possible. He's an air force general by the name of Mathews."

Clay looked bewildered. "I remember that name; he was one of the original ten. But, I really couldn't pick him out of a crowd."

The senator reached to open his middle desk drawer. "I have a picture of him with his family. Take a look, I'll bet you'll recognize him. He has a face not easily forgotten. Clay, you're on the top of their hit parade. I may very well be on the same list, who knows?"

As the senator was about to hand the picture to Clay there was a knock on the door.

"Come in," the senator said, rising from his chair.

Ms. Lazar entered the room. "Bob, the newscaster says that the roads are really bad, and they're asking everyone to stay put. Mr. Smith, it looks like you'll be spending the night with us, I trust that's not a major inconvenience."

Clay started to speak but the senator cut him off. "Better safe than sorry, Son. Anyway, we haven't had to use the guest bedroom for a long time."

"If you think I should, Senator. Unfortunately, I don't even have a toothbrush with me."

Ms. Lazar laughed. "Don't worry about it; I'll see to it that you have everything you need." She took a deep breath. "That end of the house is extremely quiet; therefore, you should be able to sleep as late as you wish. And if I know my husband you'll spend most of the night talking anyway."

Clay had been watching her every movement, and without a doubt there was much more going on behind those big beautiful eyes, more than she was willing to share at that moment.

He tried, unsuccessfully, to hold her gaze. Failing that, he turned to the senator. "Well, thank you both. How could I refuse such a gracious offer? It looks like you have a houseguest. Senator, do you think my car will be okay in this mess?"

The senator walked around the desk. "C'mon, Son, we'll see if we can move it into the one empty garage space." The senator turned and laid the picture on the desk, motioning for Clay to follow. "That would probably make you feel better. I know how important that car is to you. Hell, I was that way once about an old Bel-Air Chevy."

Clay placed his cigar in the huge ash stand next to his chair and dutifully followed the senator to the foyer. It was quite a task, but they were finally successful, the car was safely in the garage.

Upon returning to the den the senator poured them another snifter of cognac and proceeded to turn on the gas logs in the fireplace.

"This should warm you, My Boy," the senator muttered, all the time, briskly rubbing his hands together.

Clay joined him by the fire. The heat from the blaze made his face tingle.

"Senator, how could this be happening? I thought we shut the entire operation down when the general was taken into custody."

"I don't know about that," the senator replied. "However, you remember Tim Siler don't you, Clay?"

"Yeah, I like him. Damn straight shooter."

The senator returned to the desk where he had been sitting earlier. "Well, he says they only went underground for awhile. General Mathews has rekindled the fuse, and, according to Tim, they are 'bigger and badder' than ever." The senator relit his half smoked cigar, and handed the lighter to Clay. "Clay, these guys have more than a trillion dollars in the coffers; and with that much money, you can do almost anything."

The senator sat back in his chair. Clay could see the anger and frustration etched deeply in his face.

Clay sat down in the same chair as before, across from the senator. "Why do they want to eliminate me? I can't see how they could consider me a threat."

The senator almost chuckled. "If nothing else, I think General Essex wants us both dead, and even from prison he swings a big stick."

"Damn it, Senator. I told you we should've killed that son of a bitch. If we had, this situation would not exist."

The senator moved uncomfortably in his chair. "God, what kind of world are we living in when I'm forced to admit that killing someone is the only way to find peace from the demons around us. Our justice system is a joke, isn't it?"

"Yes, Senator, it surely is. When a man can go to prison and still carry on business as usual, well - - -"

Carl R. Smith

The senator began pounding on the desk. "Damn, I hate this. You know, Clay, this bunch handles more than sixty per cent of America's defense contracts, and they have almost all those corporations in their hip-pocket. Left unchecked through the next election the damage may be irreversible. Hell, in ten years they could control the known world; with their fingers in every cookie jar."

Clay stood and walked to the liquor cabinet, shaking his head. "May I have another drink, Senator?"

"Sure, whatever you like. Would you mind pouring me about a half glass of scotch, straight up? I need something a little stronger to dull my senses."

Clay poured the drinks and returned to the senator's desk with glasses in hand.

"Here, Senator. Maybe this will help."

As he turned to hand the drink to the senator, his eyes focused directly on the picture of General Mathews and his family. The glass fell from his hand. "Oh, Lord, I can't believe . . ."

The senator jumped up, his chair slamming back against the drapes. "What's wrong, Son? You look like you've seen a ghost."

Clay picked up the picture, walked back to his chair and collapsed.

"What is it, Clay? You do recognize the man, don't you?"

"Oh yeah, I surely do! Both faces are only too familiar."

The senator's eyes widened, "I didn't know you knew his wife."

"Not his wife, Senator, his daughter."

"Holy cow, Clay, how do you know his step-daughter?"

"It's Gidget. Damn it, it's Gidget. I must be the dumbest man alive. My lord, how stupid can one man be?"

"Who the heck is Gidget?" the senator asked.

"You met her at Pamela's funeral," Clay answered. "She was the short girl with black hair; the one you thought was so incredibly gorgeous. I thought she was one of my dearest friends."

"Oh yeah, I remember, and the tall one was Susan, right?"

"Right," Clay responded.

Clay continued to sit, his thoughts bouncing from floor to ceiling, and from wall to wall.

In the meantime the senator was attempting to clean up the mess. As he dumped the last of the broken glass and wet towels in the garbage, he walked over and placed his hand on Clay's shoulder. "Son, let me get us both another drink, and then, just maybe, we can make some sense out of all this."

Clay looked up, trying to mask his emotions. "Please! If it wouldn't be too much trouble, could I have some coffee and another cigar? I'm afraid I crushed this one."

The senator attempted a smile. "Absolutely, coffee would be just the thing. Help yourself to the cigars and I'll see if anyone is still up and about. If not, I'll make the coffee myself."

The senator opened the door and disappeared into the hallway. Clay cut the end off a new cigar and reached for the lighter. *I wonder how much these things cost*, Clay thought. *They're a damn sight better than the ones Johnny and I used to smoke.*

The senator appeared in the doorway. "The coffee will be ready momentarily. Are you all right?"

"Yes, Sir, I'm just kicking myself in the ass for being so stupid. Where is the closest bathroom?"

"Follow me, My Boy, I'm headed that way myself."

The senator stopped and turned to face him. "Leave the cigar in the ashtray; my wife doesn't like the smell to get into the rest of the house."

Clay complied.

"Don't lose me in this big house, Senator. They probably wouldn't find me until the spring thaw."

The senator laughed. "It's really not that large. Everything connects off the two main hallways, both, up and downstairs."

"If you say so, Sir."

The senator opened a door to his right. "Here, Son. You use this one, and I'll use the one off the kitchen. Can you find your way back to the den?"

"Yes, Sir, I'll be fine. I'll see you there."

"You got it," the senator muttered as he disappeared around the corner.

Chapter 2

Clay returned to the den just as Ms. Lazar was bringing in the tray of coffee.

"Mr. Smith, I have prepared your room. When you men are finished, Bob will show you where to go. If you need anything further, push the intercom button on the telephone and press two and I will come to your aid. Don't worry about waking the senator. We sleep in separate rooms; anyway, his number is one."

"Thank you, Ma'am. I'm sorry to be so much trouble." Clay knew that he was fidgeting, but he couldn't seem to stop. Ms. Lazar made him nervous, and he wasn't certain why. She was sweet, soft-spoken, and ever so kind. Unfortunately, in her presence he felt the need to bow.

As she was leaving the room she made a rather dramatic pause, placing one hand on the door frame and the other provocatively brushing her hair from her face.

"Oh, by the way Mr. Smith, I put some butter cookies on the tray with the coffee, you might wish to try one. They're almost sinful."

"What's almost sinful?" the senator asked, entering the room from the other hallway.

"Bob, I was making reference to the butter cookies. I put some on the tray with the coffee, and I was encouraging Mr. Smith to try one."

The senator turned his attention to Clay. "She's absolutely correct, they are quiet tasty."

Ms. Lazar turned to leave. "Enjoy the coffee, Mr. Smith. And, Bob, don't stay up all night. I'll be upstairs if you need me."

"Thanks, Darling. We'll be through shortly; I'll come in and kiss you goodnight."

She gave Clay a curious glance and left the room. "Goodnight all."

The senator poured himself a cup of coffee, and one for Clay. "How do you take yours, My Boy?"

"Black, with one spoon of sugar, thanks."

Taking the coffee from the senator Clay returned to the chair where he'd been sitting earlier.

It was quiet as the senator prepared and lit another cigar. "Wait a minute, weren't Gidget and Susan the two ladies the general tried to kidnap at the motel?"

"That's them." Clay paused for some time, gathering his thoughts. "Gidget must have been a plant all along. I'll bet money she was working for General Essex. However, if that were true she could have destroyed us, but she didn't."

The senator leaned forward, both elbows on the desk. "Puzzling! Unfortunately, she must have been the means by which they found Pamela, and her sister Janice. I have never stopped trying to figure out how that happened."

Clay looked positively intense. "I guess you're right, Sir. But, how did she know where they were? I didn't even know, and I don't think you did either. Isn't that correct?"

The senator ate another cookie. "I knew they were somewhere in Chevy Chase, Maryland, but I didn't have an address. To be honest with you, Clay, I didn't want to know."

Clay moved from his chair to the coffee tray on the other side of the room. "Would you care for some more, Senator?"

"Not just yet. But, you can bring me a couple more cookies."

Clay placed three cookies on a napkin, and carried them across the room. After placing them in front of the senator, he continued standing, sipping on his fresh cup of coffee.

"Senator, I have a few more weeks before starting at the university. I think I'll go to Chicago and visit little Miss Gidget."

The senator began to smile. "Play it cool. She doesn't know you know. If we play our cards right, we may find out a great many things."

"I'll do that, Sir. However, that's secondary to why you asked me here for dinner. What, if anything, is your plan of action?"

The senator rose and proceeded to refill his own drink. "Listen, Clay. I know you're not going to like this; however, I have secured you a new address, at least for the next sixty days. Good friends of mine own a beautiful place about two blocks from here and I have promised them you would housesit for them while they are in Europe. They'll not return until the first week of March. Maybe by then we can have this mess cleared up." The senator took a huge drag on his cigar. "Clay, you call me on my private line and let me know when you're returning from Chicago. You come straight here, and I'll show you the house. Do not go back to your place."

"Anything you say, Sir."

The senator looked pleased with himself. "My office will pay the rent on your apartment for the next couple of months as well as your telephone bills etc. And, before we part company tomorrow, I'll give you enough money to handle everything else. Can you live with that?"

Clay looked directly at the senator. "We are gonna nail these guys, aren't we, Sir? I really want to finish this, once and for all."

The senator rubbed his hands together. "Damn right we are. And, this time we're gonna do it your way, My Boy. I'm tired of living in fear; this has to end. It's not fair to my wife or my children."

Clay stood, almost spilling his coffee. "Can I have your hand on that, Sir?"

"Absolutely, we must stick together or they'll kill us all, or worse. There are some things worse than death. Right, Clay?"

"You're right again, Sir. There are a number of things worse than death."

Clay began pacing. "Senator, is John Murphy or Susan Weidenberg on that list?"

"I don't know for certain, Clay. But, I would expect Doctor Murphy's name to be high on the list. However, Susan, I'm not sure about."

Clay stopped pacing and relit his cigar. "Of course, if her name is on the list, Gidget would have been responsible for putting it there. I don't think anyone else even knew about her. Hell, even you didn't remember who she was."

The senator patted Clay on the shoulder. "Son, I think she's safe, at least for now. On the other hand, you may call the good doctor using my private line. I have to make another trip to the bathroom; you may call him now. It's only a little past ten in California."

"Okay, Senator. Where's the phone?"

"Oh, I'm sorry. You'll find it in the bottom right hand drawer of my desk. After using the bathroom, I'll go up and tell the wife goodnight, so take your time."

Clay moved toward the desk. "Thank you, Sir."

The telephone was there all right. It was in some kind of battery pack, and it had no wires. *How cool,* he thought. *This must be the coolest phone ever.* Removing the handset from the drawer he dialed Johnny's number. *Please, God, let him be home,* he mumbled.

"This is Doctor Murphy; what seems to be the problem?"

Clay chuckled. "I'm lonely as hell. You see, I'm in love with this tall handsome, black man, and he's so far away. Can you help me, stranger?"

"Boy, if I was there," Johnny laughed. "I'd help you all right. Pow, right in the kisser, that's how I'd help you. How you doing, Clay, you jerk?"

Carl R. Smith

"I'm okay, Partner. I'm on Senator Lazar's secured line and you have the number, or at least I hope you do. Call me back as quickly as possible from another telephone. Got it?"

"Oh shit, not again," Johnny exclaimed. "Give me fifteen minutes to find another telephone."

"I'll wait," Clay responded.

Laying the telephone on the desk, he went to the bar for some more coffee. The coffee was barely lukewarm. After only one sip, he went for the scotch and soda. The telephone rang. *Boy that was quick,* Clay thought, as he rushed across the room. It took him three or four rings just to figure out how to answer the darn thing.

"Hello, is that you, John?"

"Yes, Old Buddy, it's me. Were you expecting, maybe, the President?"

Clay took a swig of his drink. "Very funny! Look, Johnny, there's a new general in town and the Indians are on the warpath again. You, me, and the senator are first on their hit parade, so be careful."

Johnny was quiet for some time. "Sorry, Clay, I was trying to think. Do you guys need me? I can take some time off and be there the day after tomorrow."

"No, don't come here. Anyway, we're snowed in, and the airport is closed. As soon as the weather clears I'm headed to Chicago. I need to have a long talk with Gidget." Clay paused for a long time. "Johnny, I don't know how to say this, but, here goes. Gidget's stepfather is the new general in charge. He was one of the original ten. I didn't know because their names were different."

"I don't believe it," Johnny yelled. "She must have been the one who gave up Pamela and Janice. Wait a minute, Clay. If that's true, we should all be dead."

"I know, Partner. That's what the senator and I have been trying to figure out."

"How sure are you, Clay?"

"Pretty damn sure, Johnny."

"Look Clay, I'll meet you in Chicago, Monday night or Tuesday morning. Stay in the best hotel downtown and I'll find you. Use the name, Hockenfuss."

"Johnny . . ." Clay's voice was shaking.

"I know. Don't worry, Clay. I'll look under my bed and in all the closets. They'll probably come after you first, you're the closest."

"It's okay. The senator has me a new hiding place. One more trip to my apartment, and, I'm outta here."

"Don't go back there, Old Buddy."

"Look, the senator's already given me that speech. Don't worry, I'll be careful."

"Okay, but if you get killed I'm gonna cut your thing off and bury you naked."

Clay laughed. "I believe you would at that. I love you, John. See ya soon."

"Hey, Clay, tell the senator howdy for me."

"Okay John, goodnight."

"See you soon, Old Buddy."

The senator had not returned, and frankly Clay was a little concerned. Suddenly, there was a noise in the hallway as the senator appeared in the doorway.

"Did you get to talk to the doctor?" he asked.

"Yes, Sir, he's gonna meet me in Chicago."

"That's good. I don't think you need to face the young lady alone. Remember, she could have gotten all of us killed. I'd like to know why she didn't. Wouldn't you?"

"Yeah, I mean, yes Sir."

"Let me show you to your room. We'll finish this tomorrow before you head out. You must be tired, I know I am."

"Actually, my mind's racing at a fevered pace, but I could use some rest."

"Follow me, Son; the guest room is in the other end of the house."

Clay followed dutifully, and after a few twist and turns, the bedroom appeared.

The senator opened the door and turned on the light; then he walked across the room and turned on the bathroom light as well.

"I hope you sleep well. If you need me punch one on the intercom."

"Sure thing, Senator."

"I'll see you in the morning, Clay. Don't be in a hurry to get up; I usually sleep late on Sunday." With that having been said, the senator was gone.

Clay spent some time in the bathroom preparing for bed, and even found a new toothbrush. After a quick, 'poor mans' shower he turned off the bathroom light and entered the sleeping area. Someone had even turned down the bed for him.

A note left on the pillow read. "Sleep well, if you need me, dial two."

He turned on the lamp next to the bed. Then he walked across the room and turned off the overhead light. When he got situated in the strange bed he flipped the switch on the lamp. *Damn this room is dark,* he mumbled to himself.

Fatigue took over and he was almost asleep when he noticed the faint stream of light from the bedroom door. Someone entered the room. Lying perfectly still he waited for something to happen; eyes straining to become adjusted to the darkness.

The individual went into the bathroom, and then walked very quietly over to the bed.

In a flash, Jolene was laying on the bed beside him, with his weapon nuzzled under her chin.

"Oh me Lord. Oh me Lord," she screamed

"What the hell are you doing here?" Clay yelled, putting a little more pressure than necessary on the arm he had wrenched behind her back.

"Please don't shoot me. I was just placing some clean towels in your bathroom, and thought I would check on you. Please, Sir, you're breaking my arm."

Releasing the pressure he sat up. "You're lucky I didn't blow your head off, Young Lady. You should never sneak up on anyone like that. If I were less in control you might have been seriously hurt."

Jolene never moved, and her breathing became a little less labored. "Are you really as good as the senator says you are? Or is that just a bunch a crap?"

He looked down at her. She didn't seem the least bit unnerved by what had just taken place, or the fact that she was laying in a strange man's bed.

"I don't know what you're talking about, but I'm, so far, as good as I need to be. Is that good enough for you?"

"Of course it tis. I understand you Americans, even if I do talk a wee bit different."

Swinging his feet to the floor he reached to turn on the lamp. "I like the way you speak, and I know very little about the Scottish people, but I'm always willing to learn. Maybe you can teach me a few things."

Jolene jumped from the bed. "I might be willing to do that, but for now it's bedtime. Goodnight, Mr. Smith, see you on the morrow."

Clay was alone once again. *She sure is a Feisty Wench*, Clay mumbled, as he ran his hand through his hair. *I think that's what they're called in Scotland. Oh, who cares?*

Turning off the light, he crawled beneath the warm covers. Sleep came quickly, and so did the morning. Once fully awake he realized it was after eleven and even closer to noon. He headed for the bathroom and began his normal morning ritual. After shaving, showering, and brushing his teeth, he dressed quickly. *Now, let's see if I can find my way out of here,* he said aloud to an empty room.

Heading east from the bedroom, he knew a successful exit was somewhere ahead. He made his way to the hallway leading to the dining room. Hearing voices, he knew civilization was close by.

Ms. Lazar greeted him warmly. "Good afternoon, Mr. Smith. I trust you had a restful sleep."

Clay looked at Jolene who was sitting across the table from Ms. Lazar. "I must apologize for sleeping so long, but I was like a bear in hibernation, and you were right it is deathly quiet in that end of the house."

Ms. Lazar offered him a chair, and poured him a cup of hot coffee. "What would you like for breakfast, or brunch, if you will?"

"Just coffee, if you don't mind. Is the senator up yet?"

Ms. Lazar looked at him, and as before, he felt uncomfortable. "My husband will be down soon. I heard him in the shower a few minutes ago."

Jolene stood and excused herself, winking at Clay as she left the room. "Have a nice day, Mr. Smith."

Clay turned his attention, once again, to Ms. Lazar. This lady was, without question, a woman of class and great beauty, even in the middle of the day.

Her long black hair was brushed neatly from her face, accentuating her high cheekbones, and the face of a goddess. She was wearing white satin slacks that helped to emphasize the curve of her long legs, and the matching satin blouse could hardly contain her small but ample breasts. She was even wearing satin pumps. Her skin was as polished bronze, and her lips offered just a hint of red, with dazzling white teeth and puppy dog eyes that could deceive a priest.

Carl R. Smith

"You're staring, Mr. Smith. Is something wrong? Do I displease you?"

"Oh, no Ma'am, I mean you are a stunning woman. I didn't mean to stare. Please don't be insulted."

She smiled. Obviously this was giving her a tremendous amount of pleasure. "I'm not the least bit insulted. Thank you for noticing, I hoped you would be pleased."

"Pleased about what?" the senator asked, suddenly entering the room.

She stood and gave him a kiss on the cheek. "My coffee, Dear. Mr. Smith likes my coffee. I was attempting to get him to eat something. Maybe, you can convince him. What will you have, Dear?"

The senator looked pleased, so, Clay figured he had not been listening to the previous conversation. *Whew!*

The senator looked at Clay, and then focused his gazed on the wife. "You know what I like, and bring enough for the both of us."

Clay tried, unsuccessfully, not to watch as she left the dining room.

Reaching for the coffee pot the senator was paying no attention to the look on his wife's face. He poured himself a cup, and then refilled Clay's cup.

"Are you feeling any better, Clay? I know what a shock it must have been seeing that young lady's face in the picture, but suppose we had never found out. Wouldn't that have been worse?"

Clay nodded, "I guess so. I keep thinking that there must be a mistake. Gidget could have destroyed us, but she didn't, and Johnny said the same thing on the telephone."

"Clay, do you think you could get Sergeant Shackelford to stay with the wife and I for awhile, at least until we can get a better handle on exactly what to do? Or, until you get back from Chicago."

Clay stood and walked to the window. "I have no doubt but what he'd be more than happy to help out. I'll give him a call."

Jolene entered with the food. Serving the senator first, she spoke. "Senator, would it be okay if I built a snowman? I'll do it in the backyard so as not to embarrass."

The senator looked at her for a moment. "Hell, I don't know why not. C'mon, Clay, let's eat. My wife makes a mean omelet."

The roads were still closed, except for the main highways, and Clay wasn't going anywhere, so they talked and planned their next few moves very carefully. They did; however, move to the den so the senator could smoke. They placed a call to the sergeant and he was thrilled to comply. Although, he was not too pleased with the circumstances, and he had much yet to learn about what was actually going on. Shack promised to be there as early the following day as the weather would allow.

He and the senator began drinking, and the more Clay drank the angrier he became. "Do you ever feel foolish, Senator?"

The senator almost bit the end off his cigar. "Foolish? Have you taken a close look at my wife? I'm married to a beautiful woman, twenty years younger than me, and I'd give a thousand bucks to screw that Jolene. Foolish, I feel foolish all the time. Truth is I probably couldn't do anything even if she asked. Don't get old, Clay, it stinks."

Carl R. Smith

The senator must have been drinking more than Clay realized. "Well, the alternative doesn't sound like much fun," Clay replied, reaching now for his own cigar.

"Right, Son. At least I can still think about it."

"Senator, its going to be dark soon, maybe you'd better show me where I'm going to live for the next few months."

The senator opened one of the desk drawers and fished out a key. "Let's go. It's only a couple hundred yards if we cut through the back. Let me get your coat, and I think I have some extra goulashes you can wear."

When they were sufficiently bundled up they were on their way. The snow was up to their knees. The house was only three doors down, but facing the next street over. To get there by car, one would have to drive all the way around the block. The house was not quite as large as the senator's. It was; however, incredibly beautiful, and the cupboard and the liquor cabinet were fully stocked. The senator showed Clay to the guest bedroom. Fortunately, it was on the ground floor next to the den.

Clay looked at the senator. "Sir, I'll stay in this end of the house. That way I won't make much of a mess."

"Don't worry about it. Jolene has agreed to come over a couple of times a week to see to your needs. I hope that meets with your approval. She'll do the cleaning and the laundry, but you're on your own at mealtime. Here's the key, you can move in upon your return from Chicago."

Clay took the key. "Thank you, Sir; you're much too good to me."

"One more thing, Son, wait here, I'll be right back." The senator went into the kitchen and came back with a little box in his hand. "Here, this is the garage door opener. It will make life a lot easier, and you can use this to enter and exit the house."

It was fully dark when they arrived back at the senator's place. They were informed that dinner would be served momentarily. They each shed their outer garb and went to freshen up. When Clay entered the dining room, Ms. Lazar was the only one present.

"Join me, Mr. Smith. Bob will be here in a minute or so."

"Thank you, Ma'am, and I would be pleased Ms. Lazar if you would be kind enough to call me Clay. It feels funny being called Mr. Smith all the time. Please!"

"Whatever you say, Clay. My first name's Patricia, but my friends call me, Trish, and I sincerely hope we'll be friends."

"Yes, of course," he stumbled with the words.

The senator entered the room. "You two haven't started without me, have you?"

"Of course not, Bob. We were discussing first names, and we've decided to use them, do you mind? I know how formal you like to be."

The senator looked taken back. "No, of course not. Don't be silly. I think we should all be friends. Clay, you may call me Robert, or Bob, if you prefer."

Clay cleared his throat. "Senator, you have earned your title. I would feel funny calling you anything other than, Senator, or Sir. I hope that's all right. I want very much to be your friend, and I feel that we are friends."

"That's perfectly fine, Clay. And, we are most certainly friends." The senator looked well pleased with the decision Clay had made.

After dinner Ms. Lazar excused herself and the two men retired once again to the den. Clay drank very little, but the senator never slowed down. It wasn't long before the senator was ready to turn in.

"Clay, I think I'm going to call it a night. Help yourself to anything you want. Can you find your way to the bedroom?"

Clay stood. "Sure, Senator, I'll be fine. If you don't mind I'll turn on the television and see what they're saying about the roads."

The senator staggered toward the door. "Help yourself. See you in the morning, My Friend."

"Goodnight, Sir."

Clay watched the end of "Laugh-in" and then the News. The main roads were opened. It was simply a matter of getting to them. Using the senator's phone, he made a reservation on the earliest flight he thought he could catch, headed to Chicago. With any luck he would arrive there by eight the next evening. He decided to call Gidget to be sure she would be available.

"Hey, Gig. I'm coming through Chicago tomorrow, heading out to California to see Johnny, but I'll stay over one night if you'll have dinner with me."

"Oh my God, Clay, it's really you. Are you kidding? You bet your life I'll be here; in fact, I'll pick you up at the airport. Just tell me where and when."

The die was cast; she knew what time he would be arriving, and on what airline. He told her how much he was looking forward to spending some time with her. They talked for a while longer and then said their good-byes.

She must have told him ten times how excited she was. He felt like shit, but he played his part to the hilt.

A few more drags off his cigar, and it was time to find the bedroom. After brushing his teeth he stood in the shower for a long time trying to clear his head. Unfortunately, the more he thought about the situation the more confused and angry he became. He exited the bathroom and darted for the bed. The bed lamp was the only light on in the huge room.

Just as he got settled in there was a light tapping on the bedroom door.

"Come in."

The door opened slowly as Ms. Lazar entered the room, quietly shutting the door behind her.

"Can we talk for a minute, Clay?"

He sat up in the bed, covered to the waist. "You must be kidding. If the senator finds you here, he'll have me shot."

"Please, Clay. Bob is passed out in his bedroom; you couldn't wake him with a lightning bolt. I have to talk to someone; I think I'm losing my mind."

"Okay," Clay said, uncomfortably. "But, let's make it fast. What's the problem?"

"I'm Bob's second wife, but I guess you've figured that out by now. His first wife died almost two years ago. I have no friends here, and everyone thinks I'm a gold digger. I love those two kids and I wouldn't do anything to hurt my husband; but, I'm scared to death. I think any minute some crazy people are going to break in and kill all of us, in our sleep. We sent the children away and I stayed, hoping to prove to him that I really cared. Bob doesn't love me, I'm just someone pretty to have on his arm while he's entertaining. He'll do anything to further his career." She finally took a breath. "He's a good man and a hard worker, but he's impotent, and, because of that he's sure I couldn't possible love him. That's why he makes eyes at Jolene, hoping to regain his manhood and make me jealous. Can you help me Clay? Bob thinks the world of you. He told me last night to come to you. He thinks if you satisfy me sexually he'll be off the hook. He said you were the only person that he trusted, absolutely, and the only one he would trust with his wife."

Clay had not moved; he was dumb founded. "All you ladies want is to toy with me. This is one of the craziest things I've ever heard. Anyway, you don't want to get involved with me."

She began to sob quietly. "I understand. I won't bother you again, but please don't let anything happen to my husband. He's a good man, and he has a good heart."

Clay knew he would hate himself. "Trish, throw me my trousers, there on the chair by the bathroom door. Go on, Woman, do it."

She walked across the room and returned with his trousers. "Here, shall I turn my head?"

He grabbed them and put them on under the covers. "Wait there. I'll be with you in a minute."

Clay emerged from the bed with his trousers on, and he started across the room to retrieve his shirt as she grabbed his arm.

"Clay, you're quite a specimen. My husband has good taste, even in men," she said, pulling herself close to him.

Her hot breath raised the hairs on his neck. He took both her hands and held them behind her. That may have been a mistake for it brought her body even closer to his.

She smiled. In spite of the circumstances, she could feel his body becoming excited. "You want me, Clay. Don't you think I'm pretty?"

"Oh yeah, I think you're incredible, but this is not gonna happen. Not here, not now. Go to your own room, and I promise to do everything in my power to protect your husband. You want to be my friend? Then, do as I ask. Please!"

"Okay. But, you want me; your body can't deny it. I'll be here when you change your mind."

He released her and stepped back; however, she rubbed her body against him deliberately as she moved toward the door.

"Goodnight, Clay."

Standing in the middle of the room he was feeling even more frustration. He walked to the door and flipped the lock. It took awhile for sleep to come, but thank God it finally came.

The next morning Clay was up at dawn, attempting to remove the snow from the driveway. Having found a shovel in the garage, he had put it to good use. As he started the car and was backing out he spied the senator heading his direction. Clay rolled down the window.

"Good morning, Sir. I hope I didn't wake everyone, I was trying to get an early start."

The senator smiled; taking two steps forward, he placed one hand on the car and with the other one he pulled a rather large envelope from his

Carl R. Smith

coat. "Here, My Boy. This money will come in handy. I also thought you might want to know that Sergeant Shackelford is on his way." The senator hesitated. "Thank You, Son. Let me know what's happening and I'll do the same."

Clay took the envelope and shook the senator's hand. "Give my best to the sergeant. I'll keep in touch."

And, with that, they parted company.

Chapter 3

The plane ride to Chicago was bumpy, but they arrived on time. Clay's emotions were running amuck. His stomach was doing flip-flops. Airplane food, even in first class, was no picnic. Smiling at his choice of words he tried to gather his thoughts. Knowing Gidget would be waiting, he desperately hoped to keep it together until they were alone. He began to pray, silently. *God, you know I'm not much at praying, but give me the right words. I want to wring her cute little neck; however, I need to know the whole truth. Amen! Oh, sorry. Thanks for listening.*

The stewardess tapped him on the shoulder. "Sir, we're on the ground."

He jumped, "Sorry, Miss, but I was deep in thought."

She took his arm and helped him to his feet. "I believe you have a hanging bag in the rack, don't you, handsome?"

He smiled at her, still not all there. "Yes, Love. Yes, I do. Thank you!"

The stewardess helped him retrieve his bag, and he was quickly down the steps across the tar-mac and back up the steps to the terminal where Gidget would be waiting.

Where was she? He headed toward the baggage claim area thinking she might be waiting there, but again, no Gidget. Clay laid his hanging bag across one seat and planted himself in another. *Hell, Little One, where the heck are you?* He sat, he paced, and then he sat some more. After some twenty minutes, his thoughts had gone from anxiety and anger to fear and concern.

"Sir, are you all right?"

It was the stewardess from his flight.

"I'm okay, I guess. Someone was supposed to meet me and she isn't here."

The stewardess sat down in the seat next to him. She laid her hand on his left arm. "Have you checked with the ticket counter, she may have left you a message?"

"No, I haven't, but I suppose I should have thought of that." He stood. "Will you point me in the right direction? Oh don't bother, I'll find it. Thanks again, you're terrific."

"You're welcome!"

Clay grabbed his bag. "I hope they pay you extra for this."

"Well, they don't. Anyway, you looked as though you needed a friend. C'mon, I'll go with you. It's not the wife you're looking for, is it?"

Clay picked up the pace. "No, I don't have one of those; it's just a dear friend. Don't you have another flight?"

"Nope, this is my home, and I'm off for the next two days. Where does your friend live?"

"Forest Park. Do you know where that is?"

"Sure I do, Silly. It's not far from here, and I live in that same area." Her eyes brightened. "If you have no message, I'll take you there. We can be there in fifteen minutes. Do you have the address?"

He nodded. "Sure, it's in my wallet."

They had reached the counter and no message had been left.

She took his arm. "C'mon, I'll take you. You're starting to look concerned."

They made a beeline for the parking lot. Once in the car he gave her the address and she knew exactly where they were going. As they sped out of the parking lot it began to snow. Not much, but just enough to make it slippery.

She asked a million questions. Clay answered very few, directly. They did however introduce themselves. Her name was Stephanie, and she had been a stewardess for almost a year. She lived with another stewardess; however, they were almost never home at the same time.

Stephanie was about five four and quite tiny, with shoulder length blond hair and blue eyes, probably in her early twenties. She wore glasses while driving. It made her look like a schoolteacher. Unfortunately, Clay never had a teacher this attractive.

When they got to Gidget's apartment, the lights were on, but no one answered the door. Clay was undaunted. Knowing in his gut that something wasn't right, he decided to pick the lock. As the door opened he could hear music from what he assumed was the bedroom. He walked some twenty feet down the hallway, and there she was. Clay had to hold his breath to keep from screaming. Gidget was lying on the bed half naked, beaten so badly she was almost unrecognizable. Her hands and feet were tied with some type of wire that had cut deep into her skin. She had another wire around her neck. The three wires were strung together so that if she tried to free herself she would only succeed in strangling herself to death; or, she would cause herself to die form a loss of blood. Either way, she was dead, and in Clay's opinion it had taken her a long time to die.

My God, Gidget, were they afraid you would tell me something? Clay leaned across her lifeless body, closed her eyes and kissed her on the forehead. *I'm gonna miss you, little one.*

He backed out of the room and down the hallway attempting to retrace his steps, all the time, wiping his fingerprints from the few things he had touched. There was no need in looking for anything pertinent; if it had been there, it would be in the hands of someone else by now. Shutting the door he hurried back to the car where Stephanie was waiting.

She rolled down the window. "Is everything okay?"

Clay tried to remain calm, but every fiber of his being was screaming. He grabbed his face with his hands, trying to focus. "Stephanie, will you take me to a hotel? I can't stay here!"

He hurried around the rear of the car and got in. "My friend is dead; get me the hell out of here!"

Not a word was spoken. Stephanie swung the car away from the curb and shot down the narrow street. Clay didn't know where she was going, and furthermore, he didn't care. In a couple of minutes, she pulled into a parking garage and threaded her way into a parking space. She turned off the motor and looked at him.

"Clay, this is where I live. Shouldn't we go inside and call someone?"

He looked at her quizzically. "Are you sure you can trust me. I may have killed her for all you know."

Stephanie slid around in her seat in order to face him. "Bullshit! You weren't in there long enough to have killed anyone. Anyhow, you don't have a hair out of place. And if you had killed somebody, I don't think you would come out to my car and make the announcement."

Clay was visible shaken, but he could appreciate her logic. "You're not only beautiful, but intelligent as well. I hope you have something to drink in your place."

She removed her glasses and opened her door. "I sure do. Move it, it's cold out here!"

They were inside her apartment in minutes. Clay took a quick look around. It was obviously the apartment of two girls. It was much too neat for most men's taste.

Stephanie threw her coat across the sofa. "The telephone is on the desk at the end of the sofa. What do you want to drink?"

"Hell, I don't care!" he replied curtly. "I prefer scotch and soda if you have it; if not, anything will do."

Clay removed his overcoat and laid it beside hers. Then he sat on the end of the sofa next to the telephone, trying to organize his thoughts.

Stephanie came back from the kitchen, drinks in hand.

"What are you waiting for, call the police?" She plopped down across from him in a recliner. "Do you want me to make the call?"

"No!" Clay said, reaching for his wallet. He pulled a ten and threw it on the table. "I have to make another call first. It's long distance. Ten should more than cover the cost, okay?"

She glared at him and threw off her shoes. "Go ahead. Make your call. She's already dead, so I guess it won't matter much!"

Clay said, "Thanks," as he picked up the phone and dialed the operator. After giving the operator the appropriate information he sank back into the sofa. Just as quickly he sat up straight.

"Good evening, Senator. I'm in Chicago and I have some rather disturbing news."

He explained everything in detail. He also told him that he would contact the local authorities, but anonymously of course. Lastly, he informed him that he would contact Johnny and meet with him before returning to Washington.

Stephanie could only hear Clay's side of the conversation; however, she was somewhat impressed. When he finally hung up, she just sat there looking at him.

Clay repositioned himself on the sofa. "Is there a pay telephone close by? I want to call the authorities, but I don't want them tracing the call back to your phone."

"There's one in the laundry room in the basement, but I'm going with you. You're not leaving me here alone."

Clay stood, fishing in his pockets for some change. "Could I borrow a dime? I don't seem to have any coins."

She reached for her purse. After a moment of searching, she handed him a dime; all the time trying to put her shoes back on.

The call was made, and they returned to Stephanie's apartment.

"Clay, would you like another drink? I sure do need one. This has been some night."

"Yes, I surely would. I need to make one more call; do you have a telephone book?"

"It's in the drawer under the telephone."

Clay called the Hyatt Hotel downtown and left a message for Johnny, then laid his head back on the sofa and closed his eyes. He had a splitting headache, probably from a serious lack of nourishment. And, it could possible have something to do with the present circumstances.

Stephanie came out of the kitchen with the drinks. "I know it's late, but I need to eat something, and I'll bet you're hungry. Can I fix you something?"

He looked at her for a moment. "You're terrific, and I have been a real pain in the butt. I hope you'll let me make it up to you. Can you scramble eggs?"

Stephanie stood erect, hands on hips. "Yes, Smartass, I can scramble eggs. Will two be enough?"

Clay stood rubbing his neck. "Yes Ma'am! Can I be of some help?"

"No, I think I can handle it; however, you can come into the kitchen and talk to me while I'm cooking."

He followed her to the kitchen. While she cooked, and as they sat eating, Clay attempted to explain more than he probably should have, but he felt he owed her that much. She asked questions, and he answered, carefully. When they were through eating they retired to the living room once again.

Clay had been watching her closely; he was very good at that.

"Do your feet hurt?" he asked.

"Yeah, I was on them for about ten hours straight."

"Come here and sit on the other end of the sofa and give me those tootsies. I've been told I give a great foot massage. C'mon, a little payback. If you're displeased, I'll quit, and get the hell out of your life."

She did as he asked. Before long, she was moaning and making sounds one might hear coming from the back seat of a car, parked on Lover's Lane.

After some ten minutes she leaned forward, their faces only inches apart.

"My turn," she said, shyly. "You must have something that needs massaging."

She ran both her hands up his thighs, all the time looking him straight in the eye. She unzipped his trousers, and repaid him in kind.

He lay back on the sofa, not yet believing what was taking place. She was as good at her task as he had been with his. Leaning forward she kissed him passionately.

"C'mon, Big Boy, let's go brush our teeth and take a shower. I'll just bet I can do a much better job when we're both clean and relaxed." She stood, motioning for him to follow. "Indeed, you may wish to repay my hospitality in other ways as well; who knows?"

The repayment was lengthy and complete, each person fully satisfied with the results. Sleep came quickly for both parties.

Chapter 4

The following morning Stephanie dropped him at the hotel about eleven. As he approached the front desk, Johnny was just checking in.

Just seeing the back of his head brought a wide grin to Clay's face. "Hey, is there a doctor in the house?"

Johnny wheeled around. "Clay, you're a sight for sore eyes. Gosh, you look great; you had sex, didn't you? I'd know that afterglow anywhere."

Clay stuck out his hand; Johnny grabbed it and pulled him close. They embraced, unashamed, in front of some twenty people.

Johnny put one hand on each shoulder as if to size him up. "You wait right here, Old Buddy. Let me get my room key and I'll buy you some breakfast, lunch, whatever."

Clay smiled. "I've got to find the john, but I'll be right back, don't go anyplace."

"Got it," Johnny replied. "I'll be here!"

Some big guy from the back of the line yelled. "When you two fagots get through, there are other people trying to check-in."

Clay whipped around. "You'd better watch your mouth, Fat Boy, or you're gonna be checking in at the nearest hospital."

He started toward the man and Johnny grabbed his arm. "Don't hurt him, Clay, he's just mad at the world; anyone can see it's not been very good to him." Johnny looked at the man. "Sir, I'm a doctor, take it from me, slow down you'll live longer. And, to be honest with you this young man could destroy you with two fingers. You best believe me. Now, shape up!" Johnny put his hand, quickly, to his mouth. "Oh, sorry about that shape up crack, I guess you've heard that one before."

Everyone started laughing, except for the fat man.

Clay took care of business, exited the men's room and found Johnny in the lobby reading the morning paper.

"Get your nose out of the paper, Doc, let's eat."

Johnny looked up from his paper. "Lead me to it, Old Buddy."

When they had been seated in the restaurant, Johnny couldn't wait to start asking questions.

"How's Gidget? Why didn't you bring her with you?"

Clay was unprepared for the blunt way in which Johnny asked. "Partner, I hoped this could wait until we were someplace a little more private. Gidget's dead. I found her last night at her apartment. It's almost too horrible to describe."

Johnny reached across the table and patted him on the hand. "Let's take this to my room, we'll order something from room service."

Clay didn't say anything; he just stood up and headed for the door, Johnny close behind. When they entered the room, Johnny broke the silence.

"Damn, they put somebody else's bag in with mine; I hate it when they do that."

Clay looked at him. "Sorry, Partner, that's mine. I didn't think you'd mind, I haven't checked in yet. I'll go down and do it now, if you want."

"Don't be silly. It's okay; I didn't know it belonged to you. No sweat, Clay." Johnny continued, "I think you better sit down, you don't look so good. Let me get you a cold washcloth."

Johnny headed to the bathroom and Clay slumped into the chair closest to the window.

Johnny came out of the bathroom, wet washcloth in hand. "Here, wipe your face with this and then lay it on the back of your neck, it'll help. You have my word as a certified medical doctor."

Clay followed the doctor's orders, and then began speaking, slowly. "I guess I've kind of been in shock for the last few hours. Bear with me, Partner, this may take awhile."

Johnny picked up the room service menu. "Rest for a minute, I'll order us some food; do you want breakfast or lunch?" he asked. "How silly of me, breakfast of course."

Clay tried to smile. "Right you are, Old Friend."

Johnny placed their order and then reached in his bag and pulled out a bottle of Jack Daniels. "I think a little shooter might help. I know it's not your drink of choice, but how about it?"

Clay finally smiled. "It couldn't hurt."

As they drank, he told Johnny everything. Johnny sat quietly and listened. By the time the food came he knew almost as much as Clay.

The waiter sat up the table for them. Johnny signed the check and began pouring the coffee.

"Clay, do you think Gidget could have told them anything they could use against us?"

Clay finished his bourbon and took a drink of coffee. "I don't know. My only concern at this point is for Susan and Sydney. No one else knew about them, except us, and that makes me a bit nervous. Do you think they would go after either one of them?"

Johnny was trying to chew, swallow, and talk all at the same time. Bad move; he almost choked. "Clay, I . . . Give me a minute."

Johnny took a few deep breaths. "They might, just to see if they know anything of importance."

Clay ate the last bite of his eggs before speaking again; Johnny waited patiently.

"I'm not too worried about Sydney. He's in South Africa and he won't be back for a month. Surely they wouldn't go that far just to question him."

"Why not," Johnny stated. "Distance means nothing to them. They came to Chicago quick enough, didn't they?"

Clay started fidgeting. It was something he usually did when he was nervous or unsure of himself. "Shit, Johnny, I guess we better warn Susan. They would go after her first, don't you think?"

Johnny thought for a minute. "Yeah, I think so. Let's call her right now. But, what are we gonna tell her to do? Hell, Clay, you're always the one with the bright ideas; come up with something."

Clay picked up the telephone, punched eight, and then dialed the number. "It's ringing. She should be at the hospital. I hope she's not at lunch or---. Hello, physical therapy please. Hi, can I speak to Susan?" He looked at Johnny. "She's there thank God. Hey, Gorgeous, how's the world treating you?"

"Clay, oh my, it's great to hear your voice. How are things? Are you in town?"

"No, Babe. I'm in Chicago. Listen, Susan, can we talk for a few minutes, or are you with a patient?"

"No, no patient. I'm in the back office, fire away."

Clay hesitated. "Susan, I want you to do exactly as I say, exactly. Do you understand?"

"Oh Lord, what's wrong?"

"Just listen. Call the airport and make reservations for the next flight to Chicago. Drive your car to the airport, and then catch a taxi to the train station. Get on the first train to D. C.; I'll have Sergeant Shackelford meet you at the station. You know what he looks like, you met him at the funeral, remember?"

"Yes, Clay, I remember!"

"Okay. He'll take you to a safe house, and I'll be there no later than noon tomorrow. Be sure you're not followed. You've done this before Susan, you can handle this. Do you have any questions?"

"Yes, is Gidget all right? Let me talk to her."

"I can't do that Susan. She's not here with me; I'm with Johnny. He says hello."

He motioned for Johnny to say something.

Johnny hollered from across the room. "Hello, Beautiful."

"Clay, what should I tell them here at work?"

"Give me a minute," he responded. He didn't want to tell her that he was doing this by the seat of his pants, so to speak. "Tell them your mother is real sick and you have to go to New York, right now. Cry if you have to; you can do this."

"Okay, I'll be on my way as soon as I call and make my reservations with the airlines. I guess that's supposed to make someone think I'm traveling by air, right?"

"Right you are," he replied. "Call me back before you leave there, and let me know when you're getting into D.C. Use another phone, but stay in the public where you know people. If you can get someone there to take you to the airport that would work even better. You could leave your car at the hospital." Clay was very firm with her. "Susan, whatever you do, don't go home. Now, repeat back to me exactly what you're going to do. I want to be absolutely sure we understand each other. I'll wait here until you call me back."

Susan repeated everything, almost verbatim.

He gave her the number where they were and hung up.

Clay was fidgeting. "Johnny, what do you think? And, do you have any cigars? I promise to blow the smoke out the window."

Carl R. Smith

"No cigars, but I'll go get us some in a few minutes." Johnny said pouring the last of the coffee into his cup. "Clay, I think it's a good plan. By the time they realize she's not on the plane, she should be in D.C., if she times it right."

Clay looked rather intense. "Johnny, I don't want to tie up this phone, Susan could call any minute. But, while you're getting the cigars, call the airport and see when I can get back to D.C.; will you do that for me, please?"

Johnny put his jacket back on and started toward the door. "I'll be more than happy to. Stop worrying, everything's gonna work out fine. I'll be back in a few minutes."

Clay looked at him. "Be careful, and don't talk to strangers."

Johnny threw him the bird, and away he went.

Clay sat by the telephone, anxiously waiting. *God, it's me again. Please protect my friends. The only reason they're in this mess is because of me. Please don't let them be hurt. Let Gidget be the last. Please!*

The door opened, Johnny came in carrying scotch and cigars. He even had a bottle of soda.

"Say, Lone Ranger, you're the best friend a man ever had," Clay declared, laughing like a six year old.

Johnny laughed too. "Right, Tonto, me bring um firewater to wet whistle."

No two men ever loved each other more. They had been inseparable most of their lives. When Clay's father had beaten him severely and tied him to a tree in the yard overnight, Johnny would slip out and stay with him all night, sneaking away early the next morning so Clay's father wouldn't punish Clay further because of him. At the age of eight when Johnny's family moved to Kentucky, Clay was heartbroken. However, when they met once again, a few years ago, they swore no one would ever come between them again. When the Cubans held Johnny captive, Clay went immediately without thought for his own safety to free him. And, when Clay had been framed for murder, Johnny was there through it all; risking his life, and his career as a medical doctor for his childhood friend.

"Clay," Johnny said excitedly. "We can be in D. C. by nine thirty this evening. The plane doesn't leave for another three hours, but we can make some reservations as soon as we hear from Susan."

Clay opened the window and lit a cigar. "What's this *we shit*? I'm not gonna get you mixed up in all this again. I put you in harm's way enough last time. I'm sure you remember; although, I guess we need to see to your safety as well."

"Right, my thoughts exactly," Johnny mused, lighting his own cigar and making them both a fresh drink. "If I'm gonna get killed, it's gonna be by your side. I'm not gonna get killed while I'm all alone in California, no way."

The telephone rang and they both jumped. Clay grabbed the receiver. "Hello."

"Clay, it's me," Susan began. "The train arrives at eleven fifty. The airplane leaves at nine thirty-five. I thought that would work perfectly. By the time they realize I'm not on the flight, the train will be arriving in D. C." she paused, getting her breath. "How'd I do?"

"You did great," he replied. "That works out super. No need for the sergeant, Johnny and I will be there to meet the train. For God's sake be careful, Susan, we'll see you about midnight. Love ya, Babe."

Crash, bang!

Scotch, soda, and broken glass went everywhere as Clay hit the floor; noticing as he landed, Johnny, diving into the bathroom.

"How stupid are we?" Clay screamed. "Here we are, like idiots, standing in front of an open window?"

"Pretty dumb," Johnny replied. "Can you reach to close the curtain? I'm afraid to cross the room."

"Yeah, I can get to it, stay there," Clay replied. "There's probably a lot more bullets where that one came from."

Clay reached the cord and closed the curtain. The room was fairly dark even for mid-afternoon.

"God must love us; one of us could easily be dead," Clay noted, almost whispering, as though he could be heard by whomever was taking pot shots at them.

Johnny started throwing his things, once more, into his bag. "Something's burning," he yelled.

"No sweat," Clay assured. "It's just my cigar; I dropped it on the carpet. Fortunately, there's only minimal damage." He, unconsciously, began picking up the broken glass.

"Have you lost it, Old Buddy? Screw the mess; let the maid get that." Johnny shouted. "Let's get the hell out of here."

"No, I think we outta stay right here," Clay replied calmly. "They'll be expecting us to run. Let them come to us; I want that bastard."

Johnny gave him a look of disbelief. "What if there's a bunch of them?"

Clay grinned. "Well, in that case, I'll take two of them, and you can take the rest. Maybe, they'll let you take their temperature."

"Oh, that's real funny. What do we do when they come to the door?" Johnny asked, not trying to be funny.

Clay checked his weapon. "I don't think they'll knock; however, if they do we'll invite them in for drinks."

Johnny grabbed him by the arm and spun him around. "What's the matter with you?"

Clay dropped his head. "When I close my eyes I can still see Gidget all trussed up like a piece of dead meat. Forgive me, Partner, I don't mean to take it out on you, but I'm so mad I could scream."

"It's okay," Johnny said, frantically looking for his own weapon.

Clay walked across the room and patted him on the shoulder. "Johnny, you're right. Get your things; we're going to the airport. We have about three hours before the plane leaves for D.C."

Johnny brightened up. "Now you're talking, I'm ready, let's go. Although, I think we should be extremely cautious."

Clay looked carefully through the peephole. "Johnny, when we get to the lobby you look left and forward, and I'll look right and behind us."

Johnny threw his bag over his shoulder and followed Clay out of the room, clutching his gun tightly under his jacket. They made it to the lobby without incident. Clay stood by as Johnny checked out.

When they were safely in the cab and on their way to the airport; Johnny spoke quietly. "You know we can't take these guns on the flight. We'll have to unload and declare them."

"I know," Clay replied. "But, so will he, or they."

Johnny leaned closer to him. "I don't think we're being tailed, but there's so much traffic I can't be sure."

"Relax, there's two of us and probably only one of him. Anyway, his next shot probably won't come until we're on the plane."

"Shot," Johnny grimaced. "They can't shoot us while on the airplane, they won't have any weapons."

Clay poked him in the ribs. "Sorry, Partner, bad choice of words, I meant attempt."

Johnny pushed him away. "Boy, I sure do feel better now. What did you have in mind, anything specific?"

"No, not anything special," Clay replied, as they pulled up to the terminal.

They watched everything, and everybody, all the way to the gate. No one acted suspiciously, and nobody else came to the gate except this sweet looking, very large old lady with a huge shopping bag. Clay pointed her out to Johnny.

"Aw, c'mon," Johnny snickered.

Clay glared at him. "Don't be deceived, anything's possible. That could be a two hundred and fifty pound assassin in disguise."

Johnny glared back at him. "Well, Tonto, my scrub nurse could take her, and she wouldn't even be breathing hard."

"I need to meet this nurse; is she cute?" Clay asked, trying hard to remain stone faced and not having much luck.

He and Johnny sat as far to the rear of the plane as possible with the old woman in front of them, and in full view at all times. The flight felt as though it took forever, but they actually got to D.C. on time. They deplaned and found Clay's car, or what was left of it. Evidently the bomb that had been planted had been prematurely set off by someone, or something.

"Shit, shit, shit," Clay yelled, throwing his bag down in the snow. "I'm gonna kill those sons a bitches."

Johnny picked up the bag. "Let's go rent a car, Susan will be here soon."

Clay took the bag from him, and they trudged back to the terminal. Thank goodness the Avis counter wasn't busy. They piled all their stuff into the rental car and headed for the train station.

Johnny said, "I wonder when it happened, I would've expected the police to have towed it away by now."

"With all the snow, all the tow trucks are probably tied up. Hell, it's not going anywhere. Damn things dead, just like we'll be if we don't get this asshole first." Clay grimaced. "Somebody's gonna pay, you mark my word."

Johnny listened patiently, hoping, Clay would get it all out of his system before they met Susan. Finally, he had had enough.

"Get over it, Old Buddy. After all, it's just a car," Johnny mused.

"Just a car?!!? I can't believe you said that. That's like saying Natalie Wood is just a girl. I just can't believe you said that," Clay stammered, with the volume of his voice decreasing all the while.

"I really am sorry, Clay."

"Forget it, Johnny. I don't wanna talk about it. Is anyone following us, or have you been paying attention?"

"Yes, I've been paying attention, and we're not being followed. Maybe they think we died in the explosion," Johnny surmised.

"Could be, but not likely; however, we may have bought enough time to regroup. Then, just maybe, we can start our own offensive. I'd rather chase than be chased, wouldn't you, Partner?"

"Damn right," Johnny agreed.

Chapter 5

They arrived at the train station a little past ten. The roads in D.C. were still a bit slippery and Clay drove cautiously. The ticket agent informed them that the train from Boston was running on time, so the wait wouldn't be too long. The station café was closing so they raided the vending machines, consuming their goodies in the men's room in an attempt to go unnoticed. Deciding to a smoke afterwards, they stayed in the shadows outside the station.

"Clay," Johnny whispered. "This may sound a bit stupid, but where're we going from here? Is the new hiding place close by? We don't have to stay at the BOQ again do we?"

Clay answered quietly. "You won't believe it, but we have an entire house in the senator's neighborhood. The owners will be gone until March, so we have the place all to ourselves."

"I hope it don't take us that long," Johnny replied. "Although, Old Buddy, I do still have more than a quarter million dollars in the bank, thanks to you. I think that should take care of me until March, don't you?"

Clay looked at him. "Yeah, I should hope so."

At ten forty eight the train pulled into the station. At the thought of seeing Susan, the butterflies in Clay's stomach were jumping for joy. There must have been thirty people getting off the train, but no Susan.

"There she is," Johnny screamed.

Clay jumped up on the bench to see over the crowd. Indeed, there she was, more beautiful than ever. What a welcome sight.

Susan came running out of the crowd. "Hey, Guys, I'm here."

"Gee whiz, Susan, you look wonderful," Clay exclaimed grabbing her small bag.

Johnny chimed in. "You do look grand, Young Lady. Is that all the luggage you brought?"

"Luggage? That's a bag I borrowed from one of the girls at work; it contains my uniform and a change of shoes. Clay wouldn't let me go back home; you probably already know that, don't you? You're making a joke, aren't you, Doc?"

Johnny smiled and took her by the arm. "Let's get away from here. Your chariot awaits, My Dear. Unfortunately, it's not the one you most probably expected." He leaned real close to her. "Don't say anything about the car, Clay's still steaming."

Susan just looked at him.

Clay said, "What the hell are you two whispering about, c'mon. I want to get someplace safe and warm."

"We're coming, Master. We's moving just as fast as we can," Johnny mocked.

Susan started laughing. "Gosh, I've missed you guys. Where's Gidget?"

It got deathly quiet. Neither man knew what to say, and neither one wished to be the first to speak.

Susan stopped in her tracks. "She's dead, ain't she? Well, somebody better say something."

Clay put both arms around her. "Yes, Susan, she's dead. I'll tell you about it when we get in the car, c'mon. Johnny you drive; I'll sit in the back with Susan. Do you remember how to get to the senator's place?"

"Generally, if I'm unsure I'll ask."

They were soon on their way. Clay spent some time explaining, very carefully, everything that had taken place in the last three days. Well, he did leave out the part about Stephanie. But, that would not have been appreciated, under any circumstances.

Susan was beginning to sob. She loved Gidget; and too, she was in fear for everyone else's safety, including her own. Clay knew that she was now fully aware of the danger that lay ahead. The wake-up call had come all too quickly. She was trembling. Clay simply held her close, and gave necessary directions to Johnny.

They arrived at the house about midnight. Clay had put the garage door opener in his bag. He had meant to leave it in the car, but thank goodness he forgot. He pressed the button and the door rose. Johnny pulled the car into the garage. Clay pressed the button and the door went down. Fishing the door key from his pocket, they went inside.

Clay locked the door behind them. "I've only been here once, so we'll have to find things together. I do know this is the kitchen, and the den is that way."

Johnny spun around. "This is nice, but I don't see a pool. Well, I guess we'll just have to rough it."

Understanding Johnny's attempt at humor, Clay and Susan smiled.

"Okay, Guys," Clay said, touching Susan's arm. "Let's explore the house together. The information might come in handy later on."

"Who lives here?" Johnny asked.

"I don't remember the name, but he's the Ambassador to Great Britain," Clay replied.

"Well, he sure has a beautiful family," Susan noted, pointing to the picture over the mantel.

Clay nodded. "You're right, Susan. They're a handsome family." Clay took a deep breath. "Guys, let's try to keep this place in some kind of order."

"Which bedrooms do we take?" Johnny asked.

Clay thought for a minute. "Johnny, you and Susan take two of the bedrooms upstairs. I'll take the one downstairs. I may have to come and go at odd hours, that way I won't disturb you two."

Johnny said sternly. "If you have to come or go I want to know about it."

Susan chimed in. "That goes for me too."

They were avoiding the obvious conversation they were going to have, and they each knew. Each of them wanted to talk about Gidget, but none of them knew exactly how to begin. It was quiet for a few minutes, as they just milled around; each one, hoping someone would say something and take the pressure off the other two.

Hunger reared its head, as they, one by one, headed for the kitchen. The cupboard was anything but bare, and there was booze galore.

Susan said, "I'll fix some sandwiches. How does grilled cheese sound?"

"Great," Clay answered; as Johnny nodded affirmatively.

"Can I help?" Johnny inquired.

"Sure," she replied. "See if they have any potato chips, and you, Clay, can get us something to drink and set the table, okay?"

"Yes, Ma'am," Clay mocked.

She just looked at him and went on about her business.

"Sorry, Susan, I know better than to call you ma'am."

Johnny turned. "Is this some kind of private joke?"

"As a matter of fact it is," Susan replied. "Now, find those chips, and mind your own business."

"Got-um," Johnny said, pulling an unopened bag from the cabinet.

Clay poured himself a tall glass of milk, and one for Susan. "Johnny, what do you want to drink?"

"I'll take some milk also."

Susan had found a griddle pan and was browning all three sandwiches at once. They looked great. In a few minutes they were all sitting around the table. Again, no one was willing to tackle the subject of Gidget. Finally, Susan, spoke up.

"You know, Clay, Gidget worshiped the ground you walked on. That's the real truth. She wanted you to want her more than anything. She may have given the general the location where Pamela and her sister were, but she would never have let anything bad happen to you personally, not if she could help it."

"Maybe so," Clay said, shaking his head.

Susan glared at him. "No, maybe, that's the way it was. She adored you."

The doorbell rang. They all looked at each other; fear showing on Susan's face. Clay motioned for them to be quiet. Brandishing his weapon, he headed for the door. Johnny stayed behind with Susan.

"Clay, its Shack, are you in there?"

Recognizing the voice, he opened the door.

"I saw the lights on over here, and since the senator told me this is where you would be staying, I thought I'd check."

"Come on in, My Friend. We were just having a bite to eat. Would you like something?" Clay asked, extending his hand in friendship.

Shack smiled. "I'll take a beer, if it's handy."

They walked into the kitchen where Johnny and Susan were waiting.

"Hey, Sergeant," Johnny said. "It sure is nice to see a friendly face. How the hell are you?"

"Great," the sergeant replied. "It's really good to be back together with you guys. Who's the Young Lady?"

"I'm Susan. These bums have no manners, but I have certainly heard a lot of great things about you, Sergeant. We met at Pamela and Janice's funeral, remember?"

Shack blushed. "Aw, you can't believe these guys." He shuffled his feet nervously. "Oh, I remember. You were then, and still are the most beautiful woman I've ever seen."

Susan, who was three or four inches taller than the sergeant, bent down and kissed him on the side of the face, "Boy, Sergeant, you sure know how to turn a girl's head."

Clay stepped in. "Okay, you two. Enough of this; let's go into the den where we can talk. Johnny, will you get the sergeant a beer, please?"

"Sure, Old Buddy. Go on, I'll be right there."

Johnny came into the den carrying the beer and handed it to the sergeant. Clay, on the other hand, was fixing drinks for the rest of them. He finished and handed them out, first to Susan, and then to Johnny.

The sergeant began. "I guess you already know about the new general, don't you?"

They all responded in the affirmative.

"Well, this guy may be even more ruthless, but he's not nearly as smart. Clay, they have been training another young man. They brought him to me; however, after a few days I sent him packing. He's good, but he's mean, no heart. And he can dish it out, but he can't take it."

"Is he the one coming after me?" Clay asked.

"He probably will. He's been out of town for the last couple of days. I've been keeping tabs on him."

"Do you know where he is?" Johnny asked.

"Not really," The sergeant replied. "He caught a flight for San Francisco, on Monday. I don't know where he was going from there. He didn't buy a round trip ticket. Maybe, he's gonna be there for awhile."

Clay stood and walked to the fireplace. "I think he must have been traveling through Chicago."

Johnny concurred.

Clay dropped his head. "He must have gotten into Chicago way before I did."

"I wonder why he wasn't waiting for you at Gidget's place." Johnny said, pausing to take another sip of his drink. "That, to me, seems like the perfect place. Anyway, that's what I would have done."

Clay went on to remind the sergeant who Gidget was, and as briefly as possible how she was killed. The sergeant sat motionless through the entire explanation; every once in awhile he would shake his head. Finally, as Clay was describing the way Gidget was bound; the sergeant interrupted.

"That's him, that's his trademark. He learned that 'little trick' in Vietnam. They used to tie husbands and wives, mother and daughters, and many other combinations, together. Then they'd watch as their captives would kill themselves and each other trying to gain their freedom. They thought it was amusing."

"Those guys are animals," Susan cried. "Clay, let's go to France or England. Please, I don't want any of us to end up like that."

Clay walked across the room and knelt down in front of her, as she sat crying on the couch. "Don't you want me to get this bastard? He killed Gidget; we can't let him get away with that."

She looked straight into his eyes. "That won't bring her back."

Johnny chimed in. "Susan, if we don't get him he's gonna get us all. And I for one don't want to live in fear. I say let's go after him, he won't be expecting that, will he, Sergeant?"

"Right you are, Doc," Shack replied. "That'll screw up his timing something awful."

Clay looked at him. "Can I take this guy? Be honest, Old Friend. I need to know how good he really is."

"Face to face, one on one, absolutely," Shack replied. "But, he's gonna shoot you in the back, or blow you up, if he gets the opportunity."

Johnny headed for the kitchen, he returned with another beer for the sergeant. "Okay," Johnny stammered. "That's why we need to go after him. We need to catch him with his pants down."

Shack, thanked him for the beer. His eyes began to dance, and he spoke hurriedly. "You're gonna love me; cause I know where he lives."

Even Susan smiled at that bit of news.

Shack continued. "He lives in a trailer, in the middle of nowhere. I'll draw you a map."

"What's his name?" Johnny asked.

"Steve Bolen, he's the lowest piece of scum this world has to offer," Shack answered, seemingly pleased with his description.

Susan stretched out on the couch. Clay offered to take her to her room, but she declined. "I don't want to be alone. Can't I just stay here until you guys are finished?"

Clay took the afghan from the back of the couch and covered her. He kissed her on the forehead.

"Of course you can, Babe. We'll hold it down."

Clay focused his attention once again to the sergeant. "Does he live by himself? I don't want innocent people getting hurt."

"Yes, he lives alone," The sergeant replied, finishing his second beer. "Let me call my friend at the airport, and I'll find out when he's coming in, or if he's already back."

Johnny smiled. "Damn, Shack, you're a real treasure."

The sergeant sat his beer can on the table. "Thanks, Doc. You guys are gonna let me participate, aren't you?"

Johnny stuck out his hand. "As far as I'm concerned you've always been on the team. Ain't that right, Clay?"

"No doubt about it. Hell, if it hadn't been for you, Old Friend, we'd probably all be dead. I just wanna be sure you get better compensation this time around."

Shack's smile was so wide you could count all his teeth. "I'll have the map for you in the morning. I'll put it in an envelope and slide it under the front door. I think I'd better get back to the senator's place before I'm missed. He might get nervous."

Clay said, "Let's go out the back door, I want to show you something."

Cutting the Fringe

They all three walked into the back yard. Clay stopped and pointed to a window on the second floor. "If those curtains are closed, Shack, you come running. As you can see they're open now. That will be our signal to each other, okay, Old Friend?"

"You betcha, and I'll keep a sharp eye on that window. Thanks, Clay, and you too, Doc."

Clay gave him a hug. "I'm sure glad you're on the team."

Shack, sheepishly, returned the hug and headed for the senator's house.

Clay and Johnny walked back into the house and into the den where Susan was sleeping soundly.

"Johnny, you know that Steve guy was going to California to take care of you."

"Yeah, I know," Johnny, replied. "Do you want one more drink before we call it a night?"

"That'd be good. Make it a strong one. I intend to sleep until noon."

Johnny began making the drinks. "The three hour time change has got me all screwed up. Hell, it's only midnight in California, and I'd give ten bucks for a good cigar."

Clay said, "Follow me, Old Buddy; have I got a treat for you."

He led Johnny to an office just off the den and over the garage. Fumbling through one of the desk drawers Clay produced an attractive humidor. "Here you are, Partner. The best cigar you'll ever smoke. The senator gave them to me."

"Groovy," Johnny exclaimed. "Where can we smoke them?"

"We'll go back to the den, turn on the fireplace, and blow the smoke up the chimney," Clay replied, grabbing the box with his right hand and heading back toward the den, with Johnny in close pursuit.

He and Johnny smoked their cigars, and Susan kept tossing and turning on the couch, mumbling in her sleep.

"Get away from me, you bastard," Susan screamed, fighting the afghan with all her strength.

Clay grabbed her and shook her back to consciousness. "Susan, its me, you're here with Johnny and me. Look at me, Babe."

Susan clung to him for all she was worth. Her clothing was soaking wet, and she was shaking so hard he could barely keep from falling over. Johnny brought her a shot of whiskey, and all but ordered her to drink it down.

"It was awful. This man was gonna kill me if I didn't tell him where he could find the two of you." She had to stop and get her breath. "I knew he was gonna kill me anyway. But when he started taking this wire out of his bag, I thought of Gidget, and, I started kicking and hitting him as hard as I could. It was terrible!"

Clay raised her chin so he could look into her eyes. "This is all my fault, I'm truly sorry. I had to bring you here so we could protect you. I'll get this guy, I promise."

They were all three sitting on the couch; Johnny on one end, still puffing on his cigar, and Clay and Susan on the other, still clinging to each other.

"I'm fixing one more nightcap, any takers?" Johnny asked, rising to his feet.

"I'll take another one," Susan replied.

Clay said, "Me, too. Then I'm putting you to bed, Young Lady."

Susan frantically grabbed his arm. "Only if you'll stay with me, don't leave me alone. Please, not tonight."

Clay winked at Johnny. "Say, John. Do you want to sleep with us, or will you be all right on your own?"

Johnny grinned. "Thanks a lot, it's a mighty tempting offer, but I think I'll go it alone."

"Ouch," Clay yelled.

"Whoa," Johnny said, jerking his head sideways in a failed attempt to avoid being hit by a flying pillow.

Susan bellowed, "It's not nice to make fun of people, you jerks."

Clay and Johnny leaped for her and pinned her to the couch, kissing her repeatedly all about the face and neck.

"Okay, okay, I give," Susan stammered, trying to get her breath. "Get off me you Big Lugs."

Clay led her up the stairs to a bedroom, one that she had chosen earlier. They showered and hit the sack; too tired to think of anything else. Susan held on to him for the entire night. And, ever so often she'd jump, as though someone or something had startled her.

Chapter 6

Sleep, peaceful sleep, finally came. As luck would have it, it didn't last very long. "Clay, wake up," Susan urged. "Somebody came in through the back door. They're in the kitchen."

He rolled over. "Don't worry about it, it's only Johnny."

"Darn it, Clay, it's not Johnny. I was just in the den and he's passed out on the couch."

Clay's eyes flew open, and he sprang from the bed. "Stay here, Babe, and lock the door until I get back."

A bloodcurdling scream echoed throughout the entire house.

Susan jumped. "My God, that's a woman screaming."

Clay stopped in his tracks. "C'mon, Susan, it's okay. I'll bet money, Jolene walked in on Johnny sleeping in the den."

Susan was red-faced. "Who the hell is Jolene?"

"C'mon, Susan, I'll introduce you. She works for the senator, and she probably came by to tidy up."

Susan finally smiled. "That's cool; we have a maid. Why didn't you tell me?"

Clay just kept walking. "Well, frankly, I didn't think about it until a second after I heard her scream."

When they got to the den, Johnny was trying desperately to hold a tall thin redhead in one hand and pulling his trousers up with the other. He wasn't having much luck with either one.

Clay and Susan started laughing; however, the two combatants were not amused.

"Let her go," Clay insisted. "She's a friend; she works for the senator."

"I'll release her if she'll stop biting me," he snarled.

Shoving her onto the couch he backed away pulling at his trousers, this time using both hands.

Jolene was livid. "Mr. Smith, I declare, I walk in and this black man is sprawled on the couch, obviously drunk. I scream, and he leaps up and grabs me. I didn't see your car in the garage, but a strange one there instead. What was I suppose to think? Anyway, he scared me silly."

Clay looked at Susan, then Johnny. "Yes, Jolene, I can see your point."

Clay tried to be serious; however, the irony of the situation made him grin noticeably. Johnny wasn't amused. He continued straightening his clothing, but Clay could see his apparent frustration.

"I'm glad you're enjoying this, Old Buddy," Johnny scowled.

Clay smiled. "Sorry, Partner, but she ended up in my bed three nights ago, almost the same way. Remind me to tell you about it sometime. Right now, I think we could use some coffee." He hesitated, "Susan, would you do the honors?"

Susan cut him a look. "Yeah, I'll make the coffee, but I want to hear more about the other night, and soon." She turned abruptly and headed toward the kitchen.

Johnny, who had been trying for some time now to find his second shoe, looked at Clay, with this strange expression on his face. "You know if I didn't know better I'd think she was jealous."

Clay just passed it off and began the introductions. "Dr. John Murphy, this is Jolene - - -"

"O'Dern, Jolene O'Dern. It is indeed a pleasure to meet you, Doctor. And, for the fifth time, I'm truly sorry for having bitten you. But, you can understand why a person would do such a thing. I mean, all things being the way they were."

Johnny smiled at her. "It's okay. I think I understood what you just said. But, I loved hearing you say it. Talk some more."

Jolene dropped her head. "Now, you're making fun of me."

"No I'm not," Johnny insisted. "I really like listening to your accent."

"Me too," Clay echoed.

Susan came out of the kitchen. "C'mon you three, the coffee's almost ready. Next time you can make the coffee, Miss Prissy, or whatever your name is." And, with that she whirled around and disappeared thru the door.

Johnny said, "Damn, Clay, I've never seen her like this. What's the problem?"

"I don't know," Clay replied. "But, you guys wait here for a minute. Let me talk to her alone."

Johnny through up his hands, "Take your time; I'll get better acquainted with Jolene. Maybe, she'll help me find my other shoe."

Clay entered the kitchen, Susan, was standing at the sink. Walking up behind her he put his arms around her waist. She started to move away, but he wouldn't let her go.

"I adore you, Susan, please don't be mad. What can I do to make you feel better?"

She twisted around in order to face him, tears streaming down her face. "I can still see Gidget and it's killing me. That is, if the crazy man don't get me first." She slid her arms free and encircled his neck. "Clay, please don't let them kill me, I'm so scared I can't think straight."

He kissed her gently. "I promise I will not rest until that bastard's dead. Susan, look at me."

She raised her head.

He looked deep into her eyes. "I will not leave you in anyone else's care. I will personally see to your welfare. I love you, Babe. And, for your information, nothing happened the other night. Jolene brought clean towels for my bathroom; it was dark in the room and I tackled her, nothing more." He paused, giving her time to think. "Look, Susan, I know that sexually you prefer women; but, tell me you're still my girl, and my dearest friend."

She wiped her eyes on his t-shirt. "You know how I feel about you. There will never be another *man* in my life."

He hugged her tightly. "Well, that's comforting. Now, may I bring the others in without you poisoning their coffee?"

Laughing heartily he crossed his arms in front of his face. She punched him hard, in the stomach.

As he started to get the others she reached for him once more. "You are the greatest, and I do love you, Spook-key."

Clay squeezed her hand. "Yeah, I know; me too. And have I told you how beautiful you look without make-up, and even before my morning coffee?"

She giggled. "Go on; get Johnny, and Miss Prissy."

"Susan!"

"I'm only kidding," she assured him.

He walked into the den; Johnny and Jolene were getting along handsomely.

Clay interrupted. "Jolene, I need to explain to you about Susan. She is very upset, but it has nothing to do with you. Actually, her very best girlfriend was killed two days ago, and she's having a really rough time right now. I hope you'll try to understand."

"Certainly, Sir, I fully understand," she replied. "Is there anything at all I can do to help her?"

"No," Clay answered. "Not now, but maybe later."

She snatched her coat from the sofa. "Well then, I'll be getting back to my duties. Ms. Lazar will need me for shopping this afternoon."

She allowed Johnny to help with her coat.

"Mr. Smith, I'll stop by on odd days to clean," she stated, and away she went.

Clay and Johnny went into the kitchen for some coffee.

Susan turned. "Look, Doc, I'm sorry I acted like a fool. Where'd she go? I wanted to apologize."

"Its okay, Babe, she had to get back. The senator's wife was waiting for her," Clay said, pouring the coffee. "Also, she said she would be back to clean on odd days. I guess that means Friday will be her next visit."

All three of them sat drinking coffee, and discussing the past and present situation. They talked about their times together with Gidget, and emotions were freed. They still didn't have all the answers, but they weren't about to stop looking.

Clay jumped to his feet. "Wait a minute, I'll be right back."

He headed toward the front of the house.

Sure enough, there it was. The white envelope was lying on the floor in the foyer. Shack had slid it under the door with some force. Nonetheless, he was true to his word.

Clay returned to the kitchen, note in hand.

"Is that the directions?" Johnny asked.

"I think so," Clay replied, as he tore open the envelope.

Susan looked up from her coffee. "Directions for what; are we going somewhere?"

Clay cut his eyes toward her. "You're not," he snapped. "I have in my hand the directions to the trailer where our would-be assassin lives. Now, I can put an end to this mess."

Johnny chimed in. "You mean we, don't you, Tonto?"

"Oh yeah, right, Kemo-saabe." He then paused while reading the note. "It says here that his flight arrives at nine thirty-five this evening. Johnny, would you go upstairs and shut the curtains in the middle bathroom window? I think we need to parlay with the sergeant."

Johnny set down his cup. "I'm on my way."

Clay explained everything to Susan. He thought she might need the signal sometime, if she were there alone. *God forbid!*

He reached for her and pulled her down on his lap. "Do you still love me?" he asked. "Did you know, you big bruiser, that I think about you all the time?"

"Yes," she replied, taking his hand and laying it over her heart. "Feel my heart beating; it does that every time I'm close to you."

Clay kissed her neck. "Maybe it beats so fast because I keep getting us in these life and death situations."

"Be serious, Clay. I do love you, enough to die for you. But, please don't ask me to prove it anytime soon, okay?"

Johnny came thundering down the stairs. "Well, Master, the deed is done. Our chief slave, Master Shack, will be here momentarily."

Clay stood, lifting Susan in his arms. "Johnny, you have so many sides to your humor; regretfully, that's not one of my favorites."

"Sorry, Old Chum, a bit of bad taste on my part. I shall go immediately and wash me mouth out with a scrub bar."

Clay placed Susan in the chair. "Not bad, Old Pal. However, it could use a little polishing."

Susan stared up at the both of them. "I gotta hand it to you guys. With death staring us in the face you always keep it in perspective. God, I adore you two."

Clay and Johnny looked at her and then at each other, as if preplanned. "We love you too, Boobie."

"I'm sure glad the senator can't see us now," Clay said, trying to regain a bit of decorum.

Johnny's eyes widened. "Hell, I'm just thankful my patients aren't watching."

The doorbell was a welcome interruption.

Johnny spun around. "I'll get it."

It was, of course, Sergeant Shackelford. After giving the sergeant time to step out of his over-shoes and remove his overcoat, the meeting began in earnest.

Clay said, "Well, Guys, any comments before we get to it?"

Johnny spoke. "I have a question. Do we wanna take this guy alive, or are we simply gonna cancel his ticket?"

"I'd like to talk to him," Clay replied. "Unfortunately, that may not be the wisest move. What do you think, Shack?"

"The guy is lethal, and he's smart. I don't think we should take any chances."

Clay looked at Johnny who was nodding his agreement. "Then, let's just go to his trailer and wait for him to come home. I don't think he'll be expecting us to show up at his place. Anyway, a good offense is better than a strong defense, and he'll be expecting us to be on the defensive. That gives us the edge we need; don't you think?"

Johnny was squirming in his seat. "Question number two, how do we know he's the only one, there may be others? I don't wanna sit around waiting for someone to shoot me. How do we find out?"

Clay had this disgusted look on his face. "Shit, I guess we have only one choice, we gotta take him alive."

Shack's eyes widened. "Doc, do you have anymore of that stuff we used on those guys at the hotel?"

"No, but I can get some pretty damn quick." He looked at Clay. "Do you think I should, Old Buddy?"

"Yeah, I think so," Clay replied. "We got less than six hours until he returns and I don't think we'll have a better opportunity. Shack, do you have your car here?"

"Sure, Clay, it's at the senator's."

Clay was on a roll. "Okay, Johnny, you take our car and get what we need. How long will it take?"

"Thirty minutes to the hospital at Bethesda, and another hour to get what I'm after and drive back. I should make it back here by six."

"That should work." Clay replied. "Shack and I will have our plan in place and we'll be ready when you get here. Get moving, Partner."

Johnny grabbed the car keys from the counter. "I'm on my way."

"Hey, Shack, you wanna beer?" Clay asked. "I'm gonna fix me a drink."

"I'd love one, thanks."

Clay returned in a moment with his drink, and walked to the fridge for the beer. "Here you go, My Friend."

The sergeant smiled. "Thanks; I hope the senator won't mind, I am still on duty."

"I'm sure he won't mind." Clay hesitated, "Boy, I sure wish he was here, I'd like to have his input. I'll bet he's still at the office, isn't he?"

Shack turned in his chair. "No, Clay, he's home. If he were gone I'd be with him."

"Right you are, My Friend. Let me try his private line."

Clay dialed the number. "Good evening, Senator, I hope I didn't disturb your dinner."

"Clay, my boy, it sure is good to hear your voice. What can I do for you? And, no, no interruption at all, talk to me."

"We're putting a plan together to take down this Bolen character and I thought you might wish to be involved. Can we come there, or would you rather come here?"

"You come to me," the senator answered. "And come the back way. I'll open the patio door. Is the sergeant coming too?"

"Yes, Sir," Clay replied. "Give us five minutes."

Clay walked into the den where Susan had fallen asleep on the couch. Being very careful not to alarm her, he knelt, and gently touched her shoulder.

"Susan, it's me. Johnny has gone to the hospital and Shack and I need to go to the senator's for an hour or less. Will you be okay?"

Carl R. Smith

She came immediately to her feet. "Don't you leave me here alone. I'm going with you."

Clay knew better than to argue.

They quickly donned their winter garb and down the hedge-way between houses they went. The Moon was high in the sky, and for security, their only light. The ground was frozen, and the snow crunched under their feet making more noise than Clay had hoped for. They walked single file, with Shack in front, Susan in the middle, and Clay bringing up the rear guard. In less than two minutes they were directly behind the senator's house. And, in three, they were through the patio door and standing in the kitchen. Jolene greeted them, looking somewhat agitated at the slush and watery mess they had created.

"Get out of those rubbers afore you move another meter," she said, sharply. "Well, Mr. Smith, I see you brought the whole gang."

The senator's wife entered the room. "Jolene, where's your manners. Hush now, and take their wraps."

Jolene smiled warmly at Clay, ignoring the others. "Yes Ma'am."

Ms. Lazar took Clay's arm. "Introduce me to this big beautiful young lady."

Clay flushed. "Sorry. This is Susan Weidenberg. Susan, this is the senator's lovely wife, Patricia."

Susan smiled broadly. "It's a real pleasure to meet you, Ms. Lazar. Your husband is a remarkable man, but I'm sure you already know that."

Ms. Lazars' smile was just as fetching. "Yes, he is, and call me Trish, please." She turned her attention toward the men, her hand still resting on

Clay's arm. "Bob's waiting for you gentlemen in the den. You may go on in."

Susan grabbed Clay's other arm. "If you don't mind I'll just stay in the kitchen? That is, if you don't mind, Trish?"

Patricia flashed a huge smile. "Of course not, My Dear, we'll have a little chat."

Vacating Clay's arm and taking Susan's; Ms. Lazar was still talking as the men left the room headed for the den.

The senator rose from his desk as the two men entered the room, extending his hand to Clay.

"I'm always glad to see you, Clay. What can I do for you?"

"Senator, we thought it would be wise to keep you informed. We're about to bring down the hired assassin and we wanted to give you a chance to have some input. That is, if you wish to be involved."

"I'd certainly like to know your plan," he replied.

"Well, Sir, we know he's coming in on a flight from Chicago at nine thirty-five this evening, and we intend to be at his place when he arrives home to give him a hardy welcome." Clay paused to take a breath before continuing. "I plan to take him alive, at least until we can ask him a few questions. But, make no mistake about it; he will die, as slowly and painfully as did Gidget." Clay's voice was shaking. "That's a promise. What he did to her was beyond cruel."

The senator appeared a little uneasy with Clay's words; however, he understood the emotion, and he wasn't about to interfere. "Do you think there are others on the payroll?"

"We don't know, Sir, but we simply cannot afford to overlook the possibility."

Shack raised his hand as though he were asking for permission to speak. "I have reason to believe this Steve Bolen character is the only one. Although, I do know for sure they are training two new men at Fort Bragg, North Carolina. I haven't met them, but I trust my sources, Senator."

The senator half smiled. "That's good enough for me Sergeant."

The senator's 'vote of confidence' made the sergeant stand a little straighter, and his chest expanded considerably. "Thank you, Sir. Hopefully I'll know a lot more real soon. And, when I know, we'll all know."

Clay, looked at the senator, thumbs raised. "That's why I keep him around. He's invaluable, and he has great taste in friends."

The senator laughed, and Shack, blushed.

The senator lit his cigar. "You know, Guys, we make a great team. By the way, where's Dr. Murphy?"

"He's making a quick trip to Bethesda for some supplies," Clay explained. "You know, Sir, a little juice to make the tongue loose."

The senator nodded. "I think I understand; however, if I'm wrong please allow me to be, blissfully ignorant."

"You got it, Sir, I mean - - -"

The senator interrupted. "Its okay, Clay, I know what you mean."

Clay looked just the least bit flustered. "Senator, I have the greatest respect for you, and I would never - - -"

"Hush now." The senator said, coming out of his chair. "I'm going to the bathroom; Clay, make us both a drink. And, Sergeant, I'll stop in the kitchen and bring you a beer. We don't keep any in here, but I'm quite sure there's some in the fridge." The senator turned and looked at the both of them. "My wife likes to have one from time to time, and I think Jolene sneaks one to her room at night. But, hell, no big deal, right Guys?"

"Yes, Sir," Clay replied, heading for the bar.

In the senator's absence, and while still mixing the drinks, Clay turned to Shack. "Ever say anything really dumb?"

Shack looked at him, "Only when I open my mouth."

Clay almost dropped the glasses. "That's pretty clever; you're beginning to develop quite a sense of humor."

The sergeant adjusted himself. "Yeah, I'm a million laughs."

The senator walked back into the room, carrying a rather large mug and a bottle of beer. "Here you are, Sergeant. I hope it's your brand."

"If its beer, it's my brand. Thank you, Sir."

Clay interrupted. "Senator, we're gonna have to drink fast. Johnny should be back any minute and he'll freak out if he can't find us."

The senator re-lit his cigar. "No problem, just call me when it's over I don't care what time it is."

Clay gulped his drink as the sergeant was finishing his beer, never even using the mug.

"Are you ready, Shack?"

"You betcha," he answered. Then focusing on the senator, he continued. "Thanks again, Sir, for the beer."

The senator was still standing. "You're more than welcome, Sergeant. And, Clay, you fellows be really careful."

"You can count on it, Sir," Clay replied, sitting his glass on the bar.

The senator walked with the two of them toward the kitchen. Putting his arm around Clay's shoulder, he lean close, almost whispering. "You are well aware, My Boy, if anything bad happens to you I'm as good as dead."

Clay nudged him, playfully. "With that in mind, Sir, I'll be even more careful."

The senator flashed his most infectious smile. "Thanks, Clay, I know you will."

As the two men walked into the kitchen, they could hear the ladies yakking away, seemingly having a swell time, all things considered.

Clay grabbed Susan and kissed her on the forehead. "I ask you Gentlemen, have you ever seen two more beautiful women?"

The senator smiled, and Shack just nodded.

Before anyone could muster a response, Clay continued. "Ms. Lazar."

"Patricia," she reminded.

Clay looked at her. "Patricia, would you be kind enough to allow Susan to stay here with the two of you until we return? I'm sure she doesn't wish to be alone in that huge house. And, if we're unable to return before bedtime - - -."

"Not another word, Clay. I would be delighted to have her spend the night."

Susan looked around the room. "Are you sure it's no bother?"

"Bother? Don't be silly." Patricia stopped and turned her attention to Clay, and then back to Susan. "Susan, we both know full well, whatever Clay wants he can most assuredly have. Isn't that right, Bob?"

The senator attempted to roll with the punch. "Certainly, Dear."

Clay could see that even the sergeant was suddenly uncomfortable. He reached for Susan's hand. "C'mon, Babe, you probably need some things from the house."

"Well, I would like to get my purse, it contains the only make-up I have with me; thanks to you."

Clay pulled her to her feet, looking at Patricia. "I'll have her back in thirty minutes or so."

Patricia stood also. "Very well then, I'll have Jolene freshen-up the guestroom."

Clay, Susan, and Shack were halfway back to the house before Susan broke the silence. "What the hell was that all about?"

"Damned if I know," Clay replied, picking up the pace. "Ms. Lazar is an unusual woman."

This time bringing up the rear, Shack was totally silent.

Clay slowed. "Be careful, you two, it's very icy here."

"I got you," Shack yelled.

Clay wheeled around in time to see Susan come dangerously close to busting her rump. Taking her hand, Clay, helped steady the two of them. "You okay, Shack?"

"I'm fine," the sergeant replied. "I'm just glad to be of service."

Clay stepped back, while watching Susan's response.

"What? What are you grinning about?" she whined. "Did you want me to fall on my ass?"

"Of course not," Clay responded. "I just had a flashback to one of the greatest days of my life, remember?"

It was as though a light went on in her head. "Sure I remember, Silly, the day we met. But, that time I was covered in mud and snow."

Clay laughed. "Yeah, but you were the prettiest 'mud-pie' I ever saw."

"Oh, Clay. . . "

"Susan!"

Shack couldn't help cracking up as he helplessly watch them go down.

Susan screeched. "Now we're both a couple of 'mud-pies'."

"Yeah, yeah, anything you say, Babe," Clay grumbled. "But, would you please remove your boney elbow from my chest?"

"I'm trying to," she replied. "Sergeant, would you stop laughing long enough to give me a hand?"

"Yes, Ma'am, but I'd give anything to have a camera. I declare, I've never ever seen Clay when he wasn't in total control. Sorry, Clay, but if you were in my shoes you'd be laughing too."

"You're right, we must look pretty silly."

With everyone working together they finally reached the house, a little dirtier and little wetter, but in a much better mood.

Susan hurried upstairs to secure the few items she needed. Clay went to the back bedroom to change, and Shack headed for the fridge and a cold beer.

"Hey, Shack, would you be kind enough to escort Susan back to the senator's? I need some quiet time. Anyway, Johnny should be back shortly."

Susan and Clay walked into the kitchen at the same time. Susan was carrying the little bag she had borrowed from her friend at work. "I'm ready. But, I'm not walking back over there by myself."

"No problem, Shack's going with you. And, I'm gonna wait here for Johnny." Clay's hands went to his hips, and he cocked his head to the side. "Stop looking at me like that; you know I have a job to do."

"Yeah I know," she replied, "But I - - -"

"Look," he interrupted. "I'll come and get you first thing in the morning, I promise. Okay?"

Susan looked at him with irritation etched on her pretty face. "I guess it'll have to be, now won't it?"

Shack was sipping his beer and taking everything in, but he looked a might uncomfortable.

Clay reached for her and motioned toward the den. "Would you excuse us for a minute, Shack?"

"Oh sure," he replied, not knowing whether to stand, sit, or head in the other direction. He remained still.

When they were alone in the den, Clay took her bag and set it on the sofa. Sliding his arms inside her coat he pulled her close. "Love, stop fretting, if I get back in time I'll come and get you tonight; however, it will probably be too late."

He brushed her lips with his, and their two bodies melted together.

"Clay, I've missed you so much, even my fingernails hurt. If anything happens to you, I swear, I'll kill myself."

He looked deep into her eyes. "Well then, I really will have to be careful."

Her gazed never changed. "Please, make that bastard suffer for what he did to Gidget."

Clay gave her a half smile. "You can count on it, Doll Face."

When they re-entered the kitchen Shack was on his second beer. "Are you ready, Miss Susan?"

"Yes I am, C'mon Sergeant, and I'll try not to fall on you."

Shack grinned. "Oh darn, that Clay gets all the luck." Suddenly realizing how that must have sounded, he flushed red, and quickly headed for the door.

Clay glanced at Susan. "Way to go, Shack, I knew you had it in ya."

Susan flashed a huge grin. "Hush Clay, you're just making it worse."

She kissed Clay on the cheek, biting him gently, and then she dutifully followed the sergeant out the door.

Chapter 7

Susan and the sergeant had left and Clay was alone; the immediate silence was almost deafening. Clay shook his head and headed for the den. After mixing himself a drink he settled into the overstuffed chair by the fireplace. Closing his eyes he made a concerned effort to clear his otherwise cluttered mind. *God, it seems that I only remember to speak to you when I'm in trouble. You know how tired I am, and you know I don't want to kill anymore, but I don't know how to make this stop. If you can see your way clear to lend me a hand I sure would be grateful. Thanks, Big Guy, I think I just heard Johnny coming in.*

He headed toward the garage and met Johnny coming in. "How'd it go, Partner, were you able to get the stuff we need?"

"Sure enough, Old Buddy."

Clay stepped away from the door. "Good man."

Johnny poked him in the ribs. "Fix me one of whatever you're having, I got to pee something fierce."

Carl R. Smith

Clay smacked him on the back of the head as he passed. "Hell, don't let me stop you."

The doorbell sounded.

"I'll get it," Johnny yelled. "You make the drinks."

In minutes, and once Johnny had answered nature's call, the three of them were together in the den polishing their plan, each with a fresh drink in hand, even a Schlitz for the sergeant. Shack's favorite beer was a cold Pabst Blue Ribbon; however, Schlitz was the next best thing, and hell, it was free.

Clay began. "I want to get to this man's place with at least thirty minutes to spare, that way if something has to be changed it won't cause a major problem."

Shack was fidgeting.

"What is it Sergeant?" Johnny asked. "Speak your mind."

"Well, I was thinking. This guy's pretty thorough, and we should probably approach his place from the woods. Anyhow, Doctor, I don't think those shoes are gonna work."

Johnny looked down. "Damn, I didn't bring any boots."

"I saw some boots in the ambassador's closet," Clay exclaimed. "Let's go check it out, we might get lucky."

Although, the boots were a size to small, his overshoes did fit. Actually, Johnny could only wear them as a regular shoe.

"This ain't gonna work, Clay."

"Yes it will," Clay asserted.

Cutting the Fringe

"Here, Doc, try this," Shack insisted, tossing him a handful of socks. "Put on as many pairs as will fit comfortably."

"Yeah, that works,' he said smiling. "That was a good idea, Shack."

In record time they were warmly dressed and on the way. Now, it became really quiet, and, as had happened many times before they knew what each other was thinking, or they were at least satisfied believing they did.

Shack gave some needed direction and that broke the silence. It was nearly nine PM when they reached a secluded area in the woods. They hid the vehicle as best they could and proceeded on foot the last two hundred yards.

Shack reached out and touched Clay's arm which brought everyone to a halt. "This place is most likely booby-trapped. What's say, let's spread out and come back together at the oil drum, there, at the end of the trailer?"

"Good plan," Clay agreed.

Panic etched Johnny's face. "I'm sorry; Guys, but I have no idea what to look for."

Clay took his arm. "It's alright, Partner, you follow me. Step where I step, and only touch the things I touch, got it?"

"Got it," he replied.

Clay glanced at Shack and they nodded their understanding.

At ten past nine PM they were back together at the east end of the trailer.

"Did you see anything, Sergeant?" Clay inquired.

"There's infra-red criss-crossing the driveway; otherwise, nothing. You?"

"Nothing at all," Clay replied.

The two of them looked at Johnny. He extended both hands, palms up, as if to say, I'm just here for the ride.

Clay pulled Shack close to him. "I'm going in through the vent in the roof. Give me a hand."

Shack boosted him onto the drum and in seconds Clay disappeared on the roof. He returned in a minute or so to inform them that the coast was clear and that he was going inside. Both Johnny and Shack knew enough to wait in silence.

Fifteen minutes passed.

Shack tugged at Johnny's sleeve. "Give me a boost. I'm going inside, something's gotta be wrong."

"Wait," Johnny said. "Clay knows more about electronics and wiring than most electricians, he learned from a master. Shush, I think I hear him."

Clay appeared, head hanging off the roof. "Shack, flip the switch on the fuse box. I've disconnected the battery back-up, so we're safe for now."

"Okay, Boss. Do you want me to come in?"

"No, I'm fine. Give me another five minutes and I'm coming out."

Five, six, seven minutes passed, and then finally Clay appeared once again. When he was on the ground he began to explain what he had done.

Short of finishing, he said, "Let's get a safe distance from this place and I'll explain everything."

They retreated some fifty yards before any more talking took place.

Clay turned. "Okay, I think we're far enough."

Shack's eyes were dancing with excitement. "What'd you do? Tell me!"

"When this Steve Bolen character enters the trailer and turns off the alarm, it will reactivate in five seconds. I rewired everything, including the hatch; therefore, if he attempts to open the doors or the windows once he's inside, boom, and then its good-bye Steve." Clay took a deep breath. "Johnny, that tape recorder you gave me really came in handy."

Johnny looked puzzled. "What, you left him a message?"

"I sure did. I told him if he touched anything he would die. I further told him that if he wanted to negotiate he should turn the table lamp on and off three times, and if he did so I would come to talk, and maybe we could work something out."

Shack couldn't hold back any longer. "Suppose he opens the front door before hearing everything?"

"Then, boom, he's dead."

"Oh shit," Johnny screeched. "Here comes someone."

"I hope it's him," Shack answered, rather matter-of-factly. "I'm freezing my ass off. Johnny and I have been outside for half an hour."

"I know," Clay acknowledged. "It won't be much longer. And, if he doesn't play along so we can warm-up inside, then there'll be a nice warm fire outside, real close by."

Shack laughed out loud. "Sorry, Guys," he muttered. "I got carried away, It won't happen again."

"Is that him, Shack?" Clay asked.

Shack strained to get the best possible look. "Yep, that's Steve," he replied, softly.

Clay stood perfectly still refusing to allow any movement, but inside he was frantically pacing back and forth.

Johnny grabbed Clay's coat. "He's going inside, oh shit."

Nobody moved a muscle.

"How long is the taped message?" Johnny whispered. "Never mind, there goes the lamp. Dang, I'm not cold anymore."

Shack said, "What now, Clay?"

"I'm going in, you guys, cover me."

Johnny grabbed him. "Are you nuts, you'll blow the place?"

"No I won't," Clay explained. "I can open the door from the outside; he just can't open it from the inside."

Shack looked Clay right in the eye. "I hope you're right."

"Me too," Clay replied, as he walked forward.

The infra-red disabled, Clay moved within ten feet of the door.

"Steve, I'm gonna open the door. You had best be standing in the middle of the room with your trousers around your ankles and your arms extended outward, palms up. If you even take a deep breath you're a dead man, do you understand?"

"I understand," he yelled. "Go ahead, open the door."

Clay looked over his left shoulder, giving Johnny and Shack the prearranged signal. When he had gotten into place, he motioned for Johnny. "Hey, Partner, come here," he yelled, plenty loud enough for Steve to hear. He continued yelling. "The rest of you guys stay back. If anything goes wrong, or if this asshole makes a bad move, then, don't waste anytime, blow this place to hell."

Shack and Johnny signaled their understanding.

Clay turned his attention to Steve. "Okay, I'm coming in, Mr. Bolen, don't do anything dumb."

As Clay reached for the door he could easily feel the sweat running down the center of his back, and he could hear Johnny's breathing some ten feet away. Suddenly he swung around.

"Hey, Partner," he whispered, "Move over by that big oak. If I'm wrong I don't wanna kill anybody else."

Johnny looked cold and angry. "Bullshit, I'm staying right here. Open that door, and if that bastard moves I'm gonna put a bullet right between his eyes."

Steve hollered, frantically, "Hey, Fellows, don't shoot, I'm not moving."

Clay opened the door. Steve was standing at attention in the middle of the living room, trousers down around his ankles.

Clay turned toward Johnny. "Throw me your handcuffs."

Johnny threw up his hands. "Hell, Clay, I don't have any handcuffs."

"I have some," Steve yelled. "They're in the floor with my belt."

Clay said. "Pick them up slowly. Put one end around the arm of that chair and the other around your right wrist."

"Okay, okay," he replied, following Clay's instructions to the letter. "There, it's done, you satisfied?"

Carl R. Smith

Clay didn't respond, but instead he walked into the room and put his handcuffs on Steve's left wrist and the other chair arm. Johnny proceeded to wrap Steve's ankles with tape and then he secured them to the chair.

Clay returned to the opened door. "Sergeant, flip the switch on the fuse box and then come inside. Be sure it clicks."

Shack was already on the move, and in minutes he had done what Clay had asked, and quickly, he was in the living room with the other three.

Shack looked at Steve all trussed up like a badly wrapped package. "I tried to tell you not to go up against Clay, but you wouldn't listen."

Steve said, "I don't know what you're talking about. I haven't done anything."

Clay put up his hand to the sergeant, as if to say, I'll take it from here.

"Okay, Mr. Bolen," Clay began. "You say you've done nothing, well, the only way you're gonna see another day is to tell us the absolute truth. And, if you tell me one lie it will take you painful hours to die."

"What do you want to know?" he pleaded.

Clay said, "Who are you working for? And, remember what I told you about lying."

"Yeah, I remember," he replied, sweat dripping from the end of his nose.

Clay got this disgusted look on his face. "Well, who are you working for?"

"I work for GM."

Clay slapped his open palm against his chest. "That's it. Johnny get the medicine bag."

"What are you gonna do?" Steve cried.

Clay answered him. "I'm gonna start by cutting off your toes. How's that, you piece of shit."

"But why? I didn't lie to you. I work for GM. Please, that's all I know. I never heard anyone call him anything other than GM."

"Bullshit," Clay recoiled.

Shack interrupted. "Clay, I think he means General Mathews. That must be GM."

The sweat on Steve's brow had damn near turned to blood. "Please, I swear I'm telling the truth. We dealt mostly by telephone, and the first time I met him in person was in Chicago. That little girl; I think her name was Gidget, she was his stepdaughter. He told me that one of the reasons he married her mother was to get into that little girl's pants and boy did he ever. But, I got to tell you no matter what he did to her she wouldn't tell him anything. She wouldn't give him any satisfaction at all."

Clay's face was burning. "My God, did you molest her too?"

"No. But, I did everything I knew to make her talk. However, she was loyal to the end. Actually she was still alive when we left her, but I'm sure she didn't last very long."

Clay turned again to Johnny. "Give him the needle. I think he's telling the truth, but I wanna be sure."

Steve jerked back and forth. "What are you putting in my arm?"

Johnny grabbed him by the chin and yanked his face around. "This won't hurt you, you, son of a bitch."

In less than a minute Steve had gone limp. Clay rephrased the questions and got basically the same answers. Although, when Clay asked him again if he, Steve Bolen, had raped Gidget, his answer was affirmative. "She was incredible," he replied, "And the hottest little woman I've ever seen. But indeed she had told them nothing."

Clay was satisfied. And the fact that Steve had been dishonest made what came next much easier.

"What do we do now?" Johnny asked.

Clay answered, "Take off the handcuffs and remove the tape. Shack you go outside and flip the switch at the fuse box, but wait until Johnny and I get outside."

Shack said, "Are you gonna kill him, Clay, or are we simply gonna leave him here like this?"

"We'll talk outside," Clay urged.

"He's coming around," Johnny commented.

Clay got right in Steve's face. "You left my friend to die a horrible death; now, you will be repaid in kind." Clay took a deep breath. "You have three minutes to live. If I were you I'd make my peace with God, but, you do as you wish."

Steve tried to respond physically, but Clay cold-cocked him. "See you in hell asshole."

"C'mon, Clay," Johnny yelled.

"I'm coming," Clay responded. "You Guys, head for the car."

When they were again assembled in front of the car, Clay began to explain.

"There's no escape. He has about a minute and a half to live. And there's enough explosives in there to send parts of him to the Moon."

"My God," Johnny exclaimed.

Shack looked at Johnny, then he reached for Clay's arm. "Let's get outta here."

They jumped in the car, and, almost simultaneously, the forest suddenly became alive with color; however, in seconds they could only see a yellow haze in the distance.

No one spoke until they were pulling into the driveway back at the Ambassador's residence.

Johnny couldn't hold back any longer. "I knew Gidget wouldn't betray us."

Clay nodded, "Me too."

Soon they were warming themselves before the fireplace in the den.

Johnny started mixing drinks as Shack headed to the kitchen for a beer. When he returned with his drink the room was still silent, not one of the three of them wanted to look at the others. Finally, Clay broke the silence.

"Say something, Shack. What's on your mind?"

"I was simply wondering how many more of them are still out there."

Johnny raised his head. "Do you think there are others?"

"Probably," Shack replied.

"Geez, I thought this was the end of it," Johnny mumbled, hanging his head once again.

"Cheer up, Guys, there's a light at the end of this tunnel. I grant you it may only be a fifteen watt bulb, but it's there," Clay testified, hoisting his glass.

Johnny stood and walked over to the mantel and helped himself to his customary cigar. "Want one, Old Buddy?" he asked.

"Why not," Clay replied.

Shack spoke-up, "Hell, give me one too. We're celebrating, right?"

"Damn right!" Clay and Johnny answered, simultaneously.

Clay lit his cigar and then offered a light to the others. "I wonder if the senator's still up. We should probably let him know what's taken place."

Shack came immediately to his feet. "I'm sleeping in the spare room over the garage, let me go over there and see if anyone is stirring." He started to gather his belongings. "I'll let you know something real soon, okay?"

"Yeah, that'd be great," Clay replied. "Be careful, My Friend."

Shack smiled, "No sweat."

"I mean it, you be careful," Clay repeated.

Shack became very soulful. "Don't worry, Clay, I'll be fine."

And, with that said he was gone.

Johnny went over and flipped his cigar ashes into the fireplace. "You know, Old Buddy, you're something else."

"What does that mean?"

"Nothing," Johnny replied. "Want another drink?"

"Sure, I could take another, but if I don't get something in my stomach pretty soon I'm gonna regret it. Have you eaten anything?"

Cutting the Fringe

Johnny looked really thoughtful. "No, as a matter of fact, I don't remember when I ate last." Johnny hesitated, "We're in a lot of trouble, you know that don't you?"

"What do you mean a lot of trouble?"

Johnny handed him a drink. "There's not a Waffle House within five miles."

That's just what Clay needed to hear. The uncomfortable feelings began melting away. They laughed, and they laughed.

"You know, Johnny; somehow, one of us always seems to know the right thing to say, and when. I'm glad it was your turn."

The telephone rang. Johnny grabbed it.

"Hello. Sure, we'll be right there. Thanks."

Clay was waiting patiently, sipping his drink.

Johnny replaced the receiver. "The senator is up and quite anxious to hear about tonight."

"Let's go," Clay said, grabbing his coat and throwing Johnny his.

"Let me put this cigar out," Johnny remarked. "Oh crap, I'll just throw it in the snow. They won't find it until spring anyhow."

Clay locked the door behind them and they went trudging through the snow once again. Shack met them at the back door.

"Take those shoes off and leave them on the rug," Shack instructed.

The house seemed unusually quiet as they made their way to the study. The senator was all smiles.

"That was pretty quick," he surmised. "Did everything go as planned?"

Clay took the senator's hand. "Yes, Sir, everything went smoothly. The bastard's dead and I'm fairly certain they learned nothing from Gidget."

The senator returned to his chair and motioned for everyone to sit. "Clay, do you think there are others?"

Clay looked a bit grim. "The Sergeant seems to think so and I've never known him to be wrong, and he's sure not one to exaggerate."

The senator nodded in Shack's direction. "Well, Sergeant, why do you feel that way?"

Still bursting with pride from Clay's last remark the sergeant adjusted himself in his chair. "Sir, scuttlebutt has that they have been training two more young men and I have that on good authority. I thought that Bolen character was the only one, but now I'm not too sure. And, Sir, I trust my sources."

For a moment no one said anything. It was as though they were afraid to take the mantel of responsibility, even the senator. They just continued to look at one another.

Clay cleared his throat. "Senator, I think it's about time for me to have a face to face with General Matthews. Do you know where he lives?"

"Are you going to his house?" the senator asked.

"Yes, Sir, that's the general idea, if you'll forgive the pun."

Johnny said, nervously, "Are you crazy? Clay, I don't think that's a very good idea."

Shack chimed in. "I agree with Johnny. What purpose would it serve?"

Clay shuffled his feet, uncomfortably. "Okay, but I think we need to be on the offensive, and he won't be expecting that."

The senator popped out of his chair. "Wait a minute, Guys, he may be right. A late night call at the general's residence could really get his attention."

"Hell, Senator," Johnny injected, "I think we already have his attention."

The senator moved to the bar. "Yes, Doctor, you're correct; however, we are running for our lives because of this man. I think it's about time he realizes we can touch his life just as quickly and severely as he can touch ours."

Clay jumped in. "Exactly, I'll make him understand that if he even so much as looks our way ever again, I'll kill him, his family, and all his friends, if he has any. That should give him something to think about."

Johnny could hardly wait to speak. "Alright, I understand. Are you saying, in so many words, that if he leaves us alone, we'll leave him alone?"

"Yes, that's what I intend to tell him. Although, you know that's not what I really mean. Look, I'm just trying to save a few lives here and hopefully make everyone sleep a little easier at night."

"I got it," Johnny replied.

The senator went shuffling through some papers. "Clay, I thought I had the addresses of the whole bunch here, but it must be at the office. I'll get it for you tomorrow."

"That's good, Senator, I'm too tired to do it tonight anyhow."

That's just what the group needed. Now they all got a good chuckle and new drinks for everyone.

"Senator," Johnny said, "May I have one of those great cigars Clay's always bragging about?"

"Certainly," the senator replied. "Would you like one, Clay? How about you Sergeant?"

"Not for me," Shack answered, "I've already had my allotment this year; anyhow, I think those things will stunt your growth."

The senator glanced at him. "I guess we should have thought about that a long time ago."

Cigars lit, they gathered around the fireplace and Clay began giving out the marching orders for the next day. The senator was to get the addresses for as many of the remaining Ten Little Indians as could be obtained easily. Shack was to find out as much as he could about any other assassins still in training, and Johnny was told to get some well deserved rest. And Clay was to pay Tim Siler a call. Mr. Siler was a reporter for the Washington Post, and had played an integral part in their last assignment.

Tim and Clay had become quite close over the last few months.

The senator began to yawn. "Sorry, Guys, it's been a long day for everybody. I suggest we meet back here tomorrow night at eight."

Clay stood, "Okay, Men, let's call it a night."

Everyone agreed.

On the way out Clay asked the senator if it would be okay for him to visit the guest bedroom. He wanted to say goodnight to Susan. After receiving an affirmative answer he told Johnny not to wait up for him.

Chapter 8

The guest bedroom was rather cold, but Susan was nestled under a mountain of covers. Clay knelt beside the bed before speaking so he wouldn't frighten her.

"Hey, Babe, it's me," he said, softly touching her gently on the arm. "I just wanted to kiss you goodnight and let you know we were back, safe and sound."

She reached for him and began pulling him onto the bed beside her. "Oh, Clay, hold me, I've missed you so."

Without hesitation, he slid out of his shoes and under the covers. Susan was as warm as a good radiator on a cold winter's morning. Cuddling next to her he began to nibble on the back of her neck.

"Clay, you know that drives me crazy."

"I know," he replied. "That's why I'm doing it. Love, you drive me crazy, and I have missed being close to you."

She turned to face him. "Clay, you have your clothes on. It'd be more fun if you took them off."

Frantically, she began helping him. As he was undressing, she slid her soft yet strong hands down his chest ever searching for his manhood. It had been so long he was about to explode.

Susan knew exactly what to do, and before he could gasp for air once more she was taking him. When the explosion occurred she was well prepared and eager to taste him once more.

Clay's body stiffened, and after what seemed like forever he collapsed.

"Susan, you are the most amazing woman; give me a minute and I'll show you just how amazing."

Susan giggled, "I love to taste your essence. You're so strong and beautiful it's almost overwhelming. That's the one time I know I'm in complete control, and the rush is incredible."

Clay kissed the end of her nose. "How many times must I tell you girl; men aren't beautiful - - -"

"Well, you are," she insisted.

His hands were exploring every part of her body, stopping only to give pleasure, and then exploring further. He began tasting her throat, her shoulders, her breast, and then her taut stomach. Gently rolling her over he started down her back. She would move slightly, from time to time, gulping little bits of air. When he reached the back of her knees she began to moan. She had gorgeous feet, and Clay lingered there for a very long time, giving every toe a modicum of attention. He had learned that the foot, properly treated, could give enormous pleasure.

Now it was his turn to taste the 'essence of Susan' and he loved it maybe even more than she did. In moments, she was almost crawling up the wall backwards. After her third or fourth explosion their lips met. Softly searching each other they kissed, like eating marshmallows and sucking on a Popsicle all at the same time.

"Clay, I declare, I love you with all my heart. I could stay with you forever."

He kissed her eyelids and the bridge of her nose. "Maybe we should give that some serious thought. There is no one on the face of this earth I would rather be with. Would you have my child?" he kidded.

Susan wrapped her arms around him. "Clay, don't joke about that; you know I want a child. Oh my God, that would have to be the most beautiful child ever."

"You're right, Love, as long as it looked exactly like you."

Susan was reaching for him again and he was more than ready. They came together with great precision, and as he looked down at her and gazed deeply into her eyes he knew she adored him.

As the pinnacle came for the two of them they collapsed from sheer exhaustion. They lay there caressing each other for the longest time. Susan snuggled closer, head on his shoulder.

"You are as soft and as gentle as any woman, and then, oh my God, then, you capture me like a beast. And then you treat me with the utmost respect; what more could a woman want?"

Clay kissed her on the top of the head. "Yeah, I'm the greatest," he whispered. "And you, Babe, are incredible. Now that we've visited the mutual admiration society together, let's get some sleep, okay?"

"Yes, Sir," Susan replied. "And, Clay, thanks for coming to me tonight, I really needed you."

"Me too," he replied.

Suddenly he sat up. "Susan, I think we better go home and sleep. Johnny will be worried if he wakes up and no one's there. Do you mind the walk in the cold?"

She put her arms around him from the back. "No, Baby, I don't mind; anyway, you're probably right. Let me find my clothes."

They both dressed quickly, and Susan left a note for Ms. Lazar. In less than ten minutes they were outside in the snow freezing their buns off.

Clay took her firmly by the hand. "Let's try not to fall this time."

Susan grabbed some snow with her right hand and slapped him in the chest. He let go of her hand and attacked, snowball in each hand. He missed with both. She had by this time reloaded, and with gusto she took the shot. Bull's eye!

Clay's aim being what it was he went for the takedown. They went sprawling in the soft snow.

"Okay, okay, I give," she screamed.

He kissed her passionately and they began to regain their composure

"I love you, Clay Smith," she exclaimed. "Let's get indoors, before we both freeze to death."

"I love you too, c'mon."

As they gained their footing once more and turned homeward, a snowball came from the darkness and hit him right in the stomach.

"What the hell was that?" he yelled.

Just then another went whizzing by his ear.

"You never were much in a snowball fight," Johnny yelled, as he emerged from the shadows.

"Oh, yeah?" Clay screamed. "We'll see about that."

And the fight was on. Although, Johnny was outnumbered he made a good account of himself. The trio ended up in a huge pile, soaking wet, but happy as children.

Susan righted herself. "Guy's, somebody's gonna call the police if we don't quiet down and I don't think the senator will be pleased."

"You're right," Johnny agreed. "C'mon, let's get into the house, the family jewels are freezing."

"Oh shit, someone's coming," Clay whispered. "Johnny, you two head home and I'll handle this."

Johnny took Susan by the hand. "C'mon Beautiful, you heard the boss."

The silhouetted figure kept coming. Preparing for whatever, Clay stood his ground. Thankfully, in seconds, an all too familiar voice broke the silence.

"It's me, Shack, are you guys okay? Are you drunk or something?"

Clay could see him clearly now. "Sorry, My Friend, we got carried away. I guess we woke you."

"No sweat, I don't sleep too soundly anyway."

Carl R. Smith

"Well," Clay said, "I am sorry we woke you. It's been a long day and I guess we were relieving an inordinate amount of nervous energy."

"Don't give it another thought, Clay. But, next time, I want an invite. Heck, I'm still an overgrown kid myself."

Clay chuckled, "Aren't we all? See you tomorrow, Old Pal."

"Goodnight Clay, sleep well."

When Clay arrived at the house Johnny and Susan were changing clothes and talking about food.

"I'm hungry too," Clay declared. "But, wait a darn minute, John Wayne Murphy, why the heck are you still awake?"

"Ah hell, you know I can't sleep until all the children are home safe. But, now I can't sleep because my belly's empty."

He and Clay looked directly at Susan.

She had this puzzled looked on her face, then the light went on. "What? Oh I know, grilled cheese sandwiches, right?"

Together they replied. "Please, Babe?"

"Oh, all right you Big Babies. But, first I have to visit the ladies room again." Susan turned to face Johnny, "Fix some coffee, John, will ya?"

"Sure," He replied, and headed for the kitchen.

Clay poked his head in the door of the kitchen. "Johnny, I'm gonna get out of these wet clothes. I'll be back down in a few minutes."

"No problem, take your time."

When Clay returned, Susan was busy cooking and Johnny was drinking coffee; he looked somewhat forlorn.

Clay pulled out a chair and sat down on the opposite side of the table. "What's wrong Johnny, you look a bit weary?"

"Believe it or not I miss that little lady. You know it was because of her that I never married Francine."

"I thought as much, but we never really talked about it. Did you see her much in the last few months?"

"Yeah, and I talked to her three or four times a week. Hell, I talked to her for more than two hours on Saturday afternoon. It's cheaper to call on the week-ends."

Clay poured himself some coffee. "When I called you, you didn't tell me that you had just talked with her. No wonder you were so amazed when I gave you the news."

Johnny hung his head. "Actually, I thought that when I got to the hotel in Chicago you and Gidget would show up and everything would be explained away."

Tears flooded Clay's eyes. "My God, I'm so very glad you and Susan didn't have to see her."

Now Johnny was crying like a baby, and when Clay looked towards Susan he could easily tell she was crying as well, even though she had her back to him. He knew instinctively that it was time for a cleansing of the soul.

Susan came to the table with the sandwiches, saying nothing, but the tears were there just the same. Johnny's head lay on the end of the table, his shoulders rose and fell with each sob.

Susan put her hands on the back of his head as though she were praying for him. "It'll be alright, Johnny. I know she cared for you. In an odd sort of way, we were, and still are 'family'."

Clay looked at the two of them. "We had some wonderful times, and we had some times of simply growing together, in love and respect. I will forever believe that Gidget truly loved us, for if she didn't we might very well be dead."

Johnny raised his head. "You're right, she held our lives in her hands and we didn't even know it. She must have loved us, God, she must've."

Clay's fist hit the table and he stood straight up. "What about her funeral, Guys? Some friends we are, we just left her there. Bullshit, I just left her there."

Johnny interrupted, "You had no choice, but if it makes you feel any better, when this is over I for one am gonna have a private service of my own. I hope you'll both join me."

"I love you, John, and you have the right idea," Clay said, pouring coffee for everyone. "Guys, we'll do it right. Her step-father may be an asshole, but she was one of us."

Susan's face lit up. "I say, in Gidget's honor, let's eat. What could be more appropriate than that?"

It was as though a great sword had been wielded, and had cut its way through all the pain and sorrow. Gidget would live on, in their hearts, in their laughs, and in their very beings, but most especially in their times of nourishment. Gosh, that girl loved to eat, and she could down an entire cow and never gain a pound.

Cutting the Fringe

They all three knew this time would come, and now they could deal with the memories. They would always remember Gidget as she was when the four of them were together. The time would come someday for each and every one of them to join her. That is indeed, life in its full circle.

The sandwiches were cold by now, but they ate them anyway. Hell, what's a cold sandwich or two among friends.

Chapter 9

Sleep had come fitfully for the three; nevertheless, it did finally come. Morning, however, was a story all its own. Wintertime sunlight that glares and bounces off the snow is without a doubt the brightest light ever. Bright sunshine after a snow can darn near blind a person; it will make you squint involuntarily which causes wrinkles, and sometimes it can bring on a splitting headache. Clay knew all this but he had gone out without his sunglasses again. This time it was not by accident; unless you call someone blowing up his beautiful car an accident. The absence of his favorite sunglasses brought back the entire car debacle. Without using too many expletives, Clay was angry, and being angry always served to make him uncomfortable.

He had left early that morning in order to meet Tim Siler. Johnny was sleeping and so was Susan, they were to care for each other until his return. Clay didn't like leaving Susan with anyone. However, Johnny was pretty damned good in his own right.

Mr. Siler, like Clay, was an early riser. Although, both of them had those days that never actually begin and never seem to end; days that just keep running into each other. The morning "Bill of Fare" at the Press Club was a little fancy for someone who loved to eat at the Waffle House; but, what the heck, Tim was buying.

Clay was waiting on the sidewalk as Tim exited the cab. He looked as though his coat had been slept in, but there was actually a crease in his trousers and his shoes were shined. To say Tim wasn't a snappy dresser may have been a gross understatement. On the other hand, he was the most munificent person Clay had ever known. He would give most anyone the wrinkled shirt right off his back. Clay didn't like many people but he liked Tim Siler and the feeling was mutual.

Tim flashed a huge smile as he approached; a smile that was truly infectious. *Surely that incredible smile had gotten him in many a door,"* Clay thought, a door typically closed to other reporters.

Clay extended his hand. "Hey Tim, it sure is a pleasure. Thanks for the invitation. I hope I didn't wake you with my early call."

"Not at all, I had just stepped out of the shower. Hell, my schedule is so screwy I don't know day from night most of the time. If God hadn't given us darkness and light I would be in real trouble."

Clay laughed. "That makes two of us."

Tim put his hand on Clay's shoulder. "Come with me, Young Man, this place has the best crepes in the northern hemisphere."

Clay followed, dutifully. "I've never eaten crepes, what are they?"

Tim showed his Press Pass to the doorman. "Boy, I swear you southern boys don't know anything but grits and oatmeal do you?"

Clay stepped back and gave Tim a look. "Well, I don't like grits," he replied, handing his topcoat to the attendant. "But at the orphanage, Smartypants, we had plenty of oatmeal and I liked it just fine, thank you very much."

Tim waved and or nodded at almost everyone in the place. He was well known and well liked.

"Clay, they have one order of crepes called the 'Parisians Delight' and if you like strawberries and cream cheese; well, it's to die for."

"You talked me into it. Hell, I'll try most anything once."

Tim smiled. "That's the brave soul I knew you were."

They ate and talked for more than an hour. Tim was only too anxious to be of help. Clay asked a number of questions, some Tim could answer others, he offered to research. Clay was embarrassed when he realized that in all that had been going on he didn't even know the telephone number of the place where he was staying. Actually, he had not called the number, nor had he ever bothered to look. Although, when he told Tim that he was staying at the home of the British Ambassador Tim already had the number. Surprise, surprise!

They agreed to meet again whenever Tim could obtain the information that Clay needed. He promised it would only be a day or so. Reluctantly, Tim had to get to work, so they parted company. Tim headed off walking the three blocks to the Washington Post, and Clay returned to his vehicle for the short trip back to Chevy Chase, Maryland.

It was almost ten AM when he finally got back to the house, he wanted to stop by his apartment but he didn't. Johnny and Susan were still sleeping and he tried to be quiet. Unfortunately, the quieter one tries to be the more accidental noise occurs. In an attempt to make coffee he moved a pot, and, like dominos, everything fell. The din was extremely loud, and in seconds Johnny came rushing through the kitchen door, trousers in one hand and gun in the other.

"What the hell's going on in here?" Johnny screamed, laying his weapon on the table and pulling up his pants.

"Sorry, Partner," Clay responded. "I swear I was trying to be quiet. Want some coffee?"

"No, not if you're making it. Your coffee's terrible."

Susan appeared in the doorway. "I'll make the coffee, just stop with the racket."

Johnny said, "Then, I'll take some."

Clay hung his head. "Sorry, Susan, it was an accident, I ---"

Johnny interrupted. "Look, Susan, he's pouting, all because I said his coffee stank."

"I'm not pouting," Clay insisted. "And; anyway, my coffee is not that bad."

Susan grinned. "Clay, your coffee is pretty bad. Now, you two get out of here and let me do my thing."

Clay headed to the bathroom and Johnny went towards the den, both still mumbling. In minutes they were together at the table, drinking coffee and organizing the day's activities.

They discussed Tim Siler and what Clay hoped he would accomplish. The crepes were also mentioned, and Johnny's mouth began to water.

"Can anyone eat there?" Johnny inquired.

"I think it's for members only," Clay replied.

Johnny got this unusual look on his face. "Well, I guess that leaves me out, they probably don't allow my kind to join."

"Well, it's their loss," Susan replied angrily.

Clay jumped in. "Things are changing, Johnny, maybe they will. Hell, someday people are gonna realize, inside we're all alike, you simply have a much better tan."

Johnny tried to laugh. "Yeah right!"

"You know it never ceases to amaze me. White people try constantly to get a great tan, yet you guys' have one. I think they're jealous. Hell, I'd love to have your tan." Clay was on a roll. "You're a brilliant man, Johnny, and you have some incredible friends, black and white. Anyway, people should be judged by their character."

Susan chimed in. "He's right, Johnny, I dislike many black people, and I dislike many more white people, but I dislike them because they're jerks. I don't judge them by the color of their skin."

Johnny smiled. "Thanks, Susan, I know you mean that. Thanks a bunch."

"You're welcome," she replied. "But, Guys, that's the way it should be, and those people with an ounce of sense know it. And as far as I'm concerned the others can just kiss my butt."

Johnny really started laughing, "I'll bet they'd loved to take you up on that."

Susan gave him a look. "You know what I mean."

"Just kidding," Johnny replied. "And we both know what you mean. Also, I'm proud to be one of those who has had the pleasure of kissing your beautiful little butt."

Susan blushed. "Cut that out. Where is Gidget when I need her?"

Clay said, "She's probably up in heaven looking down and cracking up."

"Yeah, I'll bet she's enjoying this immensely," Johnny countered. "In her honor, let's have some food."

Now everyone was back on target; although, sometimes things simply need to be said and this was indeed one of those times. However, the love these three felt for each other could not be influenced by the outside world.

The scene was suddenly tranquil, three friends sipping coffee, a little befuddled, but hanging on with sheer guts and determination. Without warning Susan jumped to her feet.

"Clay, is there a telephone I can use? I need to call the clinic and let them know when I'll be back."

"Yeah, there's one in the den. It's at the end of the couch, second shelf, under the lamp."

Susan peered at him, "Under the lamp?"

Clay stood. "C'mon I'll show you."

As they exited the kitchen, Susan asked, "Will it be okay? It's long distance, should I call collect?"

Carl R. Smith

He put his hand on her left shoulder, and they turned to face each other. "You made me proud in there, Kid. The more I know you, the more I like you."

Susan flushed. "Ditto."

Clay's heart leaped. That little word had such huge significance, and the two of them were the only ones left who knew. Not even Johnny shared that bit of knowledge.

She kissed him on the cheek. "Well?"

"Well, what?" Clay stuttered. "Oh, yeah! You don't have to call collect, Babe, I think our government can afford one lousy long distance call."

Susan sat on the end of the couch and reached for the phone. Clay turned back toward the kitchen to give her some privacy.

Ring! Ring!

"Oh, shit," Susan screamed.

Clay spun around as the telephone went flying by his head and landed in the chair next to the kitchen door. Susan was reaching frantically in thin air for the phone which she had just thrown some ten feet across the room.

Clay got to the phone before Susan. "Hello, hello?"

"What's going on?" the voice asked.

"The phone was inadvertently dropped," Clay replied. "Who is this?"

"It's Tim, Tim Siler. Is that you, Clay?"

"I reckon it's me. How're you doing?"

"I'm great," Tim replied. "Hey, Pal, can we meet for dinner tonight? I've got bunches of info for you. You can bring Dr. Murphy if you like."

"Can I bring Susan too?" Clay asked.

"Hell, yes. She's that enchanting, charming, and captivating young lady you introduced me to, right?"

"That's the one," Clay replied. "She'll be pleased to know you remember her."

Tim's voice cracked. "Remember her? I've dreamed about her a dozen times."

"Down, Boy," Clay quipped. "Where do you wanna meet, and what time?"

"How about the Capitol Club?"

"Sounds good to me," Clay replied.

"Okay, Clay, I'll meet you guys in the lobby about seven. I think you're gonna love what I have for you."

Clay cleared his throat. "I'm sure I will, Tim, we'll see you tonight."

Johnny entered the room. "Are we going somewhere?" he asked. "I couldn't help overhearing. Is everything alright?"

"Everything's fine and yes we're having dinner with Tim Siler tonight at the Capitol Club."

Susan's ears perked up. "Do I get to go?"

"Absolutely," Clay replied. "Tim was so excited when I mentioned you, he could barely contain himself."

Susan said, "Yeah, I'll just bet he was."

Clay grinned. "I swear. He said he'd been dreaming about you."

Susan ignored the statement. "Damn, that's a fancy place, isn't it, and I have nothing to wear."

Johnny looked at her. "Don't worry gorgeous, make your phone call and I'll take you shopping."

Susan went for the telephone as Clay motioned for Johnny to follow him into the kitchen. When they were out of earshot he told Johnny that Tim was full of information they could most probably use.

"I sure hope it's the information we need to put a stop to this mess, once and for all," Johnny mused.

"Me too, Partner."

Susan entered the kitchen. "Johnny, I'm gonna make you some crepes, if I can find the flour and a crepe pan. Look in the cupboard and see if there are any canned peaches, or cherries, or anything of the sort."

Johnny said. "Are you serious; do you really know how to make crepes?"

"Yes, Dingy, I know how to make crepes. Now, look for something to put in them, will you please?"

Johnny's face lit up. "Give me a minute, I'll find something."

Clay was really enjoying this. He winked at Susan, and would have offered to help, but they seemed to be doing fine all by themselves.

Johnny turned around with his arms full. He had canned peaches, canned pears, cherry pie filling, and a jar of strawberry jam.

"Will any of this stuff work?" he asked.

"Yeah, Boy," Susan answered. "Put the cans on the counter, and Clay, look in the fridge and see if we have any sausage."

"Yes, Dear," he replied.

She gave him a look, and then a huge smile. They were having fun now. Susan found the flour, shortening, eggs, vanilla, and whatever else she needed. She had Clay cooking the sausage, and Johnny making more coffee. She warmed the cherry pie filling in a pan, and the peaches she warmed also, while adding a little cream and just a pinch of flour for thickening.

What a meal, it was magnificent. They ate until belts had to be loosened. When finished, Clay offered to clean up while Johnny and Susan went shopping. *Cooperation, that's the key to getting along with others,* he thought.

Clay's brain was in overdrive. *I'd better call the senator and let him know about tonight's meeting. Anyhow, he may have some information for me as well.*

Picking up the telephone he dialed the senator's private number.

"Senator Lazar here, how may I be of service?"

"Senator, its Clay. Johnny, Susan, and I are having dinner with Tim Siler this evening, at the Capitol Club. He says he has some information for us, and I thought you should know."

"That's great, My Boy. Call me when you get back, regardless of the time. Furthermore, I have accomplished my assigned task, and I am at liberty to say that the sergeant is prepared to contribute some information too."

"Great," Clay replied. "I'll call you the moment we get in."

"Right, and if it's before midnight we should meet at the house. This is way too important to be concerned about losing a little sleep."

"Yes Sir, thank you Sir. I'll call you later."

"Thank you, Son. You guys enjoy your dinner, and there'll be brandy and cigars at my place."

Clay laughed, "Johnny will love that. Good-bye Senator."

Replacing the receiver in its cradle, Clay stretched out on the couch. He was mentally exhausted. The couch was comfortable; it hugged his body like a glove, and he slept as though he hadn't a care in the world. No bad dreams, just glorious peaceful sleep.

He had removed his watch while washing the dishes; consequently, when he awoke he had to guess at the time. The shadows were long and a wee bit eerie. *It must be close to five*, he muttered. Swinging his feet to the floor he stood, and proceeded to the kitchen in search of his watch.

The time was four thirty-seven PM, and Susan and Johnny had been gone for hours. Deciding not to worry he headed for the bedroom, a quick shave and shower would make things better. He was down to his shorts when the doorbell rang.

"I'm coming," he screamed.

Pulling his trousers on, he headed through the den and the library into the foyer to the front door. Looking through the sidelights, he could clearly see Sergeant Shackelford, patiently waiting.

"Hey, Shack, c'mon in."

"Thanks, Clay. I hadn't talked to any of you guys today so I thought I would check on you. How are things?"

"Everything's fine, I think. I was just about to shave. Grab yourself a beer from the fridge and come on back to the bedroom. How's the senator?"

"The senator's okay, he's having his before dinner drink."

Clay raised his head from the sink where he'd been splashing warm water on his face. "Do I detect a bit of attitude? Are you sure everything's alright?"

Shack walked to the opened bathroom door. "Sorry, Clay, I'll tell you about it later. I understand we may be having a meeting late tonight; is that right?"

"I hope so," Clay replied. "Look, My Friend, if you need to talk, I'll shave some other time."

Shack's speech was somewhat obtuse; he was almost stuttering. "No, no, not now."

Clay grabbed a towel and walked past Shack into the bedroom. "Shack, if you have a problem, I have a problem. Tell me what's on your mind."

Shack's entire demeanor changed. "Are you here alone? Where's Johnny and Susan?"

"Shack," Clay said firmly.

Looking quite befuddled, Shack replied. "It's personal, but I promise if I need help you'll be the first one I'll come to."

Clay put his arm around Shack's shoulder. "I'm here for you, My Friend; you have my word on that."

Shack hung his head, a little embarrassed. "I know, Clay, I know, and I appreciate that more than I can say."

Totally undaunted, Clay gave him a big hug. "The others have gone shopping, would you believe?"

Shack turned sideways in an attempt to hide his face. "I really gotta go Clay. But, God, I'm glad we're friends."

Clay followed him through the house to the door. "I'll see you later tonight, My Friend. You take care, okay?"

Shack finally turned at the door, his emotions leaping from his face. He extended his hand. "Even if it's too late for a meeting when you guys get in tonight; call me, will ya?"

"Sure Shack, I'll call."

Clay shut the door, it was getting dark outside, and he began to worry. *Where the hell are those guys?* He muttered.

He headed back to the master bath to finish shaving. *Ouch, shit, where's the tissue?* Blood was running down his right cheek into the sink. He clumsily finished shaving. Luckily he found a styptic pencil in the medicine cabinet and plugged the hole in his cheek.

The hot water from the shower felt good on his back; however, his mind was racing and he began praying. *Please, God, don't let anything bad happen to my friends.*

It was five forty-five PM according to the clock radio on the bed-side table. Clay donned his shorts and ran through the house and up the steps to the guest bathroom. He turned on the light and shut the curtains, summoning the sergeant.

Just as quickly he returned to the downstairs bedroom and began to dress. He screamed at the top of his lungs. *Where the hell are you guys?*

Almost, simultaneously, the doorbell sounded. Clay began to sprint for the door.

"Are you in there?" Shack bellowed. "If you don't answer in two seconds I'm gonna break the door down."

Clay grasped the door knob and literally jerked the door open. Shack rushed in, gun in hand.

"What's wrong, Clay?" Shack's heart was pounding.

Clay's eyes were wild. "It's almost six o'clock, and we have to meet Tim in D.C. in an hour. Something awful has happened, I can feel it."

Shack shut the door. "Are Johnny and Susan not back yet? How long have they been gone?"

"They've been gone for hours," he screamed. Clay steadied himself with the stair railing and collapsed on the third step. "Please Shack, help me. If anything happens to them I can't go on."

Shack's voice was very calm. "They're probably just caught in traffic. I bet they'll come pulling in any minute."

Perking up a bit, Clay forced a smile. "You think so? God I hope you're right."

Reaching for Clay's arm, Shack pulled him to his feet. "You go finish dressing. I'll keep a sharp eye out for them. Go on now!"

Clay obeyed, saying nothing. Shack opened the front door and stepped outside.

Dressing was a task, but it was finally accomplished. Immediately Clay went to the den and began mixing himself a drink. Drink in hand he walked to the front of the house and onto the small porch where Shack was still standing. The cold air felt refreshing, and it was just what the doctor would have ordered.

Clay started speaking. "If they were in an accident the police would have no way of knowing who to contact, would they?"

"Well," Shack replied. "That's assuming they were both unconscious."

Clay touched Shack's arm. "Someone's coming. Look!"

Shack strained his eyes, peering down the alley. Indeed, someone was approaching. "I think it's the senator. He's too short for Johnny, and I know it's not Susan."

The senator spoke as he approached. "Hey, Guys, why the hell are you standing out in the cold? What's wrong?"

All three men walked back into the house, and between Clay and Shack they managed to explain everything to Senator Lazar, who listened quite intently.

"I saw them a few hours ago," the senator mused. "They were on their way to the closest shopping center. Of course, Patricia told them where to shop. It seems they were shopping for a suitable dress for Susan, am I correct?"

"That's right," Clay replied. "Where did Ms. Lazar send them; do you remember?"

"Sure I do. They were headed to the Hollandale Mall; it's a huge shopping center northeast of here." The senator thought for a minute. "I can tell you how to get there, if you wish, it's on the way to Glen Bernie."

It was now six twenty-five.

Shack was pacing. "C'mon, Clay I'll take you, I know where it is."

Clay said, "Okay! Senator, would you please call the police and see if they have been in an accident?" Clay paused. "Also, Sir, would you call the Capitol Club and page Tim Siler, let him know what's happening."

"I'll do it right away," the senator replied. "You Guys call me on my private line when you get there and I'll bring you up to date on what I've found out, if anything."

Shack said, "What if they return? Someone needs to stay here."

The senator jumped in. "I'll make the calls from here, and I won't head back to the house until after seven. And, if they're not back before I leave, I'll leave them a note on the kitchen table, okay?"

Clay said, "That'll work. Let me get my stuff Shack; I'll be right with you."

The senator went for the telephone, and Clay went to retrieve his weapon. He returned in seconds, clipping his weapon to the back of his belt and donning his coat.

"Let's go Shack. Where's your car?"

Shack said, "C'mon, I'll lead the way."

The two of them were out the door quickly.

They reached the car in record time, and before Clay could get settled in the passenger's seat they were moving. Nothing was said for some time; however, Clay couldn't help but notice that Shack wasn't himself. *Maybe it's the stress of the moment.* He thought.

Clay was almost sick from worry, but he had to know what was troubling his friend.

"Talk to me Shack," Clay pleaded. "Something's got you wired, tell me, maybe it'll take my mind off the present."

Shack looked really uncomfortable. "My loyalties have me torn. Clay you're my most favorite person in the world, but - - -"

"Bullshit, Shack. We're team members; spit it out."

"Okay, okay. This afternoon I saw Johnny and Susan leaving the senator's house. They were pulling out of the driveway and I didn't get a chance to speak to them. But…" he paused.

"But what?" Clay was almost yelling.

"Damn Clay, I overheard the senator's wife talking on the telephone, and she was telling whoever she was talking to that someone could be found at Rich's Department Store in the Hollandale Center in about thirty minutes. I didn't think too much of it, but the look she gave me when she realized I had probably overheard her; well, it was pure hate. It gave me goose bumps." Again, he paused, this time to take a deep breath. "I didn't know what to think, and I'm sure she doesn't know how much I heard. Clay, when the senator told you where Johnny and Susan were going, it scared the hell out of me. You know what I mean?"

"Damn right I do. God, Shack, are we both thinking the same thing?"

Shack turned to look at him. "Yeah, I'm sure we are."

"Where was the senator when this was taking place?" Clay asked.

"He was on his private line talking to a senator from West Virginia," Shack replied. "And Clay, he doesn't know anything about what I heard, and I was afraid to tell him. Did I do the right thing?"

Before Clay could answer Shack slammed on the brakes and went into the median. When he gained control of the vehicle once more they were headed in the opposite direction. That's when Clay saw the accident. Shack drove right down the median and slid in behind a police cruiser. They both leaped from the car and ran across the roadway and down the embankment, both men recognizing the twisted vehicle wedged against a tree.

Shack grabbed Clay's arm.

"Wait Clay, there's no one in the car."

Shack stopped a policeman who was coming from the vehicle. "Officer, what happened?"

The officer turned, "You'll hear about it on the news."

Clay took the policeman's arm. "Look, Officer, we are with Senator Lazar's office and the two people in that car work for us. Now, what happened here?"

"Someone put about a dozen bullets in that car, all from the driver's side. The man was hit three times and the young lady once. They have been taken to Bethesda Naval Hospital. It seems the driver, as you probably know, is a doctor. He asked to be transported there."

Clay interrupted. "How badly are they hurt?"

"The man was, of course, conscious; but, the lady never came around. They are at the hospital by now."

Clay's will took command. "Officer, we need an escort to the hospital. I assure you it's a matter of national security."

The officer acted like he didn't know what to do, or say. Finally he consented.

"Hey, Bart," he yelled.

A tall thin officer standing by the roadway turned. "Yes Sir, what do you need?"

"Give these two gentlemen an escort to Bethesda, and make it snappy."

Carl R. Smith

"Right away, Sir. Come with me men; where is your vehicle?"

Clay and Shack thanked the officer, and then retreated up the embankment toward their car, with Officer Bart at their heels.

Fortunately, for all concerned, Shack's car had come to a stop right behind Officer Bart's patrol car.

The officer quickly sized up the situation. "Follow me gentlemen, we'll be there in no time."

Clay and Shack jumped in the car and they were on their way. Neither man spoke all the way to the hospital; although, it took them more than ten minutes.

Chapter 10

At the hospital things seemed a bit chaotic. Shack hurriedly went to find a telephone in order to call the senator. Clay, well, he was about to blow a fuse when a doctor finally appeared and was willing to talk to him.

"I'm Doctor Lyons, and you are?"

"Clay Smith. How are my friends?"

"Actually, Doctor Murphy will be fine after some rehabilitation. Two of the bullets passed through without doing any significant damage. The other one did some minor damage, but they are removing it as we speak. I don't anticipate any complications. He was a very lucky man."

"What about Susan?"

"She's still unconscious. The bullet she took only grazed the back of her neck; fortunately, she must have been leaning forward at the time. I must tell you; however, the accident itself caused most of the damage she sustained. Her head must have crashed into the windshield, or the dashboard. She is still being evaluated. There is major swelling, and we may have to operate to relieve the pressure on her brain."

Clay simply couldn't be still. "Can I see them, Doctor?"

"I feel sure that you can see Doctor Murphy in an hour or two; the young woman, well, I'll keep you posted."

Calming a little, Clay asked, "Will you let Johnny, I mean, Doctor Murphy, know I am here?"

"He already knows, Mr. Smith." Doctor Lyons, hesitated, "Look, I need to get back. Someone, either myself, or one of the nurses will keep you posted, I promise."

The doctor walked off just as Shack was returning. Clay explained everything, or at least he made the attempt. All Shack could do was shake his head.

"What did the senator say?" Clay asked.

Shack came out of his trance. "He's on his way; he should be here within the hour. What are you gonna do about Mrs. Lazar? Have you had time to think about that?"

"I don't know, My Friend, that's a tough one. I want to wring her pretty little neck, but first I want to know who she was talking to."

"Yeah, me too," Shack replied.

A somewhat matronly looking nurse walked into the waiting area and looked straight at them. "Are one of you men named Clay?"

"Yes, Ma'am," Clay replied. "Has something happened?"

"The young lady is asking for you, and she won't stop. Come with me, if you will please."

Clay gave Shack a small hug. "Watch for the senator, I'll be back."

"Give her my best," Shack hollered after them.

Clay was ushered into a surgery prep area. Susan lay motionless, with tubes coming from almost every part of her anatomy. Approaching her bed he touched her arm. Feeling his touch her eyes fluttered and then partially opened.

"Clay, they hurt me. They . . . they tried to kill us. Is Johnny alright?"

Clay struggled mightily to hold back the tears. "He's gonna be just fine, and so are you."

"I talked to Gidget; she's waiting for me. Clay, I think I'm gonna die."

She began to fade away.

Clay fell to his knees beside her bed. "Susan, please don't leave me. Fight, Babe, fight for me. Fight for us. Please, Susan, please."

The nurse touched him on the shoulder. "She can't hear you, Sir."

Clay cried, "Oh, God, don't take another one from me. Take me; it should be me lying there."

The nurse grabbed him, "Sir, she's not dead. The drip is taking effect, she's headed for surgery."

"Oh, thank God. Is she gonna make it?"

"She has a very good chance, and the best surgical team available. C'mon, Young Man, you'll have to go back to the waiting area. But, don't worry, I will personally come and give you an update as soon as I know anything."

Two men entered the room as they were leaving.

"Who are those guys?" he asked.

The nurse nudged him on. "They're going to take her to surgery. It's okay."

When he got back to the waiting room the senator was already there. Both he and Shack stood as Clay approached.

"How's she doing?" the senator asked.

"They've just taken her into surgery, so we won't know anything for some time," Clay answered.

The senator lit a cigarette. "I understand that Doctor Murphy is going to make it. When can we see him?"

Clay said, "I really don't know. Doctor Lyons said he would come for me as soon as that were possible."

Shack had not opened his mouth; he just kept watching as though he were frozen in time. All three men became unusually quiet. It was as though each one was praying in his own special way. The senator broke the silence.

"Men, I need something in my stomach. Shack, I know you haven't had anything, and you haven't either, have you Clay?"

Clay said, "I'm not very hungry, but you guys go ahead and get something. You can bring me some coffee."

The senator stood. "Come, Sergeant, let's find the cafeteria."

Shack rose from his chair and dutifully followed.

Clay said, "Senator, do you have any cigars? I need a smoke."

Reaching into his inside pocket the senator produced a small silver humidor. "Here Son, take these, I've got my cigarettes."

Rather quickly, Clay was alone with his thoughts. He walked to the nurse's station and told them he would be outside the emergency entrance having a smoke if he was needed. The air felt good and sorely needed. He lit a cigar and attempted to prioritize his thinking. He had learned over the years that the best way to handle any group of problems was to tackle them, one at a time, head on.

The cigar tasted sweet, and he was enjoying the solitude when someone called his name.

He spun around just in time to see Tim Siler come rushing across the parking lot.

"Tim, what are you doing here?"

"I'm here because I care, and don't worry I'm not here to get a story. How are they?" he asked.

"I don't know about Susan; however, she's in surgery as we speak. I'm told that Johnny's gonna be alright. At least that's what they're saying."

Tim said, "How the hell did they find them. Do you know?"

Clay's eyes were glowing, almost as brightly as the lit end of his cigar. "Yeah, I know, and it makes me so mad I could spit."

"Tell me," Tim pleaded.

Clay spent the next few minutes explaining what had taken place, all the time swearing Tim to secrecy. Tim lit a cigarette and paced back and forth. He would stop momentarily to shake his head, and then he would pace some more. Tim could never seem to be still, he was always fidgeting one way or another.

When Clay finished talking, Tim stopped pacing and looked him directly in the eye. "Okay, Big Boy, what is our course of action? How do we handle this with Senator Lazar?"

Clay said, "I'm not altogether sure, but if you have an idea, I'll be glad to listen."

"Not me," Tim replied. "I don't have ideas, I just write about the ideas of other people."

Clay actually chuckled. "Oh, that's cute. You're a big help."

"Well," Tim said, "I think we have to tell him, don't you?"

Clay thought for a moment. "Yes we do, but I want to talk to her first. Do you think that's wrong?"

"Not necessarily. Hell, Clay it's your call. However, if you need me to be present, I'll be there. It might make it easier."

Clay took another drag from his cigar. "Hell, Tim, I knew I liked you for some reason. You're my kinda guy, and I mean that in the nicest way possible."

Tim smiled. "I know you do, and I like you too."

Clay changed the subject completely. "Tim, do you know anyone whom I could hire to stay here with Susan and Johnny. You and I both know that when the people who did this find out they're not dead they'll try a second time. I can't be in both rooms at the same time, and Sergeant Shackelford needs to be with the senator."

"I might know someone," Tim replied. "Let me think on it for a minute."

Clay poked him on the shoulder. "That would be great; I really need someone I can trust."

Before either man could say anything else an orderly came from inside looking for Clay.

"Mr. Smith, Doctor Lyons would like to speak to you. Would you follow me please?"

Clay said, "Sure, Young Man, lead the way."

"Can I come too?" Tim inquired.

"I guess it would be okay," the orderly answered.

They dutifully followed the young man to a small room where he asked them to wait. They did so, but not with great patience. In about five minutes Dr. Lyons walked in; Clay couldn't read the expression on his face.

"Doctor Murphy can see you now. But I warn you he looks a little rough. It will take some time; however, I would expect a full recovery."

"Thank you, Doctor," Clay said thankfully. "Where is he?"

"Come with me; I'll take you to him."

"Wait a minute, Doc, I want to introduce you to Mr. Tim Siler; he's a reporter for the Washington Post."

The doctor's eyes brightened. "Mr. Siler, how nice to finally meet you. You don't know me, but you helped my wife with a fundraiser for abandoned children. She talks about you all the time."

Tim smiled. "Well, I hope she had something nice to say."

"Oh, she did, she really did." Doctor Lyons paused. "Are you here to do a story on what took place?"

"No," Tim replied, "I'm here because Clay is a dear friend, and I am well acquainted with the others."

"Well then," the doctor added, "I hope we are able to return the kindness you showed to my wife. Mr. Smith is a lucky man to have such a fine friend."

Carl R. Smith

"I'm the lucky one," Tim answered quickly.

"Of course, I didn't mean - - -"

Clay interrupted. "Its okay, Doctor Lyons, take me to see Johnny, please!"

A bit flustered and somewhat embarrassed the doctor whirled around. "Follow me."

Clay took Tim by the arm. "C'mon, Tim, I'm sure it'll be alright."

"Okay, I'd love too," he happily replied.

The doctor smiled and led the way. In moments they were outside the recovery room.

Doctor Lyons faced them. "Listen, Men, it will be a couple of hours before we can move him to a regular room; therefore, please remain calm and as quiet as possible."

"Not a problem, Doctor," Clay responded. "How much time can we spend with him?"

"Try not to stay more than fifteen minutes. And, remember he's going to be a little groggy."

Clay took the doctor by the hand. "Thanks again, and don't worry, we'll follow the rules."

Doctor Lyons stammered a bit. "Of course you will," he smiled and excused himself.

Tim looked at Clay and whispered. "Nice, but a little left of center."

"Right you are," Clay agreed.

They approached Johnny's bedside carefully, he too had tubes running from all parts.

Clay took his hand. "Hey, Lone Ranger, Tonto may be late but I'm here."

"Old Buddy, I told you I was too young and pretty to die. But I gotta tell you I feel like shit. How's Susan, is she gonna be okay?"

Clay said, "I would expect nothing less. You know its funny, when I talked to her the first thing she said was, how's Johnny."

Johnny tried to smile. "How'd they know where we were? Get'em, Clay."

"Don't you fret, Partner, I will."

Johnny was obviously trying to focus. "Is that Tim?"

"Yes, Doctor Murphy, it's me," Tim replied. "Since you screwed up our dinner date, I thought I'd come to Bethesda and try the cafeteria."

Johnny almost laughed, but it hurt too much.

Tim touched his arm. "Sorry, Doc, that was a little unfair of me."

"It's okay," Johnny muttered.

Clay stroked Johnny's arm. "Look, John, we need to get going, they told us we could only stay fifteen minutes. Anyway, they are gonna have you in a private room soon, and I'll come see you there." Clay suddenly realized he was talking, but Johnny was out cold.

He and Tim walked back to the waiting area just as the senator and Shack were coming back from eating.

The senator spoke. "Tim, nice of you to come. Clay, did you get to see Doctor Murphy?"

"Yes, Sir, he's in recovery. Everything went well; he'll be in a room soon."

"Thank, God," Shack interjected. "How's Susan, is she out of surgery yet?"

"No, My Friend," Clay replied. "They said it would be four to six hours."

Shack hung his head.

"Is the cafeteria still open?" Tim inquired.

The senator looked at his watch. "They should be open for another thirty minutes. Why don't you and Clay go get something? Shack and I will stay here and hold the fort."

"Come on Clay," Tim urged. "I gotta put something in my stomach, and you look as though you could use a little nourishment."

"Yeah, I guess you're right, I could eat a bite," Clay agreed.

He and Tim took off toward the cafeteria, leaving Shack and the senator in charge of waiting.

As they went through the cafeteria line, Tim broke the silence. "Sergeant Shackelford is taking this really hard. He feels responsible, doesn't he?"

Clay said, "Yes, I think he does, but it's not his fault."

"Well," Tim said. "You can tell he sure feels like it is. We need to help him if we possible can."

They paid for their food and found a table, not a big chore this time of the evening. The place was almost deserted. There were two men sitting alone, drinking coffee, some twenty feet away, and a young woman with a baby seated next to the exit.

Clay placed his napkin across his right leg and started to take his first bite when he noticed Tim was blessing his food. He waited quietly.

Before Tim had time to complete his prayer, Clay noticed the two men walking toward them; grabbing Tim's chair Clay shoved him against the wall. The first shot rang out like a ball peen hammer hitting a metal casing. Two more shots were fired as Clay dove under the adjoining table. Tables, chairs, and the two men, hit the floor. When Clay got to them, one was dead, and the other barely alive.

Tim was trying to gain control of his life and limbs.

"Are you hit?" Clay screamed.

"No, I don't think so," he replied. "Are you?"

"I'm okay," Clay declared.

By this time the cafeteria was crawling with people, gladly some of them were MP's. Clay laid his weapon on the table and backed away, allowing the MP's to take charge. There was nothing he could do anyway; the other man had already succumbed.

Shack and the senator came rushing in. "What the hell happened?" Senator Lazar asked, frantically.

Tim said, "Clay shot them. They were trying to kill us and he shot them, unbelievable. Clay, how did you know what they were up to?"

Clay thought for a minute. "Actually, when I saw them coming this way I suddenly realized there was nothing behind us. They couldn't possibly have a reason for coming this way. And, seeing their faces, and watching their body language, I just knew somehow, that's all. I just knew; call it what you will, but I just knew."

Carl R. Smith

Shack perked up. "I've told you guys, over and over, he has an angel on his shoulder or something like that. He's incredible; it's like a sixth sense."

Tim chimed in, "You'll get no argument from me. I've seen it in action, and it scared the hell out of me. I think I wet my pants."

The senator just stood there shaking his head in amazement.

Clay had been talking to the MP's for only a moment when he turned to the senator. "Senator Lazar would you please tell the nice policemen I need my weapon, they want to hold it until they finish their investigation."

The senator put on his best "in charge" face. "Officers, I will be personally responsible for Mr. Smith, give him back his gun."

Shack leaned in. "It's called a weapon, Senator."

"Gun, weapon, whatever, give it back to him, and I'll take the heat if there is any. You got that Lieutenant?"

The officer stood erect. "Yes, Sir, anything you say, Senator."

As one of the cafeteria ladies was trying to clean up the mess, Clay asked, "May my friend and I have another sandwich?"

She looked at him with this blank expression. "Sir, if you will give me your check I will have everything replaced exactly. Give me one minute, please."

Clay smiled at her. "Yes, Ma'am, thank you very much. We'll take a seat on the other end. Bring my other two friends some coffee too; just add it to my check."

"Oh no," she replied. "Sir, there will be no charge, none at all."

Clay thanked her again.

"Shack," Clay advised, "Will you go to the nurse's station and let them know where we'll be? If they need us, I want to be found."

"Sure, Clay, I'll be back shortly."

When they were seated at the table, as far away from the mess as was possible, they all lit up. Even Clay had a cigarette.

He took a long drag from his cigarette. "They were here waiting for the opportunity to get another shot at Johnny and Susan when I walked right into their path. Boy, I'll bet they thought they had hit the jackpot."

"Do you think Johnny and Susan will be safe now?" Tim asked.

"Well, they're certainly safer, and I'm glad I was here." Clay smiled. "But I'm not glad you were, Tim, I'm really sorry."

"It's okay! Of course, tomorrow when I wake up and remember what took place, I'll probably have a stroke. That is, if I don't have a heart attack in my sleep, during the nightmares."

Clay snickered. "Well put, Tim, you ought to be a writer."

The senator reached and touched Clay's hand. "Son, you are the coolest customer I have ever come across, doesn't anything get to you?"

Clay's facial expression changed. "No disrespect intended, but yeah. When people I love die needlessly, and people are trying to kill the only other friends I have in this world; that gets to me. But over the last ten years or so I've learned to keep it inside. I'm angry as hell; I was forced to kill two men tonight, two men whom I've never even met. And, Senator, others are going to die, and I hope like hell it's not one of you. Unfortunately, it won't be me. You see, Sir, men like me don't die, we just learn to live with all the guilt, and try with little success to somehow kill the pain."

The senator's face grew pale. "Son, I didn't mean any disrespect either. I thank God for you everyday. Without you I would already be six feet under."

Tim never said a word.

Shack returned, and so did the lady with the food.

All four men were relatively quiet for the next twenty minutes, as food and coffee were consumed. Finally, they were forced to leave and return to the waiting area as the cafeteria was closing.

It had been more than three hours since Susan had been wheeled into surgery and it showed on everyone's face. Thirty more minutes passed before Doctor Scarianno showed up with some news.

"Gentlemen," he said, "The worst is over; however, the young lady will be in surgery for another hour or more."

"How is it going?" Clay asked.

"Things have gone extremely well, and the prognosis looks good. One of you can see her in the recovery room in a couple of hours."

"Thank you, Doctor," came from everyone.

Tim stood up to stretch his legs. "Senator, why don't you and the sergeant go home? I'll stay here with Clay; the Post can do without me for one day. Anyway, I know you have hearings tomorrow in the Senate."

The senator stood also. "I guess Trish would like to hear the good news."

Clay's expression froze, and so did Shack's.

"Clay, will you be alright?" the senator asked.

"I'll be fine, Sir. If you'll call me here in the morning, before you head to the Senate, I'll bring you up to date."

"I'll do that, My Boy," the senator replied. "You can count on it."

Clay adjusted himself. "I'll be in Johnny's room. They should have him in a private room anytime now."

As they were leaving, the senator turned. "Clay, you guys try to get a little rest. Shack and I will talk to you in the morning. Goodnight!"

"Goodnight, Sir," they replied.

Clay looked at Tim with obvious discomfort on his face. "I got to find a bathroom, I'm about to pop."

Tim chortled. "Hell, Buddy, I thought Superman didn't have to use the facilities."

"Well," Clay replied, "I guess this proves once and for all, I'm not Superman."

Tim Laughed. "Yeah, I guess it does."

They headed down the corridor still picking at each other. After relieving themselves, and washing their face and hands they headed back once more to the waiting room.

"Tim," Clay said, "I'm gonna walk outside and have a cigar, want to come?"

"Sure, let me tell the nurse where we'll be if they need us. Go ahead, I'll be right out."

The air was crisp and cold, but not bitterly so. They walked and talked for almost twenty-five minutes. Finally, Tim said, "Can we go back inside now? I'm freezing my ass off. Sorry, Clay, I didn't mean to be so indelicate."

Clay grinned. "You call that indelicate. You should spend more time with John and me."

"I'd like to do that; let's plan on it."

"Good idea," Clay agreed. "And I thought you didn't have ideas."

Tim smiled. "Okay, you caught me."

They hadn't been inside for more then a couple of minutes when another orderly showed up and gave them Johnny's room number. They acquired directions and headed that way. When they got to the room he was sleeping.

Chapter 11

Someone's touch caused Clay to leap from his chair. The nurse was startled, but carried on nicely.

"I'm sorry, Sir, but I was told to wake you," she explained. "The young lady has been taken to recovery, you can see her now."

"You did the right thing," Clay answered. "Take me to her, Nurse, will you please?"

He woke Tim and told him what was going on, and that he would be back in twenty or thirty minutes. Tim nodded and waved him off, trying, without success, to find a more comfortable position in the chair where he had fallen asleep. The straight back chair offered very little in the way of comfort.

Clay, on the other hand, was going to see the one person occupying his every thought. She lay quietly; the only sound was that of the monitors, watching, and marking her progress. He knelt quietly beside her bed offering a silent prayer, asking God to spare her life. In truth, he was begging, something Henry Clay Smith was unaccustomed to doing. But, in fact, he would have gladly given his own life to know she had hers yet to live. *God, how much more are you gonna take from me? You know my heart; when do I get a break? You've already taken my family, Taylor, Pamela, Gidget, and now you want Susan. When I've asked for help, you've turned a deaf ear. When my father beat me, I cried out to you. When my mother sent me away, I cried out to you. When my brothers and sisters turned their back on me, I cried out to you. When Taylor came into my life, and then Pamela, and Gidget; you took them all, one by one. Please God, hear me, don't take Susan, I - - -*

"Clay, don't cry," Susan's voice was faint, but audible. "I'm not gonna die, I'm gonna get better, Gidget told me so."

"I'm so glad, Susan; I'm so very glad." He clutched her hand like a terrified child. "Can I get you anything?"

"Some water, please; I'm so thirsty."

He found a water glass on the bedside table, and a pitcher of water. He even found a straw. He complied with her wishes, but she couldn't seem to drink much. Although, what she was able to ingest must have helped. Her speech seemed to be less labored.

"You look awful, Clay, I'll bet you've been up forever. How's Johnny?"

"Thanks for the compliment," he kidded. "And, you on the other hand, look stunning. A little like the 'Bride of Frankenstein', what with all the extra wiring, but nonetheless, stunning."

She tried to laugh, and managed a snicker. But, thank God, she was alive and coherent.

The nurse came in and told Clay he had to leave. "She'll be in a room soon, and when she is you can stay with her as long as you wish."

Clay kissed Susan's hand. "I'll be right outside the door, Babe; you rest and do what they say."

"Yes, Boss," she replied weakly.

Clay left the recovery room. He found a chair and set it beside the door. He plopped down with intentions of staying there; unfortunately, he remembered Tim. About that time a young orderly came hurrying down the corridor. Clay grabbed his arm.

"Son, sit down right here and don't allow anyone in this room that you don't personally know. Do you understand me?"

"Yes, Sir, but I can't do that," the kid replied. "My supervisor will kill me."

Clay just stared at him. "Young man, I have to check on another patient, it will take less than ten minutes. When I return if your ass is not in that chair, you're gonna wish you had been killed. Do you follow me now?"

"Yes, Doctor, I won't move and I won't allow anyone in the room that I don't personally know. I'll be here when you come back."

Clay looked at the boy's name tag, and he almost laughed out loud, realizing the young man thought him a doctor. "Good man, Stimson. I'll be back directly."

Entering Johnny's room quietly, Clay noticed Tim had found a new place to sleep, on the floor. Tim came around quickly, and immediately asked about Susan, his face showing the emotional relief when he heard the promising news.

The telephone rang. Clay grabbed it on the first ring. "Is that you senator?"

"Yes, how are Johnny and Susan?"

Clay spent about two minutes bringing him up to date. Tim listened to the details, those which Clay had yet to mention before the ringing of the telephone. When Clay had explained all aspects of the situation, he had a favor to ask.

"Senator, I need you to call the FBI. I need someone here to look out for Johnny while I am with Susan, and vice versa. I'm sure you understand. I realize this is a military hospital, were that not the case they would be on us like flies already." Clay paused to catch his breath. "Tim is still here; however, I don't feel he's the man for the job. He's wiry, and tough as nails, but he doesn't have a weapon, and he isn't trained as an observer. He's standing here shaking his head, Sir."

The senator spoke authoritatively. "I will have two Airborne Rangers, standing at attention in front of each room in less than two hours; you have my word."

"That would be even better, Sir. Thank you. Have them report to me when they arrive. I'll be looking for them."

"Got it!" the senator replied.

"Senator, one more thing before you hang up. We need to have a meeting at your place at six. Is that okay with you?"

The senator paused, momentarily. "That will work perfectly. Ask Tim to be here, if he possibly can, will you Son?"

Clay said, "Will do, Sir, thanks a lot," and they hung up.

Turning to Tim, Clay asked, "Can you make the meeting tonight?"

"I wouldn't miss it for the world, I'll be there."

"Thanks, Pal, I knew I could count on you," Clay said earnestly.

They both focused on Johnny for a second. He was moving restlessly, but he was still out like a light.

Tim actually tried to straighten his clothing. "Clay, I'll keep my wiry little person here with Johnny, you get back to Susan. I'll stay with him until reinforcements show up."

"Tim, I didn't mean ---"

"I'm kidding you, Sport. Look, I'm a lover, not a fighter. I leave the fighting to the Neanderthals."

Clay tried not to burst out laughing. "It might surprise you to know, Tim Siler, but I actually know what a Neanderthal is. And, I guess we're even."

Tim gave him a nudge. "Yeah, I guess we are!"

"I'll be in the recovery room, and if they move Susan before our relief shows up I'll let you know immediately, okay?"

"Go on," Tim urged. "The doc and I will be fine."

"Okay, Pal, I'm outta here. See you in a bit."

When Clay got back to the recovery room, Stimson was sitting there at attention, if that's possible.

Thanking him profusely, Clay relieved him forthwith.

When he entered the room, the nurse was at Susan's bedside taking her vitals.

"How's she doing?" Clay asked.

"She's doing much better than expected. Unfortunately, it may still be a couple of hours before we can move her. But, all in all, she's doing great."

"Can I stay with her?"

The nurse looked squarely at him. "I'll give you ten minutes, and then you must wait outside. When I return to get her vitals again, I'll give you ten more minutes."

"Thank you, Nurse. I appreciate your kindness."

Clay looked at his watch, walked around the nurse, and took Susan's hand. The nurse smiled at him and left them alone. Susan was sleeping peacefully, and for that he was incredibly grateful. He just stood there for the entire ten minutes holding her hand as she slept.

He exited the room and seated himself in the chair beside the door. In less than five minutes the nurse showed up with a breakfast tray.

"I ordered this for you, Young Man; you look as though you need it. I will bring you some milk and coffee in a few minutes. Now, be a good boy and eat this."

"I most certainly will, and bless you," he exclaimed. "You may act tough, but deep down you're just a sweetheart, aren't you?"

"Don't try me, Son. Now, eat!"

Clay downed the food in record time. In fact, he was nearly finished when the milk and coffee arrived; although, he still took it gladly. As the nurse was leaving Clay stopped her. "Please, Ma'am. I don't mean to be ungrateful, but in Doctor Murphy's room there is a reporter named Tim Siler, could you see that he gets a tray also?"

The nurse's smile reappeared. "Certainly, I'll do it straight away. Heck, we can't have someone from the 'fourth estate' starving on my beat, now can we?"

Clay said, "I reckon not."

She retreated hurriedly through the corridor, as if Tim's life were hanging in the balance. That's the military for you. Hurry up and wait, and then hurry some more.

Through with his milk, he sipped his coffee. *The nurse should be returning any moment,* he thought; and within seconds she was approaching. Her gait was unmistakable, she walked like a linebacker. Again, Susan slept through Clay's entire ten minutes; although, the time with her was precious to him.

It was nearly eight AM when the rangers arrived. There were four of them and Clay stationed two men outside each room. Tim's butt was dragging. He was ready to go home and get some badly needed shuteye.

They rode the elevator to the first floor; both men totally exhausted. Not much was said, until Tim broke the ice.

"Thanks for sending me the breakfast tray, it was a welcome surprise, and the coffee wasn't half bad."

Clay said, "Somehow I think you earned it, along with my undying gratitude. I won't forget this."

Tim bumped into him playfully. "No sweat, Good Buddy, that's what friends are for."

Clay bumped him back. "Well, that's the way I think it should be, between friends. Rest assured I'll reciprocate someday."

"Yeah, yeah! Did I do it right?" Tim asked.

Clay just stopped and stared. "Do what right? What are you talking about?"

Tim got this glint in his eye. "You know! No sweat, good buddy, did I sound southern? Did I pull it off?"

The light finally went on in Clay's worn out brain. "Southern, you say, southern New Jersey, maybe."

"Damn," Tim said. "I've been trying to emulate you and Johnny; I guess it needs more work."

Clay grinned. "Wait til Johnny gets well, he'll give you lessons."

They walked out of the hospital. The sun was bright, and it was rather nippy. Clay stopped next to this two tone blue Chevrolet Malibu. One of the soldiers had delivered it for him, compliments of the senator.

"Where'd the new car come from?" Tim asked.

"I think it's from the rental car company," Clay replied. "It sure is pretty, isn't it?"

"Damn, Man. That's a 'super sports', it'll run like the wind," Tim mused. "We're talking speed to burn, Baby."

Clay opened the door and they shook hands. "As long as it gets me back to the house I'll be happy. I'll see you at six. Go home and get some sleep."

"I'll be there, Pal," Tim replied.

Clay sat in the car for a minute before starting it; it smelled new. He pushed in the clutch and turned the engine over. Vroom! *Wow, this thing sounds powerful, it must be a three ninety-six,* he surmised. It handled like his GTX; it really felt good. It had bucket seats, AM / FM radio, and a tape deck. In the passenger's seat was the garage door opener. *How'd he do that?* Clay thought.

It took him a little over twenty minutes to drive to the house. He could have made it a bit faster, but the route was unfamiliar. He pulled into the garage and turned off the engine. Upon entering the house there was a strong smell of pine. *Jolene must have been cleaning.* He thought.

He was undressed and in the shower in record time. There was that feeling; he couldn't shake it this time. As he stepped from the shower he heard someone screaming, the screams were coming from outside the house. The back door opened.

"Mr. Smith, are you here? Oh me Lord, Mr. Smith, please answer me."

Clay ran from his bedroom, half-dressed. "What's wrong, Jolene?"

Frantically, she tried to explain. "It's the Missus, I think she's dead. Her eyes just stare at me, and she don't move. Come quickly."

"Wait here, Jolene, don't move I'll be right back."

He was back like a flash, coat on, and weapon in hand. "Take me to her, Jolene. C'mon, girl."

They flew out the door and sprinted all the way to the senator's residence. Ms. Lazar was still in her bed. Only one bullet hole was evident, and it was right between her eyes. Her body was ice cold; she had been dead for quite some time. Clay turned to Jolene, she was thunderstruck. No tears, just absolute mortal fear had taken total control of her person. She could barely speak, and when she did it was nearly inaudible. He took her from the room, down to the study and poured her a stiff drink, literally forcing her to down it. That seemed to help.

"You didn't touch anything in the bedroom, did you?" he asked.

"No, Sir. I saw her lying there, and I ran. Thank God you were home."

Clay picked up the telephone and dialed the senator's number. His mind was racing.

"Senator Lazar's office, this is Clarisse, how may I help you?"

"Clarisse, this is Clay Smith, I need to speak to Sergeant Shackelford. Can you find him for me?"

"He's right here, Mr. Smith. Hold just one minute please and I'll get him for you."

When Shack got on the phone, Clay chose his words carefully.

"Shack, the senator's wife has been shot, execution style. Bring the senator home, and be gentle, if that's possible. I'll contact Tim Siler and the FBI." Clay paused for a few seconds. "Shack, I wish I could tell you how to handle this but I can't, you're on your own, my friend."

"I'll bring him home," Shack replied. "I'll see you in thirty to forty-five minutes."

"For God's sake, and your own, be careful My Friend."

He pushed the button, popped it up and dialed Tim Siler.

"Hello."

"Tim, it's Clay, I'm sorry to wake you, but the senator's wife has been killed. Jolene found her; she was killed in her bed."

"Holy jeez," Tim exclaimed. "Does the senator know?"

"I called the office and talked to Sergeant Shackelford. He's bringing the senator home as we speak."

Tim said, "Have you called anyone else?"

"No, I'll call the FBI when we hang up."

"Don't do that Clay; let me call them. Stay put, Pal, and I'll see you in less than an hour."

Clay placed the phone back in its cradle and turned to Jolene. She was damn near catatonic. She didn't know the world she was in. He took a cigar from the senator's desk, snipped the end and lit it. When he sat down beside her on the sofa, she laid her head in his lap and the sobbing began.

He sat there for more than five minutes, stroking her hair and letting her cry. Finally he spoke. "Jolene, I need you to go into the kitchen and make a strong pot of coffee. The senator and the sergeant will be here soon. Shortly thereafter the house will be crawling with people. I need your help, will you help me please?"

She sat up and looked at him. "I'll help; I'll do whatever needs to be done." She hesitated, "They could have killed me too, why didn't they?"

"Ms. Lazar knew something, that's why they killed her. Luckily, you know nothing that would in any way threaten them. You are perfectly safe; I'm sure of it."

She stood, straightened her clothing, and headed for the kitchen. The cigar had extinguished itself. He flicked the ashes into the fireplace and relit it. He made himself a double scotch and soda, without the soda.

The senator walked in, eyes puffy, but in total control of his wits. Shack, on the other hand, looked terrible.

The senator looked in Clay's direction. "Where is she?"

"In her bedroom," he replied. "Sir, she's been dead for quite some time."

The doorbell rang.

"Answer that, Sergeant," the senator ordered. "Clay, give me five minutes to say good-bye to Trish before you let them come up. Can you do that for me please?"

"Certainly, Sir," Clay replied.

Shortly there were policemen and FBI agents standing in the foyer. The older and taller of the men spoke first, introducing himself to Sergeant Shackelford.

"I am agent Taylor, and this is my partner, agent Butts. Show me to the body."

By now Clay was beside the sergeant.

"Gentlemen, my name's Clay Smith. Thank you for coming so quickly; however, you cannot go upstairs just yet."

The shorter and stockier of the two stepped forward. "Step aside, Mr. Smith, we'll take it from here."

Clay didn't budge. "I promised the senator five minutes to bid farewell to his wife, and five minutes he shall have."

The taller agent took his partner's arm. "Another minute or so won't matter Fred, it's his wife for God's sake."

"You're absolutely correct, Ron," the shorter man replied.

Agent Taylor inquired. "Who discovered the body? Was that you, Mr. Smith?"

"No," he answered. "Ms. O'Dern found her; she works for the senator. She is in the kitchen if you wish to speak to her."

He said, "Later perhaps. Can we go up now?"

"Most certainly," Clay replied, walking ahead of them.

As they approached the room one could clearly see the senator kneeling by the bedside of his departed wife. The sight alone caused Clay to relive, the recent, and also the distant past. He allowed the agents to go in ahead of him. Then, not wanting to intrude, he hurried back downstairs. Tim had just arrived, and he was talking to the coroner who came in directly behind him. When he saw Clay he motioned for him to join them.

Tim started the introductions. "Doctor Goode, this is Clay Smith, the man we've been discussing. Clay, Doctor Goode."

Clay extended his hand. "Nice to meet you, Doctor Goode."

"Likewise, Young Man, I wish; however, it could have been under better circumstances."

Incredibly, his demeanor did a one-eighty. Clay assumed, this face, must be his coroner's face.

"Is she upstairs?" he asked.

"Yes," Clay replied. "Two agents just went up and the senator is with them."

Doctor Goode was fumbling for something. It soon became obvious; he was looking for his glasses, which he found perched on the top of his head.

"Sorry," he mumbled. "I can never seem to find those things when they're in the most obvious place. Must be 'old age'?"

Putting on his glasses, he looked, first at Tim, and then at Clay, as if for the first time. If the circumstances had indeed been different, it would have been amusing.

Gaining his composure, he continued. "Who found the body? Was it you, Mr. Smith?"

"No, Doctor Goode, it was Jolene, and she came looking for me immediately."

The doctor looked over his glasses. "And where were you, Mr. Smith?"

Clay didn't care for the accusing look, but he decided to answer directly. "I was some three hundred yards away on Winfrey Street, taking a shower."

Tim spoke up. "Doctor Goode, you sound more like a detective than a coroner."

"Its 'osmosis'," the doctor declared. "When you're around these guys as much as I am, it rubs off. Now, show me to the bedroom, will you, Mr. Smith?"

Clay and Tim exchanged glances. "Come with me doctor, its right this way."

Tim said after them. "I'll wait for you in the study, Clay."

Looking back, Clay replied. "No sweat, Old Man, I'll be right back."

Leaving the doctor in the same area where he had left the agents, Clay returned to the study where Tim was already smoking and drinking.

Cutting the Fringe

"Where's Shack?" Clay asked.

"He's outside directing traffic," Tim replied. "He'll be back in shortly; do you want a drink?"

"Please!" Clay replied. "Scotch and soda, and not much soda."

Clay was headed for the cigars. As Tim was mixing Clay's drink Shack walked in. He had the look of a man who had lost his best friend. Both Clay and Tim knew he was feeling some responsibility for all that had taken place. They also knew it was in no way his fault, or his doing.

"Shack," Clay acknowledged, "Let me get you a beer."

"I don't think so," he mused. "I'm kinda on duty, and I don't want to cause anymore problems."

Tim interrupted. "Listen to me, Sergeant. This is not your doing, and you could not have stopped this."

Shack hung his head. "Maybe I could have. I should have tried."

"No, Sergeant, you've got to stop beating yourself up. Clay needs you now, and so does Senator Lazar. Get your head on straight, or someone else may die."

"He's right," Clay began, "Shack, you'd cut off your arm for these people, and they know that. I've been in your shoes. When I allowed Pamela and her sister to go into protective custody I thought I was doing the right thing. But they were killed, and I almost didn't come back from that. However, if I hadn't, with the help of my friends, we would probably never have gotten the general."

Shack tried to smile. "I see what you mean. I don't want to get anyone else hurt. Tell me what to do, Guys."

Clay sipped his drink. "First of all, those two men at the hospital, do you know who they were? Are they the ones you were talking about, you know, the ones from Fort Bragg?"

"I don't know," he replied. "They looked a little too old for trainees. But, Fellas, I'll find out before the day is over, I promise."

Tim jumped into the conversation. "There you go! That's the Sergeant we all know and love."

This time, Shack couldn't hide the smile. "Thanks, Mr. Siler."

Putting his arm around Shack's shoulder, Clay began, once more. "Shack, we're gonna have to go it alone for the next couple of days. The senator cannot be relied upon to help very much; he has other things on his plate."

"I know," Shack replied.

"Also, My Friend, if someone could walk in here and kill the senator's wife, they could just as easily kill the senator, but not for my man Shack. You've got to be ungodly careful. The senator's life depends on you, and for the most part, you alone."

Shack perked up. "I'll do my job."

"Okay then, go find the senator and don't leave his side for any reason. In order for me to do what I have to do, I need to know the senator is safe. Do you fully understand me?"

"Yes, Clay, I understand."

Tim had been listening all this time and just shaking his head.

Clay gave Shack a small hug. "Tell the senator that Tim and I are going to the house to get a few hours sleep, we will be back here at six. The meeting still must happen, do you follow me?"

"I follow you, Clay. I'm going upstairs right this minute and I won't let the man out of my sight. I'll see you at six."

Clay threw the remains of his cigar into the fireplace. "One last thing, My Friend, if it is at all possible, you need to look out for Jolene, she is really spooked. She can be a lot of help to both you and the senator. I will speak to her on the way out. Okay?"

Once again, Shack stood tall. "I will do my best to make you proud. Do you think Susan and Johnny will be alright?"

"I think they will be fine," Clay said, with confidence. "I have a lot of faith in the rangers. Anyway, after the meeting, I will be back there. Everyone has to do their job, and do it well. If that happens, we'll get through this together, and alive."

As they went through the kitchen Clay spent a number of minutes trying to calm Jolene. He told her how much they needed her, and that she could be a huge help in the coming days.

Chapter 12

The awful clanging of the alarm clock was not a welcome sound. Although, tired as he was, Clay was ready for the meeting, and he couldn't wait to see Susan and Johnny. *Hell, they might even be awake this time,* he thought.

Tim had been asleep on the sofa, and he was trying to stand up.

"Is it five o'clock already?" he yelled.

Clay peeked around the bedroom door. "Yes, Sport, I'm afraid it is. You go take a shower and I'll make us some coffee."

Tim was already undressing as he passed through the bedroom, clothes going everywhere.

When Tim entered the kitchen, Clay had the coffee made. He had also prepared some brown sugar cinnamon toast.

"What is that awesome smell?" Tim inquired.

Clay grinned. "It's the cinnamon; I made us some toast. I hope you like it; we didn't have time for much else."

Tim poured the coffee and took a sip. "Whoa! That is some bad coffee. Shit, I hope the toast is better."

Clay had this look of dejection on his face. "Damn, nobody likes my coffee. What am I doing wrong? I'll get you some milk."

He poured the milk and set it on the table in front of Tim.

"Clay, my man, this toast is scrumptious, it more than makes up for the horrible coffee."

"Now, it's horrible," Clay declared. He raised his cup and took a long sip. "Well, I think it's . . . Horrible!"

Tim laughed. "Have some milk; it's great with the toast."

Clay headed for the fridge. "I gotta learn how to make coffee," he mumbled.

"I'll teach you," Tim offered. "But later, when we have more time. You better go take your shower? I'll clean up in here."

"Done," Clay muttered, and away he went.

They were out the door at ten til six. The snow was almost gone, and the ground was a little muddy. When they got to the senator's house, Clay instructed Tim to take off his shoes and leave them on the screened-in porch.

Jolene welcomed them. She looked better, but she was still pretty shook up. Clay knew this was so, because she never mentioned the muddy shoes.

"The senator is waiting for you in the study, Mr. Smith."

"How is he?" Clay inquired.

She appeared a little glassy-eyed, as though she had had a few too many.

"He's as well as he could be, I suppose. I don't know if I can ever go back into that bedroom." She just stared off into space. "I guess I'll have to though, won't I?"

Clay gave her a hug and kissed her on the cheek. "Don't fret, Sweetheart, we'll get through this together."

He and Tim walked down the hall from the kitchen to the study. The senator was seated on the sofa and not at his desk. Sergeant Shackelford was standing by the fireplace, and he looked somewhat stoic. Clay could tell he was back in charge, once again.

The senator stood and welcomed them. "Clay, I just got off the telephone with the hospital. Johnny and Susan are doing even better than was expected. We should all be very thankful, Trish wasn't so lucky."

Tears began to flow, and the senator's hands were shaking.

Clay was unbound by convention; he put his arms around the man and held him close.

"Those bastards are gonna pay for this. You have my word on that, Sir." Clay continued to speak, "I'm gonna pay the general a visit this very night. Whether he lives to see another sunrise will be his decision."

The senator stepped back and almost fell into a sitting position on the sofa. With his head in his hands, he cried. "Why, Trish? She couldn't hurt them."

Tim interrupted. "Senator, I think we had better get down to business. It will help take our collective minds off the present situation; at least, I hope it will."

Clay breathed a sigh of relief. He wasn't at all sure what Tim was going to say, for he had a habit of being rather blunt. Bringing up the overheard conversation, in Clay's opinion, could wait for a better time.

The four of them exchanged information, and decided on a plan of action. Well, nothing was set in stone, but they did have a direction in which to begin. Clay was going to the hospital; Tim was going home to do some more digging. He had been working with a friend of Johnny's from Andrews Air Force Base, one of the first real computer geniuses. They were following the money trail. Shack and the senator were never to be separated from each other. There were FBI agents stationed at the house also; two in the front and one roaming the property at all times.

Tim patted the senator on the shoulder and made his exit, giving Clay and Shack the 'thumbs up'.

Clay sat with Senator Lazar for some time, talking mostly to Shack, and listening to the senator sob. Giving the man one final hug, he made his exit through the kitchen looking for Jolene.

She was busily cleaning an already spotless room, and mumbling to herself. He tried not to startle her, but she jumped anyway.

"Oh, Mr. Smith, can I be of some assistance?"

"I just wanted to check on you," he replied. "I have to return to the hospital, and I have a small errand to run; however, I will return before morning."

She reached for him. "Please don't go! I don't feel safe without you here. Please!"

He held her tightly; those words still ringing in his ears. He had heard them before, and the memory was almost overwhelming. Gaining control, he raised her chin and looked through her eyes, deep into her soul.

"Listen to me, Jolene. Shack will be here, and the FBI has men stationed outside the house." Gathering his thoughts, he continued, "Shack will be sleeping inside the house. Stay close to him and he'll protect you, I promise."

Her eyes were pleading with his. "Will you let me know the minute you get back?"

Clay looked at her. "I don't even know what room you're in."

"Don't worry about that," she screeched. "I'll be wherever the sergeant is."

Clay almost laughed. "Okay! I'll find you."

She seemed to calm, somewhat, and Clay made his departure.

He arrived at the hospital before nine PM and went straight to Johnny's room. When he entered the room Johnny wasn't sitting up but he was awake, and the smile on his face when seeing Clay, spoke volumes. Trying to hide his tears of joy, and sorrow, Clay approached his dearest friend.

"Hell, you don't look so bad," he quipped.

Johnny tried to adjust himself, but it proved to be too painful. "Give me a hand, Old Buddy."

Clay helped him get settled, and just touching his friend brought happiness to his heavy heart.

"Damn, Partner, you scared the shit out of me."

Johnny tried again to smile. "Sorry, Tonto, it was unintentional. How's Susan?"

"I'm told she's doing even better than expected." Clay took Johnny's hand. "She was in surgery for hours, but they told the senator she was improving rapidly."

Johnny squeezed Clay's hand. "Go on, get out of here. She needs you more than I do. Anyway, I'm kinda tired."

"Yeah," Clay replied. "You get some rest and I'll be back soon."

Clay spent a few minutes talking to the two rangers who were on duty before heading to Susan's room. He instructed them to be ever vigilant.

Upon reaching Susan's room he had the same discussion with her protectors. The men were alert and responsive. Clay liked that, and it made him feel better.

Susan looked weary. Her entire headed was wrapped in bandages. The tubes were everywhere, but her breathing was not labored. Clay bent down and gently kissed her cheek, no response. He stood and looked at her for the longest time, hoping she would wake up.

The nurse entered the room and began doing her thing. It was as though he didn't exist. Finally when she finished she took him by the arm.

"Come with me, Young Man," she whispered.

They left the room and he followed her to the nurse's station. When they were out of earshot of the rangers she spoke.

"Are you Clay Smith?" she asked.

"Yes, Ma'am, is something wrong?"

"Visiting hours are from 1900 hrs until 2100 hrs." she said firmly. "However, I am told that you are something special."

"Ma'am, I - - -"

"Don't interrupt," she scolded. "You may be here as often as you wish, as long as you are quiet and stay out of the nurses' way. Do I make myself clear?"

Clay stuck out his hand. "I will be on my best behavior at all times, and if there is any service that I can render while I'm here, please don't hesitate to ask."

He smiled.

She wasn't sure how to respond, but she took his hand. "Fair enough," she replied.

Reading her name tag, he responded, "Thank you, Nurse Ford."

She stood, trying not to smile. "You may go. And, by the way, she is doing better with each passing hour."

Clay took her hand once more. "Thank you for the kind words, she means a lot to me."

Nurse Ford maintained her authoritative control. "Go sit with her, she's asked for you every time she's awakened."

Clay did an about-face, and walked away. As he reached the room once again one of the rangers stopped him.

"Did Nurse Ford read you the riot act?" he asked.

Clay grinned. "Nah! Well, maybe a little."

"I thought so," he whispered. "She sure sat us straight in a hurry."

Still grinning, Clay responded. "Yeah, I'll just bet she did."

As he entered the room, Susan was moaning. It was almost as though she was having a conversation with someone. He walked softly to her bedside and listened, straining to make some sense out of the words.

The words were inaudible, and no matter how hard he tried they made absolutely no sense. Suddenly, as if on cue, her eyes opened.

"Clay, I'm so glad you're here. Say hi to Gidget; she misses you terribly."

"I miss her too," Clay replied.

Her eyes shut once more, and she reached for his hand, pulling him close. The air in the room became cold. Her grip was so strong it was almost painful.

In Gidget's voice, words began to pour from Susan's body. "Come closer, Clay, I can't come to you."

He leaned over the bed laying his right cheek against hers. And he could feel her stroking his hair.

"I will love you for all time," the voice continued, "Although, we never made love, you are my champion. I would never have hurt you, you must believe that. I died protecting you."

"I do believe that," he answered.

She released her grip, slightly. "I talked to your Aunt Ella, she loves you too."

Clay felt frozen in time.

"I must go now, Clay."

Susan's hand fell limp. The room temperature changed dramatically, as a stiff breeze blew across his face. He gazed at Susan; she was sleeping peacefully, one hand on the bed and the other strapped to a board with an IV stuck into her vein.

Remembering the hand stroking his hair, forced an involuntary smile to his face. *Oh my,* he thought.

Nurse Ford came through the door quickly, almost without making a sound.

"How are you Mr. Smith? It looks as though our patient is doing well. Her recuperative powers are astounding."

"You don't know the half of it." Clay caught himself. "I mean, you're right, she's amazing."

Ms. Ford nodded and continued to do her job. Seconds later she was finished and out the door she went.

Clay stood in the middle of the room, unwilling to move, and not wanting to think. He pondered, *maybe I'm hallucinating. Dang, I know I haven't had much sleep, but this is unreal. Oh good, Clay, great choice of words.*

Susan began to speak, and Clay's heart jumped into his throat.

"What, Susan? What did you say?"

"I said get over here, why are you standing by the door?"

"Oh, I just got here, and the nurse was in here doing her thing so I was trying to stay out of the way."

"Well, she's gone now. Come closer so I can touch you."

Clay felt as though he was standing in cement, and he had to summon all his courage to make his feet move. *Get a grip, Clay, you're losing it.*

Once by her side, she touched his arm, and the uneasiness disappeared. She looked astonishingly beautiful, even with her entire head wrapped in bandages; a bit pale, but the face of an angel.

Susan said, "You're staring at me, do I look that hideous?"

"No, Babe, you are still the most beautiful woman I know."

Susan pulled the hairs on his arm. "Oh, yeah? Well, did you not tell me that I looked like the 'Bride of Frankenstein'?"

Clay grinned. "You must have dreamed that. I would never be so cruel."

"Liar, they didn't remove my brain, you know?"

"Okay, I give," he pleaded. "But I was only kidding. I was trying to take your mind off the problem at hand, and you know that's the truth."

"I know," she responded. "Although it warms my heart to see you squirm. And I love to pick on you."

Clay wanted desperately to talk to her about what he thought had just taken place; however, he wasn't sure how to begin. Before he could find the right words, she started asking questions.

"Johnny's doing well, isn't he?"

A bit relieved, he answered. "Yes, Susan, he's coming along nicely. He asked about you when I was last in his room. We have all been concerned, but you are doing great."

"Yes I am," she asserted. "You know, Clay, God sent me back to watch over you, and that is what I'm going to do." She hesitated, "I adore you, and I'm going to give you a son."

Clay's mouth fell open. "What did you say?"

Carl R. Smith

"I said, I'm going to have your son. I don't know how I know, but, I know. So there!"

He leaned forward and kissed her gently. "That's wonderful, Sweetheart, nothing would make me happier. Actually at this very moment you need to rest, and I'm gonna get out of here for a little while so you can do just that."

Susan's eyes were getting noticeably heavy, and he knew it was time to leave.

"I love you, Babe," he whispered. "I'll be back real soon. You rest now."

"Ditto, and I'll be here waiting for you, Spook-key."

Before he could say another word she was in slumber land. He was sorry to have to leave, but at the same time he was glad she was resting so comfortably. The conversation they would have sometime in the not too distant future would be a thing of beauty, and he knew it.

He had to return to Johnny's room; he had a favor to ask. Johnny was wide awake and in control of his faculties.

"Well," Johnny said. "Two visits in the same night; I must really rate."

Clay perched himself on the foot of Johnny's bed. "I need to talk to you for a minute."

"This sounds serious. What's wrong?"

Clay reached to hold his hand. "Nothing's wrong, I need to ask you a couple of questions."

"Ask," Johnny replied.

Clay began. "I am going to visit the general in a little while and I need some help. Do you have anything in your medical bag that I could use to put a dog to sleep? And, if so, can you tell me how to administer it safely?"

Johnny caught on quickly. "No I don't, but I can get you something from here. And I can show you how to use it rather easily. Shall I?"

"Yes, please."

Johnny pushed the button for the nurse.

"What do you need Doctor Murphy?"

"Nurse, would you please send the on-call doctor to my room as soon as possible?"

"Is there something wrong, Doctor?" she inquired.

"No, Ma'am. But I do need to talk to him now."

"I will page him immediately," she replied.

"Thank you, Ma'am, I'll be waiting."

"Boy, you doctors sure have a lot of clout," Clay said admiringly.

Johnny chuckled. "Yeah, in a hospital we're as powerful as senators."

Before Clay could even respond a young doctor entered the room,

"What can I do for you, Doctor Murphy?" he asked.

Johnny went through this amazing story, and this young doctor was hanging on his every word. The story centered on this female dog and a huge litter of pups, a vicious male dog and the need for removal of two pups that were desperate for medical attention. When Johnny had ended his story, even Clay was confused.

The young doctor asked, "Who's going to administer the chloroform?"

"I am," Clay replied. "That is if Doctor Murphy will show me how."

The doctor wasn't sure; although, it was obvious he wanted to be of service.

"I'll get you what you need," he assured. "Give me about fifteen minutes."

"That'll be fine," Johnny acknowledged.

And the doctor left the room.

Clay looked at Johnny. "Even Tim Siler would have been proud of that work of fiction. And you say I can think on my feet. That was incredible; I'm in the company of true genius, and I am truly humbled."

The doctor returned with the supply of chloroform. They thanked him profusely and he returned to making his rounds, but not before wishing Clay good luck on his project; whatever that was.

Johnny spent some ten minutes demonstrating how the chloroform was to be used. Listening carefully was a must; otherwise, Clay could end up minus an arm, a leg, or some other body part he wasn't anxious to part with.

Clay was ready to go, but he wanted desperately to talk to Johnny about what had taken place earlier in Susan's room. After chit chatting for a few minutes Clay decided this was not the time; Johnny was showing signs of exhaustion. Clay knew it would be better if his friend was on top of his game. The discussion could get lengthy and very involved, and he needed Johnny's full and undivided attention.

Chapter 13

Clay was about to come face to face with the man who had raped and killed Gidget, one of his three dearest friends. The adrenalin rush was mind boggling, and he found himself enjoying the feeling.

The general lived in Sterling, Virginia some twenty-five minutes away, and when Clay arrived there it was just after midnight. Parking some distance away, he circled the entire property on foot just to get the lay of the land. Afterwards, he moved his car into a different position to afford him a more direct and speedier getaway if that became necessary.

He neither saw nor did he hear the guard dogs. Regretfully, he was certain they would appear sooner or later, and he hoped he was adequately prepared. Climbing the fence and dropping to the ground on the other side, he waited. After what seemed like ten minutes he moved to a clearing, thinking this would offer him a better vantage point. From here he could see in all directions for more than ten feet. Suddenly, ninety-five pounds of vicious Doberman came from his right. Catching the dog in mid-air he went flying backwards. The canvas bag containing the chloroform rags was of no use to him; however, with the strength of Samson, he snapped the dog's neck and jaw. *One down, and one to go,* he thought.

The next one came for him and clamped onto his forearm. This time he stuck his arm and the dog's head into the bag. In seconds the animal went limp. *Damn,* he thought. *I'd rather not go in there bleeding all over the place.* Dumping the soaked rags on the ground next to the sleeping animal he wrapped the plastic bag around his injured arm, split the top, and tied it securely.

The house was dark, with the only light coming from the perimeter lighting. Placing the surgical shoe covers over his sneakers, he began to pick the front lock. Very little sound could be heard, as he gained entrance to the foyer. The only audible sound was that of his heart beating in his ears, and his shallow breathing.

Having studied the layout of the house he went left, entering the general's study. He removed the tape recorder from his jacket and set it on the desk. Then he pushed the on switch to the recorder. "I'll be seeing you in all the old familiar places," a famous tune by Tommy Edwards began to blare from the recorder.

Choosing a seat across the room; he waited. In moments he heard someone coming down the stairs. "It's alright, Honey," the general yelled back toward his bedroom. "That darn cat must have turned the radio on. I'll get it, you go back to sleep."

"Are you sure that's all it is?" she yelled.

"If it were anything more than that the dogs would be raising hell," the general replied, seemingly irritated. "Now, go back to sleep. I'll be up in a minute."

As the general entered the room Clay eased up behind him, resting his weapon against the nape of the general's neck. The general stiffened.

"What the hell - - -"

"Shut up, you sadistic bastard. Turn off the recorder, walk around the desk and take a seat. If you make even one unnecessary move, or if you make any sound of any kind, I'm gonna splatter your brains all over that beautiful desk."

The man never moved.

"Do it now, Asshole," Clay demanded.

The general did as he was told. When in place, he carefully seated himself in the leather chair in front of the desk, obviously suited to his large posterior.

Clay said, "With your feet, push yourself away from the desk and toward the fireplace, then fold your arms across your chest."

The general complied. "Now what?" he said angrily.

Clay began. "You and your cohorts have killed, or have tried to kill, everyone I know and care for. What you did to your own stepdaughter was beyond reprehensible; it was sordid and depraved."

"I don't know what you're talking about."

Clay's face burned with rage. "Did I tell you to speak? Did I?"

"No."

Clay calmed. "Lay your right hand on the desk, palm down."

Nervously, the general replied, "What are you going to do?"

Swiftly, Clay took a note spindle from the desk and drove it through the general's hand and deep into the desk.

The general leaped to his feet, screaming.

Then, without saying a word, Clay grabbed the other hand and slammed it on the desk; but this time he chose a double-edged letter opener. Almost as quickly, he stuffed his handkerchief into the general's mouth to muffle the noise.

"I didn't come here to kill you General Matthews; although, when thoughts of Gidget cross my mind the anger overwhelms me." Clay paused. "I'm gonna give you a better chance than you gave her."

He proceeded to wrap the general's ankles with duck tape, stretching the tape some two feet on each end in order to secure each one to opposite ends of the fireplace. Now, the man was spread-eagle between the desk and the fireplace.

Clay pulled the desk chair to the front of the desk and seated himself. "Pay close attention, General, I'm only gonna say this once. If you send anyone else to harm me or my friends, or if any of my friends have an accident, I'll personally kill each and every one of you; all ten, do you understand? I'll kill each member of your families, your pets, and I'll burn your houses to the ground."

The general's eyes were so wide Clay could almost see his reflection in them.

Clay stood. "Do you fully understand me General Matthews? Nod your head, General."

He nodded vigorously.

As Clay was about to leave, the general succeeded in freeing his left hand from the desk; pulling the handkerchief from his mouth he began to scream.

"Helen, help. Call the police, I'm - - -"

Clay reached him and secured his hand once more, and stuffed the handkerchief back in his mouth.

"The phone lines have been cut General. Helen will be of no help, and you have sealed your doom. I gave you the opportunity to live."

Hearing footsteps on the stairs Clay moved to the right of the doorway and waited. When Helen entered the room he grabbed her from behind and put her in a head lock; within seconds she went limp. Clay knew when the brain is denied oxygen one becomes incapacitated almost immediately. He laid her gently on the floor and returned to the general. She was only unconscious; when she woke up she would have a major headache, nothing more.

Clay returned his attention to the general. "It's time to die, General."

Taking his knife from its sheath, Clay stepped over the outstretched tape. Now he was behind the man; reaching under the general's crotch with the precision of a surgeon he made the cut. The blade of the knife was so sharp it was like cutting soft cheese. When the Femoral Artery is severed a man will bleed out in less than two minutes.

He wiped the blade on the general's robe. "You can die in a puddle of your own blood, just the way you left Gidget. You, General, are a lewd and lascivious bastard, and you're gonna bust hell wide open."

Clay jerked the gag from the general's mouth.

"Any last words, General?"

"Don't let me die. Please, I'll give you anything you want."

Clay smiled. "I have what I want. I believe it's called 'sweet revenge'. Anyway, someone said, 'revenge is a dish best served cold'. And, General, as your life's blood is rapidly oozing from your body; in moments, you will be as cold as a stone."

With his last breath, and hate pouring from every part of his almost lifeless body, he uttered. "I'll see you in hell, Boy."

Clay was checking on the woman. She was breathing and about to come around. He looked up. "You better hope not, General, for if that happens we'll repeat this over and over again for eternity."

In only minutes, Clay was out of the house and in his car, headed northeast. His arm was beginning to hurt, so he wanted to see Johnny first. The vehicle the senator had gotten for him to drive was almost as much fun as his GTX. It was so responsive he had to be extremely careful not to overdo. This would not be a good time for a speeding ticket.

The hospital was as quiet as a morgue. When he got to Johnny's room it was almost two AM. The two guards were alert and talking to each other in whispers.

"What happened to you?" Smelcher asked. At least that was the name on his uniform.

"I had a bit of an accident," Clay replied.

"Do you want me to get the nurse?" he asked.

Clay just looked at him. "I need to see Dr. Murphy first."

The other ranger spoke up. "He's been asleep for hours, Sir."

Clay said. "Well then, he won't mind my waking him up."

The two rangers just looked at each other, as Clay opened the door and walked into the room moving quickly to Johnny's side.

"Hey, Johnny, it's Clay, I need some help."

It took a minute but Johnny finally came around.

"What time is it?" He asked.

"It's a little past two," Clay replied.

Johnny reached back and flipped on the smallest light. Startled to see his friend's arm wrapped in a plastic bag he tried to sit up. Failing that, he pushed the bed control and raised the head of the bed.

"Are you alright, Old Buddy?"

"Yeah, I think so. One of the dogs got a piece of me before I could put him out. I don't think it's too bad; but, I thought you should take a look at it."

Johnny pushed the button for the night nurse. While they were waiting for her to arrive he began removing the plastic bag from Clay's arm.

"It doesn't look too awful, but you'll need a tetanus shot. Where's the dog?"

"I don't know," Clay answered. "He's probably still out, if not, he's running around the general's yard trying to find me, I guess. Why?"

Johnny looked concerned. "We have to test the dog for rabies. Otherwise, you'll have to take a series of injections."

Clay chuckled. "Hell, Partner that dog received better care than most children. Just give me the tetanus shot and get the nurse to clean the wound."

The nurse, a Ms. Reynolds, came in.

"What's wrong, Doctor, can't sleep?" She hesitated, "Doctor Murphy, I know you are somewhat privileged, but this man should not be in your room at two-thirty in the morning."

"It's okay, Nurse," Johnny declared. "I want you to take him to the treatment room and see to his arm. He needs a tetanus shot, and the wound needs to be cleaned, sterilized, and bandaged properly. Nurse Reynolds, will you do that for me, please?"

She looked at Clay, then at Johnny. She then took Clay by the hand and led him from the room, down the corridor to the treatment room.

Clay finally broke the silence. "I'm sorry to be such a bother. Although, Doctor Murphy assured me that you were such an angel of mercy you wouldn't mind in the least."

"Don't try snowing me, Young Man."

"I didn't mean - - -"

"Just be quiet and drop your trousers," she insisted. "This will be less painful in your backside."

"Anything you say, Nurse," he answered, unbuckling his pants.

"Stop shaking," she said. "It's not gonna hurt that much."

"Sorry, but it's your hands, Nurse. They're as cold as ice."

She snickered. "Well, I can't help that."

Cutting the Fringe

By the time she was finished, she and Clay were getting along handsomely. She even gave him some hot coffee, and some kind of coffee cake that was sinfully delicious. They talked for a few more minutes, and Clay even wrangled some coffee and cake for the two rangers and Johnny.

It had been nearly thirty minutes; however, Johnny was still awake and wanting to talk when Clay got back to the room.

"Are you alright?" he asked. "Do you need something for the pain?"

"No, I'm not in any pain, at least not physically," Clay replied.

"Tell me what happened. Did you talk to the general?"

Clay spent the better part of an hour explaining everything to Johnny; although, Johnny did interrupt once in awhile just for clarification. Even though Clay was quite graphic, Johnny hardly batted an eye.

"Did the woman see your face?" Johnny asked.

"No, and the general died before I left the room. Also, I wore surgical gloves and shoe covers. Many will know it was me, but there will be no proof, and if need be the senator will swear that I was with him for the entire evening."

Johnny pushed the button to lower his bed.

"Forgive me, Tonto," he muttered. "I think those painkillers I took when the nurse was helping you are kicking in. Can we finish this tomorrow, Old Buddy?"

"Sure, Lone Ranger, you get some rest and I'll see you later."

Johnny was out like a light. Clay wasn't feeling any too good either, but he was determined to visit Susan before he left for Chevy Chase.

Outside her room the rangers were walking the corridor. He greeted them and then went in to see Susan. She was sleeping soundly and hugging the shaggy dog Clay had bought for her the previous day. He sat beside her bed and wrote her a fairly long note. He had no intention of waking her, but he wanted her to know he had been there. At the end of the message he wrote, *I wish I were the shaggy dog you are holding so tightly.*

When Clay reached the senator's circle driveway, the FBI agents were quick to check him out.

"Is everything calm and peaceful?" Clay asked.

They had no problems to report.

Before he could move his car Sergeant Shackelford emerged from the front of the house.

"Clay, are you headed to the house to get some rest?"

"Yeah, Shack, I'm beat. Is the senator coping?"

"He's doing remarkably well, all things considered," Shack replied.

"Is that Jolene sitting on the steps?" Clay asked.

Shack grinned. "Where I go she goes. She's like my shadow."

"Let me talk to her," Clay said, shutting off the motor and exiting the car.

"Please do, she won't even let me go to the bathroom alone."

Clay was met halfway. The minute Jolene got within earshot she began blurting.

"I have stayed as close to the sergeant as possible; but, Mr. Clay if you're going home, I'm going with you. I think the sergeant is tired of having me around. In fact, I'm sure he would like to be rid of me."

Clay placed one hand on each of her shoulders. "Slow down, Jolene, you're gonna pop your cork."

"I'm fine now that you're here, Mr. Clay," she insisted.

He was too tired to argue. "Go get what you need, and I'll wait for you."

She hurried off.

Shack was about to find out about the general when Jolene came flying out of the house at a full gallop.

"I'm ready," she said, breathlessly.

"Get in the car, Girl. I'll be right there, as soon as I have a word with the sergeant."

Turning his attention to Shack, he said. "Look, Old Friend, don't be surprised by anything you hear. Things went a bit crazy with General Matthews. Actually, except for a dog bite, I'm fine and he's not."

"Did you punch his ticket?" Shack whispered.

Clay's expression changed. "An 'eye for an eye,' 'blood for blood'."

The sergeant smiled. "You know, it's more dangerous being your enemy than it is being your friend."

"I hope you really believe that," Clay replied.

"I do, Clay, I really do."

"One last thing, Shack. Late tomorrow afternoon, I want to meet with you and the senator in Johnny's hospital room. Set it up, and let me know the time; but, do not wake me before noon, unless Jesus returns."

"Do you want me to get hold of Mr. Siler?" Shack inquired.

Clay hugged him. "Please do and I'll see you later."

Carl R. Smith

Shack hugged him back, unashamed. "I'll take care of everything. You get some sleep, and thanks for taking Jolene with you."

"No problem!" Clay smiled sheepishly. "That's what friends are for."

Shack poked him. "Well, don't do anything I wouldn't do."

Clay laughed. "She's all yours, My Friend. Hell, I'm too tired to even think. Goodnight Shack."

"Goodnight Clay."

Chapter 14

The garage door shut behind the car and Clay just sat there. Jolene had not stopped talking. He knew that it was nervous energy. He also knew that sometimes talking to Sergeant Shackelford was like talking to a stone statue, and that she was desperate for someone to pay her some attention.

When she paused to take a breath, he seized the opportunity.

"Jolene, please calm down, you're giving me a headache. Let's go inside and have a drink, then maybe, if I'm lucky we can get some badly needed sleep. Okay, can we do that?"

"Absolutely," she replied, opening the car door.

"Great," he muttered.

Jolene headed up the steps, key in hand.

Clay went flying through the air. "Wait . . ."

Wrapping his left arm around her waist they went tumbling off the three steps and landed against the west wall with a great thud.

"What the hell are you doing?" she screamed.

Clay was still holding on for dear life as gravity took over, and they slid down the wall and safely to the floor.

"Be still, Girl," Clay said calmly. "That door may be wired. You might have gotten us both killed."

"I didn't know, I'm sorry," she replied.

Clay just looked at her, totally exasperated. "I know."

"Well, what are we to do?" she asked.

"If you'll get off me, I'll check it out," he answered.

When they were safely inside he got her a beer and mixed himself a drink. Jolene sat on the sofa sipping her beer.

"Where do we sleep?" she asked.

"C'mon," he said, reaching for her hand.

As he was leading her from the sofa to the downstairs bedroom, some twenty-five feet away, he couldn't help noticing how cold her hands were, and she was still shaking.

"You can have the bed, and I'll sleep on the sofa in the other room," he explained.

She encircled him with her arms, like a frightened child. "No way, I'm sleeping with you, and that's final."

Clay was entirely too tired to argue. "Whatever," he replied. "Crawl in the bed, if you want? I've got to take a shower and brush my teeth."

She started with him towards the bathroom. He stopped her.

"I don't need any assistance," he stated.

"Clay . . ."

He picked her up in his arms and carried her to the bed.

Cutting the Fringe

"C'mon, Jolene, I'll tuck you in. I'll leave the light on, and I'll leave the bathroom door open. Please, Honey, I won't be five minutes, I promise."

"Okay," she replied. "Go on, I'll sit right here on the bed and wait."

He grabbed some pajama bottoms and was in and out of the bathroom in record time, and she was still sitting in the same spot, wide-eyed, and legs crossed.

"Are you gonna sleep in your clothes?" he asked. "You know, you don't have to worry, I'm not going to attack you."

"I know that," she said. "You must think I'm awfully stupid."

"Not, at all. I don't think you're stupid. I just meant . . . Oh, to heck with it, let's get some sleep."

Jolene hopped off the bed and began to undress.

Clay, paying her no attention, turned off the bathroom light and got into bed. In a matter of seconds she was right beside him. However, when he turned off the lamp by the bed she darn near crawled inside his skin.

"Thanks, for keeping me safe, Clay," she whispered.

"You're welcome, Sweetie. Now, can we get some sleep?"

Snuggling close, and kissing his neck, she said, "Yes, Sir, absolutely."

They slept soundly, and when Clay opened one eye to peek at the clock it was five minutes after eleven in the AM. Jolene was still wrapped around him, kinda like a Python holding its prey. He tried to ease away without waking her, but it was useless.

"Sorry, Jolene," he said. "I've gotta go to the bathroom. You can go back to sleep for a few minutes if you want."

"What time is it?" she asked.

"It's after eleven." Clay paused, looking for his slippers. "I've gotta shave and shower; I'll wake you when I'm finished."

She grunted, and he headed for the bathroom.

When he exited the shower she was not there, but he could smell the coffee, and it brought a smile to his face. *She must not be as scared in the daytime,* he surmised.

She came rushing from the kitchen, handed him a cup of hot coffee, and began disrobing on her way to the shower.

"I'll be out in two shakes," she declared.

Clay sipped the coffee, carefully, and began getting dressed.

Just as he was retrieving his watch from the bedside table the telephone rang, and his heart nearly stopped. He lifted the receiver.

"Hello."

"Clay, it's Shack. It's right at noon, and I thought you might need a nudge."

"Thanks, Old Pal. Is the senator alright?"

"Well, he's been better," Shack replied. "Do you think you might be able to get Jolene to come over and fix him some food? He's totally helpless."

"Yeah," Clay responded. "We'll be there in a few minutes."

Jolene was true to her word; she was out of the shower and ready to go in minutes.

Clay explained everything to her as they walked between the houses. When they got inside the senator's place Jolene went straight to work. She was really quite the professional. She attended to the senator's personal needs and had lunch on the table in less than forty-five minutes. Clay tried to help, and he did actually set the table.

When the senator came to the table, his greeting was warm; otherwise, the entire meal was somber. As usual, Clay broke the ice.

He began, "Senator, will you be available for a meeting at the hospital early this evening? We need to discuss some things, and your input is needed most of all."

The senator seemed to brighten up a little. "I told the sergeant that I would be there about six-thirty; will that be okay? I'm trying to get the final arrangements settled for the internment."

Clay looked at Shack, and then focused on the senator. "Yes, Sir, that'll be fine. I'll meet you there."

The senator nodded. "Oh, by the way, we'll be receiving friends tomorrow evening from six until eight here at the house. I certainly hope you will have time to make an appearance."

"I'll be here, Sir. You can count on it."

"Thank you, Son. I know it would mean a lot to Trish, she liked you an awful lot."

"Are the children coming back for the service, Senator?" Clay asked.

The senator perked up once more. "Yes, but I'm sending them right back to their aunt's until this mess is over. Don't you think that's best?"

"Probably," Clay replied.

The senator started to get up; therefore, Clay and Shack both came to their feet immediately.

"Relax, Fellas. I'm going back upstairs to lie down. Shack, wake me at five o'clock, if I'm not up by then."

"Yes, Senator."

The senator turned back toward the table. "Men, would you thank Jolene for all the trouble she went to?"

"Yes, Sir," they replied.

Clay and Shack sat quietly until the senator was out of earshot.

They continued to look at each other, each one, waiting for the other to speak.

"He looks bad, doesn't he Clay?"

"Yes, Old Pal, he does. You stay close to him, Shack."

"I will, Clay, don't you worry."

Clay stood, "Let's go into the den. I want to talk to you about Jolene, and I need a cigar."

As Clay was lighting up, Jolene walked into the room.

Clay motioned to her. "Come, take a seat on the couch, I need to explain something to you."

Complying with his wishes she moved in that direction.

"Is there another problem?" she asked.

"No, it's not a problem," he explained. "We, that is the senator, the sergeant, and I have a meeting at the hospital at six-thirty this evening. I think it would be best for all concerned if you came to the hospital and stayed in Susan's room until the meeting is over. What do you think?"

She got this weird look on her face. "Well, I'm sure as hell not going to stay here by myself."

"I didn't think so," Clay replied. "Then it's settled, you will come to the hospital with the sergeant, okay?"

"Yes, Sir."

Clay took a deep breath. "Everything's settled then. I'll see the both of you at the hospital."

Jolene jumped from her seat. "Wait a darn minute. If you're leaving, I'm going with you."

Clay backed up. "Look, Jolene, I think you should stay here with the senator and the sergeant. I know you have things that need to be done. Anyway, they need to eat about five-thirty, before coming to the meeting."

"But, Mr. Clay - - -"

"Hush," Clay scolded. "The sergeant will be here with you, and I trust him with my life. Please, Jolene, you'll be at the hospital by dark. These two men need you, c'mon now."

"Okay, I'll do as you asked. Be warned, Mr. Clay, if I get killed my blood is on your hands."

Heading for the door, Clay whirled around. "That's all I need, another person's blood laid at my feet." He hesitated, "Well, don't you fret, Sweetie. The pile is much too high already, and I don't think there's room for anyone else."

He looked at Shack, who nodded knowingly. Then he departed rapidly, not waiting for any other comments.

Getting to the hospital was foremost on his mind; however, the traffic was incredibly bad. It was nearly two PM when he pulled into the parking lot. Finding a place to park was another pain, but to be honest he simply couldn't wait to see Johnny and Susan.

Susan came first, and when he opened the door to her room she was lucid. She even had a smile for him. That told him she was feeling much better, and nothing could have made him happier.

"Oh, Clay, I've been waiting for you to get here. You don't look as tired as you did the last time you were here."

He kissed her on the cheek, and quietly thanked God for their good fortune.

"You still look a little like a pin cushion, Babe; although, your smile is as beautiful as ever. I miss you Susan, and I'm sorry I haven't been here more."

She squeezed his hand; another good sign. "It's no big deal. I know you've been working. Can you tell me what's been happening?"

"Not right this minute. I have to go see Johnny for about fifteen minutes. When I get back I'll stay with you until after supper. Rest and think good thoughts. You know you're still my best girl, right?"

"Yes Clay, I know. Go on now, and give my best to Johnny. I'll just take a short nap."

She was almost asleep before he got out of the room. Johnny, on the other hand, was wide awake and being a little difficult to deal with. Nurse Ford was about to clobber him when Clay walked into the room.

"Mr. Smith," she said. "If you don't calm the good doctor down I'm gonna give him a sedative."

"Johnny, quit giving this beautiful lady a hard time, or I'm gonna tell her how you got that big scar on your behind."

"You wouldn't dare," Johnny yelled.

Clay started toward him. "Get the needle Nurse; I'll sit on him for you."

"Alright, you two," Johnny said. "You guys ought to be ashamed of yourselves; the two of you, ganging up on a wounded man."

"Are you gonna quiet down, Doctor?" the nurse asked, winking at Clay. "If you will I'll get outta here and leave the two of you alone."

Clay winked back. "I can handle him, Nurse Ford; you go on and see to the rest of your patients."

"Thank you, Mr. Smith," she replied. "I'll leave him in your care, but if you need me I'll come running."

Clay thanked her and she left the room. Now, Johnny was pouting.

"I need to talk to you, Partner," Clay requested. "Get a grip. Anyhow, what the heck is wrong?"

"Oh, hell, I wanna get out of here, and I'm told it will be at least two more days. How are you gonna survive without me, Old Buddy?"

Clay tried to give him a hug; unfortunately, Johnny, was a might tender. They both started laughing. Johnny first, and then Clay joined in.

"Listen, Partner, Senator Lazar, Shack, and Tim Siler are going to meet me here in your room at six-thirty. I need to fill them in on the general, and afterwards we're gonna have a long talk, okay?"

"Sure," Johnny replied. "You get out of here and go see Susan. Hey, Clay, tell her that if they will let me up tomorrow I'll come see her. Oh yeah, give her a big kiss from me."

Clay patted his hand. "She sends her love to you too. And, Johnny, please stop being such a pain. I declare, you doctors make the worst patients; in fact, I believe you told me that yourself, remember?"

Johnny's big smile returned. "Killing me with my own words, now that's cold-blooded."

Clay walked to the door. "I remember what you say even when you don't think I'm listening. Bye John, I'll see you after six."

He went by the nurse's station, and asked them to send an extra supper tray to Susan's room. That way they could eat together.

The room was quiet. Susan was sleeping soundly. He sat in the chair by the bed, laid his head back and closed his eyes. Simply being in the same room with Susan felt good to him, and knowing she was going to be alright caused his emotions to surface. *Thank you God, I won't forget this one. God, you can call in your marker any time you want, and I'll be there for you. Not that you couldn't handle things by yourself Lord; but, if you ever need my help, well, I'm here.*

Clay must have fallen asleep. When he opened his eyes the nurse was in the room doing her thing.

"Sir would you like something to drink?" she whispered. "We have soda, milk, coffee, and juice. I would be more than happy to bring you something."

"Not right now," he replied. "Although, maybe I'll walk down that way a little later, would that be okay?"

"Of course," she answered. "I'll be glad to show you where we keep things; just ask for me, I'm Karen."

Clay smiled broadly. "Thank you Karen, I'll do that."

Without making a sound, she walked across the room and out the door. As the door was closing he could see one of the rangers peeking in to check on things. Clay gave him the high sign, and he returned it, looking very professional.

He was not about to disturb Susan's sleep, but oh how he wished she would awaken so they could talk. However, he fell back to sleep once more waiting for that to happen.

Clay was startled by a young girl entering the room with a dinner tray in each hand. He leaped to his feet to offer some assistance.

The young girl smiled at him. "Thank you, Sir, but I do this all the time."

She set the trays on the table at the end of the bed. Then she rolled the table to the proper height and moved it into place. After she had completed her task, she strolled away without another word.

Susan was coming around. "Supper huh, I'll bet they brought me more Jell-O," she mumbled. "Gosh, I hate Jell-O."

Sure enough she was given some kind of chicken broth, tapioca pudding, apple juice, and Jell-O. Clay raised the lid on the other tray. It contained two medium pork chops, peas, rice, a dinner roll, coffee, milk, chocolate sponge cake, and a small container of vanilla ice cream.

Carl R. Smith

He looked at her soulfully. "I'll share, Babe. You can have the cake, the ice cream, and the coffee. I don't think your stomach is ready for meat and veggies yet. Anyhow, later I'll go downstairs and have them make you a huge milk shake. Don't be sad, Doll Face."

She grinned. "I'm not sad, not as long as you're here. Tell you what, I'll take the ice cream and the coffee, you eat the cake and drink the milk."

"Sounds like a fair deal to me," he answered.

He got a towel from the bathroom and laid it across her chest. Then he rolled the bed up as far as he dared, and offered to assist her. She would have no part of it.

"I can do this myself," she declared. "You eat your own dinner; I'll make out, you just watch."

He sat on the end of the bed facing her, and prepared to eat. They ate, they giggled, and they enjoyed each other's company.

"Why do you keep looking at your watch?" she asked.

"Well," he replied. "I'm meeting Senator Lazar, Tim Siler, and Shack in Johnny's room at six-thirty. However, I will return with your milk shake in an hour or so. And, by the way, Jolene is going to stay here with you while we're having the meeting."

Susan's expression never changed. "You mean she wanted to come visit me? Is Patricia coming too?"

Clay's insides did a flip-flop. He was seldom at a loss for words, but this was one of those times. Not wanting to lie to her, he answered. "Ms. Lazar was not at home, and quite frankly, Jolene was afraid to be alone in the big old house. So, she thought she'd come and stay with you. Please say you don't mind," he entreated.

"Mind? Not at all, it will give us a chance to talk and get to know each other. Look, Clay, I know we got off on the wrong foot; but heck, she seems like a very nice person. I'll be glad to see her."

He just stared at her in disbelief. "Susan, when I expect it the least you always impress me the most. I guess that's just one of the many reasons why I love you so darn much. It doesn't hurt that you are one of the two most beautiful women in the world today."

Her mouth flew open. "One of two? Alright, Buster, who's the other woman?"

"Aw c'mon Susan, you know who the other woman is."

She threw the towel at him. "No I don't, but you better come clean, Big Boy."

"Natalie Wood," he said shyly. "You know, I've always said she was maybe the most beautiful woman in the world, or at least she was till you came along."

She grinned. "You're right, I forgot, it must have fallen out during surgery."

"Actually," he continued. "I guess I'm saying, she's the most beautiful brunette, and you're the most beautiful blond. Now, did I clean that up sufficiently?"

"Yes you did. Now, you may get me a little water, and a cup, along with my toothbrush, and I will plant one on you that will make you forget all about Natalie Wood."

"Susan, I'll have to go downstairs and purchase you a new toothbrush, I'll - - -"

"No, you won't," she interrupted. "They gave me one. It's in the drawer right there beside you."

Clay did as she asked. Luckily, there were four toothbrushes in the drawer, three still in their wrapper. He took one for himself, and went to the bathroom to make use of it. Upon his return she handed him the bowl of used water and asked him to dump it. When he exited the bathroom for the second time she was indeed ready for him. She was puckered like a fish, and motioning for him to come to her. He cracked up, but he got the kiss he so desperately wanted.

Looking at his watch, he knew he had to be going. He wanted to catch Jolene before she got to Susan's room. Otherwise, he might have a lot of explaining to do, and he didn't really mind that, but he wanted to wait for a better time.

He kissed Susan good-bye and promised her he wouldn't forget the milkshake. The door to the room closed behind him, and he spent maybe thirty seconds talking to the rangers when the elevator opened and the entire entourage came strolling down the corridor.

Clay explained everything very quickly to everyone with his focus being on Jolene. The whole bunch had come to see Susan. Afterwards, the men were going to leave Jolene with Susan and visit Johnny's room where they could conference.

Chapter 15

It was like old home week when Clay, Shack, and the Senator finally assembled themselves in Doctor Murphy's presence. It was even better because Johnny was still feeling rather feisty. That gave the entire group immediate hope for the future.

Clay spent the next few minutes telling Johnny about Patricia. He carefully avoided the part about Shack overhearing her phone conversation. The senator sat in the chair beside Johnny's bed with Johnny's hand on his shoulder. Clay walked the floor most of the time he was speaking. Sergeant Shackelford sat by the door in one of the two chairs they had brought in from another area. Tim Siler sat on the other side of the door. Everyone was content to be silent as Clay continued to explain. When he was finished, Johnny spoke first.

"Senator Lazar, I am so very sorry for your loss. It doesn't help you to know that Clay and I know exactly how you feel. We both lost loved ones. Clay may have lost more than the rest of us, but we must remain strong."

"I really never thought of that," the senator replied, his eyes moist from newly shed tears. "Clay, I now know how you felt when you walked into my office that night after Pamela and her sister had been killed. I keep thinking that if I had done something different Patricia would still be alive. That's how you felt, isn't that right, Son?"

Clay knelt on one knee in front of the man. "Yes, Sir, and I still think about it. I guess I always will, and you may too."

Senator Lazar leaned forward and they hugged. "Clay, help me get those bastards."

"You can count on it, Sir. Hell, Senator, I think I already have."

The senator leaned back in his chair, eyes wide. "What do you mean?"

Clay patted him on the knee, stood, and parked himself on the end of Johnny's bed.

"May I speak?" Tim asked.

Senator Lazar, and Clay, both answered yes, simultaneously.

Tim stood, and began to pace. "I was there when you got the two men in the cafeteria, and on my way over here I heard that General Matthews was found dead in his home, by some woman, whose name they haven't released yet. Paul Kingery is covering the story, and he'll fill me in later this evening, I'm sure."

Clay said nothing; but, the look on the faces of the other three men in that hospital room would have been impossible to impart to an outsider, even for such a gifted writer as Mr. Siler. Fortunately, he would never have to make the attempt.

Johnny poked Clay in the hip with his left foot. "Old Buddy, I think you better tell them what happened."

It was quiet for a couple of minutes as Clay organized his thought. Then, as if he was painting a word picture, he began. There were no questions, only mouths, wide open. A very subtle smile crossed the senator's face; a smile no one had seen for two days.

When Clay had said all he had to say, he took a deep breath and asked if there were any questions.

The senator looked around the entire room, and stopped at Clay. "Well, I'm glad the son of a bitch is dead. I wish I could have seen his ugly face."

"Well, Gentlemen, where do we go from here?" Johnny asked.

The senator took the mantel of responsibility. "After receiving friends tomorrow evening, we'll all meet again, at my place."

"What about me?" Johnny asked, dejectedly.

The senator patted him on the arm. "Sorry, Doctor, we'll come back here, but we'll have to be fairly quiet. Lights go out at 2200 hrs around here, and we sure as heck don't want to draw any attention to ourselves."

"There's nobody on either side of me, so that shouldn't be any problem," Johnny interjected.

The senator rose from his chair. "Then it's settled. Gentlemen, I feel some better, and Doctor, you get better real soon. Come Sergeant, let's get Jolene and head to the house. I have a ton of things to get done before bedtime, and I could use a drink and a cigar."

Shack held the door for him. "See ya fellas," Shack said as he and the senator left the room.

Clay quickly followed after them. "Senator, would you be kind enough to tell Susan that I will be with her in about thirty minutes?"

"Certainly, Son, consider it done."

"Thank you, Sir," Clay replied, stepping back into Johnny's room.

Tim was standing by Johnny's bed and they were chatting. When Clay re-entered the room Tim turned to him. "I really need to be going, I'm two days behind also, but I'll see you at the senator's tomorrow night, and I'll see you back here afterwards, Johnny."

Clay pulled the door open and extended his hand. "Thanks for coming, Tim."

Tim took his hand, and a tiny grin appeared on his face. "I wouldn't have missed it for anything. Clay, don't let anything happen to you." He hesitated, "Actually, I'll call you sometime later, after Kingery fills me in on the general, okay?"

"Yeah, that'd be great, Old Pal."

The door closed, and Clay and Johnny were alone.

"How are you holding up, Partner?" Clay asked.

"I'm doing pretty well, all things considered. Are you alright?"

"Yeah, I'm better than I deserve."

Johnny pushed the button for the nurse. A voice came back. "How can I help you, Doctor Murphy?"

"I need something for pain," he replied.

"I'll be there in a minute, Doctor."

"Thank you Nurse."

Johnny grimaced. "My butt hurts."

"Sorry, Partner, but I'm not gonna rub it for you, if that's what you're hinting at."

Johnny laughed. "Just tell me how Susan's doing. I get reports on her, but so far I haven't been able see her, maybe tomorrow."

"She'd like that. Also, Johnny, I think it might do your heart some good. I was afraid we were gonna lose her."

The night nurse came in with a couple of pills, filled his water glass, and handed them to him. "Would you like some juice or something before you conk out?" she asked. "I'll get some for your friend too, if you like."

"No, I'm fine," Johnny replied. "Would you like something to drink, Clay?"

"Not for me, thank you, Nurse," Clay answered. "I've got to be going soon, but I do appreciate the offer."

As she was leaving, she turned. "If you change your mind let me know."

Johnny lowered the head of his bed, just a tad. "She was flirting with you, Old Buddy."

"Oh bullshit, she was not flirting with me."

Johnny smiled, "Yeah, right."

"Oh hush," Clay demanded. "I'm gonna go to the cafeteria and get Susan a milk shake, and I'll see you tomorrow."

"Okay, if you must, but give her a big kiss for me, and tell her I'll try to come and see her tomorrow. Will you do that?"

"Of course I will. I'll give her a big wet kiss, just for you."

Johnny said, "I hope she has the strength to bite your tongue. Now, get the hell out of here, I'm tired."

Again, Clay was torn. He wanted to talk to his friend about the ghostly incident that took place in Susan's room. Unfortunately, he would have to wait for a more opportune moment. He wasn't a patient man, but he didn't have much choice.

Thank goodness he got to the cafeteria in time to get a large chocolate milk shake. He always liked to keep his promises, and this was, to him, a very special promise.

Susan was awaiting his arrival. She was much more alert than she had been earlier.

"I knew you would remember," she exclaimed, as he entered the room, milk shake in hand.

He smiled. "How could I forget a promise made to my best girl? Johnny sends his love, and he might actually get to come see you tomorrow."

She took his hand. It was cold from holding the cup. She laid it against her left cheek and kissed his palm. "That would be terrific. I would really love to see him." She paused, "He must be doing great then, huh?"

"Yeah, he seems to be doing pretty well, but he sure is ornery. I think it must be the pain, and knowing while he's in here I'm on my own. Also, Sweetheart, I think he's feeling guilty. I reckon all three of us have a serious problem with that."

Susan's face showed her concern. "Hell, Clay, if he hadn't had the good sense to get off the highway where he did, we would both be full of bullets. He even tried to cover me with his body after the car came to a stop. Darn it, he has nothing to feel guilty about. You just wait til I see him; I'll straighten him out, but quick."

Clay smiled broadly. "That's my girl. You still got that fire in your stomach, don't you, Susan?"

"If you mean it makes me mad when someone is used and abused, or when someone is hurting needlessly. Yeah, things happen. It wasn't his fault. Actually, if I hadn't been so concerned about what kind of clothes to wear, or what I looked like he would not have been shot. So, I'll take the blame."

Clay sat on the bed, facing her. "The fault lies with the assholes of the world. Maybe, I'll just rid the world of the whole damn lot. What do you have to say to that, Cutie Pie?"

She reached for him with her one free hand. "Have I told you today, how great you make me feel? I love being with you, even when my head hurts."

He kissed her. "Ooh, your lips are cold, but the chocolate tastes good. I thought we were going to share?"

She giggled. "We are sharing. I drink the milk shake, and you kiss my lips. That way, I get the best of both worlds."

"Did you enjoy Jolene's visit?"

"Yeah, I did. She was very nice. Did you know that she has no family in this country?"

"No," he replied.

"Well, she doesn't. She's here on a work visa, and all the money she makes goes back to Scotland to her family. She has to survive on forty dollars a month; I spend that much on a pair of shoes."

"Bless her heart. I had no clue," Clay answered. "I thought she came from a well to-do family. She certainly seems well-bred, don't you think?"

Susan smiled. "I thought she was a bit uppity the first time we met; she acted a little high-brow. I guess that's just her nature."

Clay thought for a moment. "It may be a fence she's built around herself; we all tend to do that."

Susan suddenly became serious. "What is she so nervous about, Clay? She couldn't be still the whole time we talked. I would think it would be a snap working for the senator and his family. Is Patricia a bitch or something? She didn't act like a bitch when I was around her."

Clay wasn't sure how to answer. He hated lying, but he wasn't sure Susan was strong enough to hear about what had taken place in the past couple of days.

"Maybe she's got something going on you know nothing about," he replied, totally skirting the real issue.

"Well, you be nice to her," she urged. "If she needs a shoulder to cry on, lend her yours. You can put people at ease better than anybody, and I can tell she likes you. Her eyes lit up when I mentioned you, and she must have asked me a hundred questions about you."

"And did you tell her I was a jerk?"

"No. I told her you were amazing. I also told her she couldn't find a better friend, and I encouraged her to confide in you. She may try to do that, if she

Cutting the Fringe

does, just listen. I really think something is eating at her." Susan paused. "You don't think the senator is making her uncomfortable, do you?"

"I don't think so," Clay answered.

Susan was beginning to squirm a little. Clay knew she must be experiencing some pain. "Do you want me to ring for the nurse, Babe?"

"Maybe you better," she replied. "I need a shot of joy juice."

"Joy juice, what is that?"

She tried to smile. "That's what the nurse calls a pain shot, joy juice."

Clay pushed the button and summoned the night nurse. Within minutes she came and administered the shot, and before long, Susan, was starting to get groggy.

"Susan, I'm gonna sit with you until you fall asleep."

She looked at him through weary eyes. "You can go on, if you need to. I'll be alright."

He leaned forward and kissed her once again. "I'll stay, you rest, and I hope you have wonderful dreams."

"Thanks, Spook-key, you're the greatest . . ."

She was out for the night.

Clay went back by Johnny's room, and he was sleeping peacefully. Having tucked everyone in for the night, he decided, it was time to go home. It was almost eleven PM when he got to the house. He went straight for the bathroom and a hot shower. The hot water felt magnificent, and he just stood there for maybe five minutes. He turned off the water and stepped out of the tub. *What the hell was that?* It was coming from the outside of the

Carl R. Smith

house. He secured his weapon and flipped off the light, just as the doorbell rang.

Shack would have called first. Who the hell . . .

He went out through the garage. There was another door leading from the garage to the backyard; he took it. Creeping quietly, he circled the house. Standing on the porch was Shack and Jolene. When Clay spoke, Jolene almost jumped out of her skin.

"What's going on?" he asked. "Damn, Shack, why didn't you call?"

"I did, but you didn't answer. I was about to break down this door."

"I must have been in the shower," Clay surmised. "Well, c'mon. We'll have to go back the way I came, because I don't have a key to the front door."

Jolene said. "I do."

"Then why didn't you use it?" Clay asked incredulously.

"I was afraid you might shoot us," she answered nervously. "But, I would have said something before the sergeant broke the door down, I swear, I would have."

Clay just shook his head. "Whatever. Shack, you guys go on in. I'm going back the way I came and lock up the garage."

Shack looked somewhat befuddled. "Sure, Clay, I'll see you inside."

When everyone was finally reassembled in the den Clay got drinks for them. He got beer for Jolene and Shack; scotch and soda for himself. Lighting himself a cigar, he sat down on the hearth so he could blow the smoke up the chimney.

Shack finished his beer in about three sips. "Clay, I really better get back; the senator will wonder what's happened to me."

Laying the cigar down on the edge of the hearth, Clay walked him to the door.

"Shack," Clay whispered. "She can't stay with me every night. What am I going to do?"

"Don't look at me," Shack replied quietly. "You'll figure something out, Clay. I have all the confidence in the world in you."

He poked Clay on the arm and away he went. Clay locked the door, and turned toward the den and Jolene was right there, not two feet away.

"Holy shit Jolene! What the hell's going on?"

Jolene covered her face and cowered back a couple of steps. "I'm sorry," she cried. "I couldn't stay in the den by myself."

He reached for her and pulled her to him. "It's okay. I didn't intend to frighten you, and I'm sorry I raised my voice."

They began walking back to the den. When there, Clay retrieved his cigar and put it out.

"Do you want another drink?" he asked.

"Yes, I'll have another, if you will. Are you mad with me, Mr. Clay?"

"No, I'm not angry. I'll get the beer, stay put. I won't be two seconds, you have my word."

"Yes, Sir, I'll stay right here," she answered meekly.

Clay was back in a flash with her beer. He made himself another drink and joined her on the sofa. They sat quietly for a few moments, but she was still trembling. Sliding his arm behind her back and around her waist, he kinda picked her up, turned her, and set her on his lap. She laid her head on his left shoulder and began to calm down.

"Mr. Clay, I feel safe when I'm with you. I don't mean to cause you any trouble."

"I'm glad you're here," he replied. "I hate being alone anymore."

She cuddled in his arms, "Me too."

Clay looked across the den to the little bag that was sitting by the door. "What's in the bag? Are you moving in?"

She raised her head. "No. But, I do need to bathe. That is, if you'll allow me to use your bathroom. Also, I need to be back at the senator's by seven-thirty in the morning. I need to fix breakfast for the guys. Do you have an alarm clock?"

"Yes. Now, why don't you go do your thing? I've already taken my shower, so, I'll fix me one more drink, and we can hit the sack, okay?"

"Okay," she replied. "Will you come into the bedroom while I'm taking my bath? We can talk through the door. Please!"

Clay stood up with her still in his arms. "Pick up what's left of our drinks from the table, I'll finish this one and quit for the night."

Jolene picked up the glasses and they were off to the bedroom. After setting Jolene on the bed, he had to go back to get her bag. He set the bag on the chair beside the bed. Then he just flopped down on the side of the bed closest to the bathroom.

"If you need me, I'll be right here," he explained.

She lay back, and slid her body toward the head of the bed. When they were face to face, she kissed him.

"What was that for?" he asked.

"I wanted to kiss you. Are you mad with me?"

"No," Clay answered. "I'm not angry with you. Why do you always think I'm angry? Do I look angry?"

"You don't look anything. I get on people's nerves sometimes, and I so much wish to not get on yours."

Clay wasn't at all sure he understood. So he kissed her. He knew that would shut her up. "You worry too much, Little Lady. Now, go take your bath."

In seconds, Jolene was off the bed and in the bathroom.

Every few seconds she would holler something, soliciting an answer from him, so she would know he was still close by.

Clay thought it was amusing, but he played the game, knowing it was her fear, fear that he felt responsible for. Regardless of the circumstance, he was certain that much of the blame lay on his shoulders.

When Jolene entered the bedroom she was wearing a white nightgown, it had little straps across the shoulders and resembled a woman's slip. In fact, the picture that crossed Clay's mind was that of a movie he had recently seen. The movie was "Cat on a Hot Tin Roof" starring Elizabeth Taylor and Paul Newman. There was a bedroom scene in the movie where Ms. Taylor was wearing a white slip. To Clay, that was about as sexy as a woman could ever be, and Jolene looked scrumptious.

"I'm gonna fix me one more nightcap," he explained. "Shall I bring you something?"

"Not for me, thanks. I've already brushed my teeth."

Clay looked at her; she was shivering. "Do you want to come with me? I'll only be one minute, I promise."

Jolene jumped onto the bed, and almost dove under the covers. "I'll wait right here, under the covers. I'm freezing."

"I reckon so," he replied. "You're damn near naked."

"I'm sorry, Mr. Clay. You don't like what I'm wearing?"

As he started for the den he shook his head. "I didn't say that."

"Then you do like it," she said, gleefully.

"No comment," he answered, just loud enough to be heard.

He returned with his drink in hand and began to undress. When he was down to his trousers, he excused himself and went to the bathroom. His pajama bottoms were hanging on the back of the bathroom door. He donned them before flossing and brushing. Once he was through running a brush through his hair, he washed his hands and made a beeline for the bed.

"Look," he said. "You can sleep here if you want, but you're gonna have to share the covers."

"I'll share," she replied.

They lay there for the longest time, and he could hear her rhythmic breathing. Thinking she was asleep, he slipped out of the bed and went back to the bathroom. With all the drinking, he suddenly realized he had to drain the main vein. He washed his hands once again before returning to the bed.

"Are you alright, Mr. Clay?"

"I'm fine, Jolene, I thought you were asleep."

She rolled toward him. "Wow, you have muscles in your stomach, how do you do that?"

"It's called exercise, Jolene. I like to keep in shape, is that okay with you?"

"Yes, of course. Why are you angry with me? Have I done something to upset you?"

Clay voice calmed considerably. "Sorry, it's not you. I'm just worried about everything and everybody."

She moved her hand up to his face and ran two fingers across his forehead. At the same time she raised her body, using the other arm, enabling her to come to rest on her elbow. Now, she was looking directly into his eyes.

"I thought Susan was your girl, but she's not. She told me how much she loves you. Frankly, I was delighted to discover her secret. She likes women, but, of course you are aware of that. I also found out that you do not have a girlfriend."

Clay sat straight up, shoving Jolene to one side. "Jolene, I'm not looking for anyone. Did Susan tell you that every time I fall for someone, something bad happens? Well, it seems to work out that way." He hesitated. "I don't want to cause anyone else to get hurt."

Jolene smiled. "From what I've seen, you may very well be worth the risk. Susan says you're the most incredible man she's ever seen. She made a point of telling me that you can turn a woman on, so quick, it makes her blood boil sometimes."

Clay, never answered, he got out of the bed, walked across the room and entered the den.

She followed.

He walked to the fireplace and picked up a partially smoked cigar, moistened the end, and looked for a match. Before he could find a match, she spoke.

"I could light that for you, I'll bet. Damn, Mr. Clay, I'm so hot, I'm wet all over. Don't you want me?"

He walked over to her. They were so close together he could feel her hot breath on his chest. Taking her face in his powerful hands, he kissed her top lip, sucking on it gently. Then came the bottom lip, and, by the time he parted her lips with his tongue he was carrying her to the bed.

Desperately, she was reaching for him. However, he had other ideas. He laid her on her back and pulled her to the edge of the bed, where he was already kneeling. Starting at her toes, he kissed every part of her lower body. He was in no hurry, and by the time he reached her womanhood she was screaming loudly.

"Oh, Me Lord, I can't stand it. Please, please, please."

All at once she lost it, and her strong and powerful legs nearly crushed his head. Finally, she went limp. But, Clay was just getting started. He flipped her to her stomach. Sliding his powerful right arm under her waist, he pulled her to him, once more. She was dripping wet, which made the next part much easier. Without warning, he took her, and she made every effort to take him.

She was no stranger to what was happening. It took a bit of time; however, it wasn't long before she was slamming her body back against his, using the last once of strength left in her tall thin muscular frame.

Cutting the Fringe

Clay would not let it end; although, it took every ounce of his strength he could muster to hold back. She had lost control several times, each time becoming more moist, making it easier and less painful for the both of them. After some time and a lot of perspiration, he exploded.

He went into the bathroom and brought back badly needed towels. They dried each other, and after a few moments, Clay picked her up and retreated to the shower. As they washed, first her, and then him, she couldn't take her eyes off him.

"What?" he said. "Is there something wrong?"

"Wrong, absolutely not, Mr. Clay. You are the most beautiful - - -"

"Stop it," he scolded. "I am not beautiful. Men are not beautiful, they may look nice, they may even be handsome, but they are not beautiful."

"Fiddle Sticks, I know beauty when I see it," she argued.

"Okay," Clay surrendered. "Then you are one of the most handsome 'Little Fillies' I have ever come across."

When daylight came they were still finding ways to please each other. They were dog-tired, but incredibly satisfied.

Chapter 16

Breakfast at the senator's was pretty somber. Except for a few pleasantries, nothing much was said. Clay was almost sure that Shack knew what had taken place over the last few hours, and Shack was trying hard not to let it show.

Shack and the senator left for the office within minutes, it seems the senator had some pressing matters to dispose of. They promised to be back by early afternoon.

Clay walked into the kitchen where Jolene was. He proceeded to pour himself some additional coffee.

"Are you as tired as I am?" he asked her.

She put her arms around his waist, pulling herself against him. "I am really sore, but I could start all over again."

He kissed her on the forehead. "You're kidding."

She put her arms around his waist and pulled herself against him. "Do I feel like I'm kidding?"

"I gotta go. Will you be alright here with the FBI agents surrounding the house, or do you want to come with me to the hospital?"

She looked a bit uneasy. "As long as it's daylight I'll be okay. You will be back by nightfall won't you?"

"Yes, I will, and I'll give your best to Susan."

She wrapped herself around him once more, and kissed him tenderly.

Clay returned the kiss and headed towards the house.

The telephone was ringing as he rushed through the door.

"Hello."

"It's Tim. Are you going to the hospital anytime soon?"

"I most certainly am. With any luck I'll be on my way in thirty minutes."

Tim said. "How about I buy your lunch at the cafeteria? Say, about noonish."

Clay laughed. "That's fine with me, but I didn't think you would ever want to see the inside of that place again. Not after what happened the last time."

"Ah, tish tosh. I'm a big boy; anyway, you'll be there to protect me."

Chuckling, Clay responded. "Yeah, and I work real cheap too."

"I'll see you at noon," Tim replied. "I'll be the little guy hiding beneath one of the tables."

"See you then," Clay replied, placing the receiver in its cradle.

Clay, quite literally, ran through the shower once more. He brushed his teeth, washed his hands, and was out the door in twenty-six minutes. Not a record, but a damn good average.

He had begun to learn the feel of the car the senator had gotten for him to use. It may not have been his GTX, but it had a lot of muscle, and the music system was amazing.

Arriving at the hospital at a little before ten he went straight to Johnny's room. When he got off the elevator he noticed that the rangers were not in their usual places. His steps quickened, and his heart skipped a beat. Johnny's room was empty, and with that piece of knowledge Clay's heart fell to his stomach.

Sprinting to the nurse's station, he grabbed the first nurse he could find.

"Where is Doctor Murphy?" he yelled.

"Sir, you must quiet down."

"Don't tell me to quiet down. Where's John Murphy?"

"Have you checked his room, Sir?"

Clay was on the verge of blowing a fuse. "Of course I've checked his room. Where are the two rangers who were guarding him?"

"Oh, those guys. Some senator called and relieved them more than two hours ago."

Clay put one hand on each of the nurse's shoulders. "Nurse, I would advise you to find Dr. Lyons, before I start taking this place apart. Do you understand me, Lady?"

The nurse finally began to realize the urgency. "Sir, I'll have him paged."

"You do that, and do it right now," Clay demanded.

As the first nurse hurried away, Nurse Ford rounded the corner headed his way.

Now we'll get to the bottom of this, he thought.

Before she got to him she began speaking. "Is there some sort of problem, Mr. Smith?"

"Yes Ma'am. Doctor Murphy is missing. I was told that Senator Lazar called and dismissed the rangers who were guarding his room."

Paging, Doctor Lyons. Paging, Doctor Lyons.

Nurse Ford hurried ahead of him to Johnny's abandoned room.

Once Nurse Ford realized the gravity of the situation, she attempted to remain calm. "You wait right here, Mr. Smith. I'll get to the bottom of this, and I'll be right back."

"No way," he replied. "You can find me in Susan's room, number 311. I must warn you Nurse Ford, if Susan is not in her room, this hospital will be history by tomorrow."

Nurse Ford's eyes widened. "I'll find out what's going on, and I'll report to you in room 311 as soon as possible."

They both took off in opposite directions.

Not wanting to wait for the elevator, Clay took the steps three at a time. When he exited on the third floor, the first thing he saw were two rangers outside Susan's room, one standing, and the other one sitting in a chair by the door.

Relief calmed him some, and he rushed toward them. Upon reaching them, he asked. "Have you men been here all morning?"

"Yes, Sir, we came on at 0600 hrs, and we'll be here until 1400 hrs."

"Do either one of you know anything about the other two rangers who were guarding room 626?"

"Yes, Sir, we rode in together," the standing ranger explained. "But, Sir, the other two men left a couple of hours ago. I think their man got released from the hospital this morning."

Clay looked at him sternly. "Do you know who I am?"

The ranger came to attention, and the other one stood and came to attention as well.

"Yes, Mr. Smith," they replied simultaneously.

"Good," Clay said. "Do not leave your post no matter what anybody tells you, and if you are asked to leave, or if you are told to leave by anyone, do not do so. You are to remain here until I tell you otherwise. Is that perfectly clear?"

They both answered, "Absolutely, Sir."

Leaving them Clay went into Susan's room, and she was resting comfortably. Not wanting to wake her, he eased back into the corridor to wait for Nurse Ford. He didn't have to wait long. She got off the elevator within two minutes, tops.

They met half way. "Mr. Smith, I can't seem to find out what has taken place. I am told that Senator Lazar called this morning and removed the guard from Doctor Murphy's room."

"He didn't do that, Nurse. I was with the senator less than two hours ago."

Nurse Ford, who had seen almost everything, was nearly dumb-struck. "I have talked to Doctor Lyons, and he hasn't a clue. I just don't understand. Why would Doctor Murphy leave the hospital?"

Clay took her by the arm. "He didn't leave of his volition. Someone took him by force from this place."

Her lip began to quiver. "No, you don't mean - - -"

"Yes, I'm afraid I do mean." Clay paused to think. "Here's what I want you to do. Get on the intercom and ask if anyone saw someone being taken from this hospital by force, or if anyone saw anything suspicious. Tell them to come to, or to call, the sixth floor nurse's station, immediately."

"No, Mr. Smith."

"What do you mean no?" he was almost yelling.

"I'm stationed on the third floor. This is my floor. I just happened to be upstairs when all the commotion began. I'll tell them to call the third floor nurse's station. That's okay, isn't it?"

Clay put his hand to his forehead. "I'm sorry, Ms. Ford, that is fine. Forgive my lashing out. I should have been here."

She put her hand to his chest. "No one can be everywhere. Stop beating yourself up, Young Man."

"You're right, of course. Can I have the use of a telephone?"

Taking him by the hand, she led him to the nurse's station and found a phone for him to use. While he was making his call to the senator, Nurse Ford got busy on the intercom.

Senator Lazar's office, may I help you. "Clarisse, this is Clay Smith, may I speak to the senator?"

"Certainly, Mr. Smith, one moment please."

"Yes, Clay, what's going on?"

"Senator, Johnny has been kidnapped from the hospital. The nurses said you called over two hours ago and took the guards off his room."

"I did no such thing."

"I know that, Sir. However, someone called using your name. Thank God they didn't hurt Susan. And, by the way, the guards are still at Susan's door."

"Clay, I can't leave here just this minute, but I'll be there before noon."

"Thank you, Sir. If you will, Senator, please come to room 311. Tim is supposed to meet me here at noon, also."

"Do you need the sergeant?"

"Hell, no; you tell him that I said he had best stay close to you at all times."

"Alright, Clay, see what you can find out, and I'll see you as soon as possible."

"Thank you, Senator Lazar. I don't know what I would do without your help."

"Likewise, Son," the senator replied as he hung up the telephone.

Clay went looking for Ms. Ford. When he got to her she was talking to one of the orderlies.

"What's going on?" Clay asked.

Nurse Ford looked up from her chair. "Pete, here, says he saw three men literally dragging another man to a green van this morning, sometime before 0800 hrs. He had come on duty at 0700 hrs, and, at about 0730 hrs he went

Cutting the Fringe

back to his car to retrieve the lunch bag he had inadvertently forgotten. On his way back from the parking lot he saw the three men."

"They were dragging and carrying him, like he was drunk or something," Pete said, excitedly.

Clay went to his wallet and pulled out a picture of Johnny. "Was this the man they were dragging?"

"Yes, yes, that is the man," Pete vowed.

"Did you see the license plate, by any chance?" Clay asked.

Pete hung his head. "I'm sorry, Sir, but I did not." Then his eyes lit up. "But, there was a vacuum cleaner on the side of the truck, and it was red. There was also some writing, but I don't know what it said. I don't read so well."

Clay patted him on the back. "That's okay, Pete, you did real well. Thanks for coming to talk to us; and if you think of anything else, give us a holler."

"I will, Sir, and you too Ma'am."

Clay and Nurse Ford watched as he walked away.

The telephone rang.

Nurse Ford answered it, and immediately handed the receiver to Clay. "It's for you, Mr. Smith."

"This is Clay Smith. Who - - -"

"Mr. Clay, its Jolene. This man just called the house and he said he's gonna kill Doctor Johnny. He said he would call back in one hour. He said you best be here to talk with him or the doctor is a dead man."

"Clam down, Jolene. Did he say anything else?"

225

"No, Mr. Clay, you better come quick. Please, I'm scared to death."

"I'll be there as fast as I can. Don't hang up the telephone, but lay the receiver down, then go to the front door and holler for one of the FBI Agents and put him on the phone, I want to talk to him. Will you do that for me?"

"Yes, just a minute."

Clay could hear her lay the receiver on the desk, and then he heard her hollering. In a minute or so, a man's voice, was on the other end of the line.

"This is Talbot. Do you need to talk to me Mr. Smith?"

Clay explained everything in detail. He told Talbot to please stay in the house with Jolene until he arrived, and if by any chance the people were to call back before he got there; Talbot was to pretend to be him.

Talbot agreed, and Clay took off, but not before, once again, telling the rangers at Susan's door not to move. He explained, in some detail, what had taken place with Doctor Murphy, and they quickly got the picture. He also asked Nurse Ford to call the senator, and then she was to call Tim Siler.

As he hurried toward his car he heard a female voice call after him.

"Mr. Smith! Wait, Mr. Smith!"

Clay turned quickly recognizing Nurse Ford's voice. "Yes, Ma'am, what is it?"

Out of breath, she began. "Mr. Smith, call me if there is anything I can do. I promise I'll do anything that I can to be of service. You will call me, won't you?"

He gave her a quick hug. "I will let you know, if there is anything you can do to help."

Hugging him back, she ushered him on his way.

When he arrived at the senator's house, Jolene and Talbot were drinking coffee in the kitchen. It had been exactly thirty-seven minutes since the first call, and there had been no others.

He thanked Mr. Talbot for his help.

Talbot nodded. "I have taken the liberty of having a trace put on the senator's phone. Maybe when they call again, we'll get lucky."

Clay was pacing. "I sure hope so; I could use a break about now."

The telephone rang, and Talbot jumped to attention. "You pick up when I say three," he ordered.

"Got it," Clay replied.

It was Tim. "Clay, I'll be there in twenty minutes, please stay put if you can. We need to talk."

"I'll certainly try," Clay replied.

"See you in twenty. Keep the faith, Sport."

Clay hung up, and collapsed in the chair. Before he could adjust his position the telephone rang a second time.

Talbot held up his hand, "On three, Mr. Smith."

"Right," Clay replied.

"This is Clay Smith, may I help you."

A husky voice came from the other end of the line. "Come to the west end of the warehouses on Glen Allen Street, at midnight tonight, if you want to see Doctor Murphy again, alive that is. If you are not alone, or if you're late, we'll slit his black throat and dump his body into the bay. Do you understand?"

"I understand," Clay replied.

The line went dead.

Talbot hung the receiver back in place. He displayed this nasty look on his face. "Well, that was a waste of time. What are you going to do, Mr. Smith?"

Clay said. "I don't see that I have any choice, but to do exactly what they tell me to do. Do you?"

"I know that area," Talbot explained. "We can get cameras into place, on the other side of the dock. At least we'll get a look at them."

Clay responded. "That's okay with me, but I don't want you guys within a hundred yards of that place. Johnny's life depends on my being alone. If they spot you, it will be all over for Johnny. I know you understand that."

"I understand, Mr. Smith. But, you know they're gonna kill both of you. You do know that, don't you?"

Nodding his understanding, Clay began to plot.

"Talbot, can you get me some maps of that area, and if possible, some schematic's of the warehouses?"

"I think I can do that. Let me get on it." He hesitated. "I need to talk to my partner, he's still outside. Give me a few minutes. I'll let you know something; although, it may take me a little time."

Clay grimaced. "Well, don't take too long, or it won't make any difference. I don't want this to become an act of futility."

Talbot began moving toward the door. "Roger that."

Throughout the entire conversation, Jolene sat motionless. Now, she was in Clay's face. "Mr. Clay, please don't do this, they will kill you."

Tears flowing, she held him close.

Clay returned her embrace. "Honey, they can't hurt me, I'm impenetrable. Any way, I can't just leave Johnny to die. If it was me out there, he would come for me, I know he would. Fortunately, I'm better at this than he is."

Jolene clung to him. "I know nothing I can say will stop you."

"Look, Jolene, Johnny does his operating, and I couldn't do what he does. I can do this; this is what I do best."

A faint smile crossed her lips, as she looked up at him. "I know what you do best, and that's not it."

"Cut it out," he said. "Make me some coffee, Woman."

She walked away, after poking him in the gut. "I'll make your coffee, Man. Do you need something to eat?"

"Not right now. Maybe after Tim and everybody else gets here, you can fix us some lunch, if you don't mind?"

"Why should I mind," she answered wryly. "That is what I do best."

He walked across the room and smacked her gently on the rump. "Bullshit! You may do it well, but I too know what you do best."

Jolene turned coffee in hand. "Here, drink this."

"Thank you."

"You're welcome."

Chapter 17

The entire group was together in the senator's den, minus Johnny of course. This time the senator started.

"Clay, I called the base and I talked to the base commander. He said the adjutant took the call at 0712 hrs this morning. The man identified himself as Senator Lazar, and he told them that Doctor Murphy was being released from the hospital this AM. He told them that the guards were no longer needed. We should have had a password."

"Is it fair to assume that we now have one for the guards on Susan's room?" Clay asked.

"Yes we most certainly do," the senator replied. "But that doesn't help Doctor Murphy."

Clay took a quick sip of his coffee. He almost spit it back into the cup. "I hate cold coffee. May I fix myself a drink, Sir?"

"You don't have to ask, My Boy. You can have whatever you want."

Tim said. "I'll make them, I know what everyone likes. I'll go to the kitchen and get you a beer Sergeant, and then I'll fix our drinks."

Shack said. "I'll go get the beer; you make the drinks for everyone else."

Clay waited for Shack to return before going on. He had a plan, but Shack was an integral part of that plan, and he didn't want to get started and then have to repeat himself. So he waited.

The sergeant came back into the room just as Tim was passing out the other drinks. As Clay was about to begin, Talbot walked through the front door, grinning.

"Mr. Smith, I'll have everything you asked for in about an hour. Also, with any luck, we can have sharpshooters in place by nightfall. From the vantage point we will have to take, they will be prepared to hit a moving target at a distance of better than eight to nine hundred yards."

Clay said "Thanks, Talbot. Just be sure that Johnny or I are not one of those targets, okay?"

Talbot was still grinning. "No sweat. I have two men who could light a match at more than a thousand yards. You have nothing to worry about from our end; you have my word on that."

"May I meet with those guys?" Clay asked. "I'd like to set up a signal of some kind, and I want them to be the only ones who know my signal."

"Will do, Mr. Smith, I'll have them here as soon as possible."

"Thanks Talbot, I owe you one."

Talbot headed back to his assigned post.

Clay stood. "With your permission, Senator, I'm going out to the kitchen and ask Jolene to fix us some lunch. By the time we've eaten, the information I asked for should have arrived."

The senator stood as well. "I'll go to the bathroom while you're doing that. Help yourself to another drink, Tim. Sergeant, I'll bring you another beer from the kitchen."

In a few minutes they were all reassembled in the senator's den. Clay and the senator lit cigars and the planning session was on.

"Here's what I'm gonna try to do," Clay began. "If I can get the schematics on the surrounding warehouses, I'm gonna go in as soon as darkness comes. If I'm extremely lucky maybe I can surprise them."

He looked over in the direction of Sergeant Shackelford. "Actually, Shack, I thought we'd surprise them."

"Hell yes, Clay, I'm a player," Shack replied, almost gleefully. "You already know that we work well together."

"You bet I do, and they won't be expecting us to hit them first. Surprise could be our best weapon."

Tim said. "I like the idea. It sounds like a plan that should work. Of course, that's easy for me to say, considering I don't have to be in harm's way."

Clay punched him on the arm. "Hell, Tim, I thought you were gonna be the third musketeer."

Tim's head flew around. "I know you're kidding, right?"

The senator almost laughed out loud. That was a welcome sight, considering all he had been through in the last few days.

Clay said, "Actually, Tim, you could loan us a camera. Do you have one that will flash more than once?"

"Yeah, I have one that will flash up to six times without reloading. But, I thought you were gonna shoot them, not take their picture."

"Frankly, I hope that Shack and I can do both, and I hope we can do it at exactly the same time."

Jolene walked into the room. "Gentlemen, lunch is served. Please, wash up, and come to the table."

The senator rose. "C'mon, Men, we can finish this at the table."

Clay and the senator put out their cigars, and everyone took their respective turns in the wash room.

The senator took his usual seat at the head of the table. Clay sat to his immediate right, Tim to his left, and Shack to Clay's right.

They were quiet for a moment. Clay was the first to speak.

"Here is the entire plan. Shack and I will go in and locate the kidnappers. If there are four or less, then we can make this work. After we locate them, I will slip back outside. I will get far enough away so when I appear to be approaching at midnight, they won't be suspicious. The sharpshooters will take out whoever comes to meet with me. Hopefully, there will be no more than three. If there are three, one man will take out the man on my left, and the other, the man on the right, and I will take out the one in the middle. If there are only two, then I will hit the deck."

Tim said, "When will they know it's time to shoot?"

"Shack will point the camera towards the window. When he hits the flash, the fun begins. The sharpshooters will take out their men, and Shack will take out his. Then I will get back inside as soon as I can, and I will assist Shack. Lastly, I will carry Johnny to safety."

The senator was fidgeting. "Is there nothing I can do to help?"

Clay looked in his direction. "As a matter of fact, you can, Sir. You can be sure that an ambulance gets there no later than twenty past the hour. Senator, they must be certain not to use their sirens, or it could give us away."

The senator acted pleased. "I can see to that. Thanks for including me, Son."

"You're always included, Senator," Clay assured. "In fact, everyone at this table is joined at the hip in some way or another. We've all put our butts on the line, including you Tim."

"Right you are, Pal," Tim said. "Let us not forget; however, I have the smallest butt in the room."

Everyone got a chuckle out of that one. They were still laughing as Talbot entered the room.

"Tell me the joke; I need a good laugh about now."

Clay said, "No joke. We were just laughing at Mr. Siler's butt."

Talbot got this weird look on his face. "On second thought, maybe I don't need to hear the joke, or whatever."

Everybody laughed again.

Talbot continued, "Mr. Smith, I laid the plans on the senator's desk. Also, the sharpshooters are on the way here."

The senator moved his chair back and stood. "Everyone grab your plates and carry them into the kitchen. I'll have Jolene clean off the table. Talbot, bring the plans in here; we can spread them on the table."

"Yes, Sir, I'll be right back, Sir."

The guys did as they were asked. Clay helped Jolene clear the remainder of the dishes from the table.

In no time they were perusing the plans, with great care. Fortunately, they were able to decipher them with little or no trouble. Clay took a tablet and began simplifying what he had seen. He wanted to make the routes they were going to take easier to follow. The print needed to be a great deal bolder, so as not to be confusing.

Shack was especially pleased, for he was having a hard time understanding what he was looking at.

Tim watched Clay with great interest.

"How do you do that?" he asked. "You never once looked back at the plans as you were making your sketch."

"I don't know," Clay replied. "I've always been able to remember things. It's a gift, or a curse, take your pick."

Clay and Shack went over that piece of paper again and again. By the time they were finished, everyone in the room felt they could have walked the line in the dark, and that is precisely what Clay and Shack had to do.

Feeling reasonably sure that every detail had been accounted for, Clay handed the copy he had made to Shack.

Clay said, "I need a stiff drink."

The senator took Clay's arm. "C'mon, Son, let's go back to the den. We can finish our cigars."

Shack said. "I'll be there in a minute. I'm going to the kitchen for a beer. Is that okay, Senator?"

"Of course, Sergeant, we'll wait for you in the den."

Tim began making the drinks. "What will you have, Talbot?"

"Nothing for me," he replied. "I'm still on duty."

Just as Shack arrived, the doorbell rang.

Talbot said, "I'll get it, it's probably my men."

Indeed it was, and Clay wasted no time. He explained to them, in the most miniscule detail, the exact plan, and the part they were to play. It was nearly two-thirty, and Clay began pacing, trying hard to think. He wanted to be absolutely sure he had missed nothing; after all, Johnny's life depended on it.

Suddenly, he remembered something. "Tim, you said you had something to tell me, and I clean forgot. What was it?"

Tim gulped his drink. "I guess its okay to say it here, in front of everybody. Clay, the President wishes to speak with you, and you can thank the Senator for this one. After I got the call about Johnny, I called his office and told him it would be Thursday, at the earliest."

Clay's eyes got as big as saucers. "You told the President of the United States that he would have to wait until Thursday?"

Tim chuckled. "I told him you were a very busy man. And, of course I explained about the senator's wife's funeral." He looked at Senator Lazar.

"I hope that was proper, Sir. It was as much of the truth as I was willing to divulge."

The senator cleared his throat. "Not a problem, Tim. That was, at least, partially true."

"Thank you, Senator," Tim said. "I knew you would understand."

Clay still couldn't believe it. He was, if he didn't die that very evening, going to get to have a conversation with the President of the United States of America. What a thrill.

It was almost three PM, and Clay felt that he and Shack might need a little nap. What he really wanted was a chance to be alone with his thoughts. Sometimes he just had to get his mind right. He could usually do that around Johnny, but without Johnny present, he wanted to be left alone, at least for the short haul.

Tim was talking to the senator, while Clay, Shack, and Talbot went over the plan one last time.

"Guys," Clay said, "I need a short respite, and if Talbot will agree to stay here in the house with you Senator, Shack should rest for a couple of hours also. Is that okay with you, Sir?"

The senator quickly agreed, and Talbot was amenable to the plan.

Tim said. "Clay, I'll get a camera for Shack, and I'll show him how to use it. I have one in the car that is pretty small. I think it will do the job for you."

"Thanks, Tim," Clay responded. "Shack, My Man, I'll see you back here at five-thirty sharp." Clay dropped his head, and then he slowly looked at the senator. "Senator Lazar, you know how much you mean to me. I am truly sorry that I cannot be here for you this evening. I would give anything if circumstances could be different. Unfortunately, we must play the hand we're dealt."

Senator Lazar walked around the desk, eyes moist, and in front of everyone he put his arms around Clay. "I care for you, too. Losing you would be impossible for me to deal with. Please, be extra careful, Son."

"I will, Sir," Clay replied. "Heck, with my man Shack at my side, nothing bad could possibly happen."

Shack stood tall.

Clay shook Tim's hand, and gave him a little hug. He then shook hands with Talbot. "Thank you, Talbot you've been a God-send."

"You're welcome. And I honestly wish I could be going with the two of you, but, trust me; you have my two best men backing you up."

"I believe that," Clay said smiling. "Just be sure they know where to set up. I won't have time to do that."

Talbot returned the smile. "Count on it."

Clay looked at Shack. "We are, aren't we Shack?"

"Right, Clay."

The senator intervened. "Go on Clay, get some rest, and you too, Sergeant."

Tim headed to his car to get the camera, and Clay headed to the house, but not before asking the senator to have someone ring his phone at five-fifteen.

Clay's thoughts were on Johnny, as he walked toward the house.

"Mr. Clay, wait."

He turned. "Jolene, what are you doing?"

"I'm worried about you. I have been praying for you all afternoon." She took something from her pocket and placed it in his hand. "Take this; it will keep you from harm."

It was a Saint Christopher Medal.

"Thanks, I may need it. That was very thoughtful. Let me walk you back to the house."

Jolene gazed into his eyes. "You go on, I'll be alright."

Clay couldn't believe his ears. "Honey, you've been scared to death for two days now; why the sudden change?"

Her eyes became moist. "I guess my feelings for you are stronger than my fear. When I came running after you, I didn't even think about being afraid for my safety."

Clay took her in his arms. "That is the greatest gift you could have given me. I'll use those feeling to increase my courage."

She kissed him, and then she turned and ran away. She yelled as she ran. "Come back to me, Mr. Clay. I'll pray for you all night, and I'll light a candle for you."

Clay stood there for a moment, almost dumbfounded. Indeed, his spirits were raised, and he felt a sudden calmness. Jolene had unselfishly given of herself; something he did not expect.

Lying on his bed, eyes closed, he could still see the glow on Jolene's face, and the sincerity in her beautiful green eyes. *When someone displaces their fear for the well-being of another*, Clay thought, *that must put a huge smile on the face of God.* With that thought in mind he fell peacefully asleep.

The ringing of the telephone was not a welcome sound. Although, Clay was somehow anxious to get to the task of saving his dearest friend, Susan was in the forefront of his mind at that very moment. He made a quick call to the hospital and left a message for her at the nurse's station; knowing full well, that if he got her on the phone he would have to explain his absence and the time constraints prohibited that from happening.

He slipped into his shoes, secured the weapons he felt were necessary, and out the door he went. It was almost five-thirty, so he sprinted the last fifty yards.

Sergeant Shackelford was waiting patiently in the kitchen when Clay arrived.

"Are we ready to do this?" Clay asked.

"I was born ready," Shack answered. "Let's do it."

Clay smiled. "I had better say good-bye to the senator."

Shack grabbed his arm. "I don't think that's a good idea. People are already arriving for the wake. There must be fifty people here already."

Clay nodded. "Let's slip out the back. I sure as hell don't wanna cause a scene. Anyway, my car's in the senator's driveway. I hope we're not blocked in."

They weren't. The die was cast, and Clay was in an attack mode. In minutes they were out of the neighborhood and on the main highway.

Chapter 18

It was getting dark very quickly. However, they were almost at the docks on warehouse row.

Looking over at his friend, Clay asked, "Are you scared, Shack?"

"Not really," he replied. "I am a bit anxious though. A lot of what we're about to do depends on correct timing. That frightens me more than anything else."

"Right you are, My Friend, but there is no other man who I would rather have by my side. Thank you for always being there for me. You, Sergeant, are the epitome of what friendship is all about, and I will not forget that you entrust your very life to me. I honestly can not think of anyone else with whom I would feel safe at this moment, not even Johnny."

"Thanks, Clay. That means a great deal coming from you; because, I know you don't trust many people, and neither do I."

Shack was about to display some real emotion. That was not something he felt comfortable doing. He was basically the ultimate soldier. Hard as nails, never flinching, and so proud of his country that it showed in every fiber of his being. Sergeant Shackelford was what young soldiers called a "Lifer"; although, in Shack's particular case, the word "Lifer" carried a whole new meaning. It meant, honor, integrity, commitment, and an unwavering love and devotion for the United States of America.

Both Clay and Shack knew what their country meant to them. They also knew that even though there were some bad apples in the military and in politics, the vast majority of those men and women were above reproach when it came to serving their country and doing their respective jobs.

Considering an immediate need for the vehicle they were driving could happen at most any moment, Clay parked as far away from his supposed meeting place as he could, yet leaving the two of them a quick retreat, if that became necessary. He and Shack had dressed so as to camouflage themselves. Clay had donned a dark jumpsuit that he could discard before meeting with the kidnappers if that were indeed to happen.

They entered the long row of warehouses from the east end. Clay's midnight meeting was to take place at the extreme west end. Following this approach, they could systematically search each and every building before midnight; at least that was the plan.

The warehouses were mainly wide open. There was nowhere, at least in the first one, where they could have been holding Johnny.

"We need to move on," Clay whispered.

"Right you are," Shack answered. "Let's go."

There were half a dozen warehouses just like the first one, nothing. In the next row; however, things were a might different. Those warehouses contained many coolers, all of which were open and easy to inspect. At some time in the past they must have been used for the storage of perishable items, maybe even meat.

Continuing on, they talked only when it was absolutely necessary. Finally, reaching the last three buildings they encountered two vehicles parked inside. The hoods of the vehicles were cold, telling them that they had not been moved for quite sometime. Unfortunately, there was no one anywhere to be found, and the place was as solemn as a tomb.

As they were leaving the third to last warehouse, Shack touched Clay's arm.

"What do we do if they're not here?"

"I don't know," Clay replied. "We'll cross that bridge, when, and if we come to it."

Shack nodded his understanding and they moved on.

Before they even entered the next to last building, they knew they had hit the jackpot. Being incredibly careful, they were able to get inside. There was a light coming from a small room about halfway down, and there were three men playing cards and drinking beer. The men were making no attempt at being quiet.

Clay whispered, almost inaudibly, "I don't see Johnny anywhere. You stay here; I'm gonna look for him. If I'm detected, kill one or more of them, and I'll attempt to handle the others."

Shack gave him the high-sign, signifying that he understood. With that, Clay was on the move. Fortunately, from Shack's vantage point he could watch Clay until he disappeared behind one of the coolers.

To Shack it seemed like an hour, but finally Clay's figure showed up in the distance. In another minute or two they were side by side once more.

"What did you find?" Shack whispered.

"Not very much; although, I'm pretty sure there is no one else around."

Shack looked puzzled. "Did you see the doc anywhere?"

"No, I didn't."

"Well," Shack said. "What now?"

Kneeling, Clay shifted his weight from one knee to the other. "I think we should work our way close enough to take them. We've got to take at least one of them alive, or we may never find Johnny."

Shack said. "If we can get the drop on them we can ask all the questions we want."

Being incredibly careful they got themselves in place. The door to the little room was already opened, so all they had to do was get inside quickly. The basic problem was that the doorway was very small and whoever went first had to get completely inside the room and go left or right, giving the man behind a clear shot.

Clay went first, gun in hand. "Okay men," he screamed. "One false move and you're dead."

He stepped quickly to his left and Shack came through the door, stepping to his right.

As luck would have it, there is always one idiot in most every group. The man to the far right grabbed for a gun, and when he made his move, Shack shot him, clean through the head. The other two men never batted an eyelash.

Clay reached into his jacket and produced the old reliable duct tape. "Keep them covered Shack."

"Will do," Shack replied.

They bound both men. Clay taped one wrist at a time, and then he threw the roll of tape over a huge pipe some foot and a half above the men's head. In five minutes or so the two men were hanging, arms spread, like two sides of beef.

The questioning began in earnest.

"Where is Doctor Murphy?" Clay asked the first man.

The man answered with a Spanish accent. "I tell you nothing; he is probably dead anyway."

Clay took his knife and cut the man's belt, causing his trousers to drop to the floor. Then he said. "This is your last chance, fella, where is he?"

"Screw you," the man screamed.

Clay stuck the blade of his knife between the man's legs, and with one decisive move he cut the Femoral Artery. Blood began spurting, and the man began screaming. Backing up, Clay looked at the fear in the eyes of the other man.

"He'll be dead in less than two minutes," Clay said, rather matter-of-factly.

Shack's expression never changed. However, as the dying man's head fell forward, gasping his last breath, Shack had something to say.

"Can I do the other one, Clay?"

Clay smiled, purposefully. "Sure, My Friend, but I warn you, stay behind him, and cut from front to rear, or you'll get blood all over your clothes."

"I'll be careful," Shack replied.

Clay and Shack were both watching the other man's expression, out of the corners of their eyes. After a minute or so, Clay handed the knife to the sergeant.

"Get it over with," Clay ordered. "Look at him; he's too stupid to talk."

"I'll talk, I'll talk," the man yelled. "Please don't kill me."

Shack walked toward him, knife at the ready. "Where is the doctor?"

"He's in the cooler; the one with the lock on the door."

"Where? Which cooler?" Clay yelled.

The man nodded violently to his right. "Over there. You had better hurry, he's probably dead, there's not much air in there."

"If he's dead," Clay said. "I'll come back and kill you myself. Watch him Shack."

Clay went running for the cooler, stepped sideways, and shot the lock off the door. Johnny was lying on the floor, but, thank God he was still breathing.

Johnny looked up at him. "Hey, Old Buddy, I guess you saved me again. You're not getting tired of saving my ass, are you, Tonto?"

Clay put his arms around his friend and helped him to his feet. "Not as long as I live and breathe," he replied. "That's Tonto's job, you know?"

Johnny tried to smile. "I love you, Old Buddy, and I knew you would come get me. I'm glad you didn't wait, I don't think I could have made it too much longer."

Shack saw them coming and he began smiling from ear to ear.

"Are you alright, Doctor Murphy?" he asked.

Johnny said. "I'm okay." Then he pointed at the dead man hanging from the huge pipe. "What happened to Poncho Villa?"

"Low blood pressure," Shack replied.

Clay brightened up. "Damn, Shack, you're developing a sense of humor. I think I like it."

Johnny said, "Me too."

Clay looked at his watch; it was almost ten-thirty. "Guys, I'm going outside and see if I can get the attention of the sharpshooters."

"What sharpshooters?" Johnny asked.

"Tell him Shack," Clay answered. "I'll be back in a minute."

Outside Clay waved and waved, hoping the guys were already in place, and would come running. He went back inside.

"Shack," he said. "Go get the car. I'll stay here with Johnny and our hanging friend."

"Will do," he answered, and sprinted away.

The front door to the warehouse opened. "Mr. Smith, are you in there?"

Clay hollered, "We're back here fellas."

Within seconds two men came into view. "I guess you didn't need us after all, Mr. Smith," one of the men said.

"I do need you," Clay declared. "I need you to take this man into custody." He pointed to the man still hanging from the pipe.

"We can do that," the blonde-headed agent said. "Is it over, or is someone still coming to meet you here?"

Clay scratched his head. "I don't know. I guess it would be nice if one of you could take the guy in, and the other one could stay here with me, just in case."

They talked it out as Shack returned with the car. When everyone was finally together Clay went into his planning mode.

"Okay, Shack, you take Johnny back to Bethesda, and don't leave him alone."

Putting his arm around Johnny's waist, Shack started for the car immediately.

Clay began again. "Now, Fellas, you make the decision. One of you take this man in, and the other one can stay here with me."

The two agents cut the man down, handcuffed him, and took him to their vehicle. In a minute or so the blond-headed agent returned.

"I told Harry to send another car for us. But, I told him to be sure the car did not arrive before twelve-thirty."

"You did good," Clay responded. "I hope they bring something to haul off these dead bodies, they're beginning to give me the creeps."

The agent looked at his watch. It was eleven-forty. "Well, we don't have long to wait, Mr. Smith."

The two men tidied the place a little, in case the man who was supposed to meet them showed up and came inside. They stood on either side of the front entrance, waiting quietly; hoping to hear a car pull up, but no one came. At twelve-twenty they heard a vehicle.

"That's probably Harry," the agent said, as he started for the door.

"Wait," Clay screeched. "Let him come to us. I can't see outside, can you?"

There were no windows and only a tiny crack in the door, and you could see almost nothing.

They waited for two minutes, and nothing.

Clay looked at the agent. "You stay put unless you hear a commotion. If you do, come running."

"Will do," the agent replied.

Clay hurried down the inside wall of the building until he found a side door. He exited the warehouse and crept in the shadows to the end of the outside wall.

There was an ambulance, and Harry, leaning against the car smoking a cigarette. Clay approached him.

"What in the hell are you doing?" Clay snapped.

"I came to pick you guys up, and the ambulance was sent here by Senator Lazar. We were waiting on the coroner. He's supposed to come and view the bodies before they haul them off."

Clay turned, disgustedly, to holler for the other agent; but, having overheard the conversation he was already exiting the building.

"Harry, you dumb bastard," the agent screamed, "I ought to knock your block off."

"What are you guys so pissed about?" Harry asked, innocently.

Clay and the agent looked at each other. "Forget it," they said in unison.

Fortunately, the coroner and the police arrived at that very minute. Otherwise, Harry might have gotten a punch in the nose from his partner. The police wanted to question everybody, but thankfully the agent told them that he would file a complete report later. Reluctantly, Clay and the two agents were permitted to leave.

As they drove off, Clay said. "Fellas, would you be kind enough to drop me off at the hospital?"

"Certainly, Mr. Smith," they replied.

Harry got a smack on the back of his head from his partner.

"What was that for?" he yelled.

His partner said, "Shut up and drive, Harry."

Clay almost burst out laughing. Actually, he was so happy about Johnny being safe he wanted to shout, but he controlled himself. There would be time for shouting at another time. Under his breath, he said, *Thank you, God. That's two I owe you.*

The agents dropped him at the Bethesda Naval Hospital at a little before one-thirty in the morning. He went straight to the front desk and asked for the room of Doctor Murphy.

"He's in room 626, but you can't go up there now."

"Why not?" Clay inquired.

The man looked at him with an immediate dislike. "Because, it is past visiting hours, and no one is allowed to visit after 2200 hrs."

"Young Man, my name is Clay Smith and I work with Senator Lazar. I'm going to room 626, and I'm in no mood to be messed with. Do I make myself perfectly clear?"

The man began standing, which took a few seconds; he was a very large young man. "Maybe I didn't make myself clear. You are not to leave this floor."

Clay looked up at his nametag. "Chamberlain, don't let your big mouth write a check your big butt can't cash."

Chamberlain put both hands on the counter, which was a huge mistake. Clay grabbed the index finger of the man's right hand and almost took him to his knees, which was no small task.

Leaning in real close Clay spoke quietly. "If you push this any further I'm gonna break something important to your manhood. Do we understand each other now?"

Perspiration was actually falling from the man's chin onto the counter. "Yes, Sir, you may go up."

"Thank you," Clay said, giving the man's finger one last nudge. "A little advice, Chamberlain. Do something about that bad breath, it's a killer."

Chamberlain just looked at him as he walked off.

When he got to Johnny's room Shack was asleep in the chair, and Johnny was resting comfortably. Not wanting to wake either one of them he hightailed it to Susan's room.

The rangers were on duty as usual, and were actually glad to see him. They had heard about Doctor Murphy, but they had said nothing to Susan.

"Is someone coming to guard Doctor Murphy's room?" he asked.

"I believe they are on their way," the taller one replied.

"How is our patient doing?" Clay asked.

Again the taller one answered, "The nurse says she's doing real well."

"Thank you," Clay said, as he gently opened the door.

She was sleeping soundly, as well. He walked over and kissed her on the cheek. Susan opened her eyes, and smiled.

"Where the hell have you been? Don't you love me anymore?"

"You know I love you, Babe. There has been a lot going on while you've been lying here on that pretty little butt of yours. I will explain everything to you tomorrow, I promise. Now you go back to sleep; I'm gonna check on Johnny."

"Alright, Spook-key, I'll give you one more chance."

Clay stared at that beautiful face. "I will always love you Babe. Goodnight."

He went back to Johnny's room, and, low and behold, the rangers had arrived and were on duty. After a lengthy introduction, they finally allowed him to enter the room. He wasn't angry, but rather pleased that the two men took their job seriously, and he told them so in no uncertain terms.

Johnny was still asleep, but Shack was tossing and turning. He woke up and came to his feet. "Everything work out okay?" he asked.

"Everything's fine," Clay replied. "Have you talked to the senator or Talbot?"

"Yes, I talked to Senator Lazar, and he said for you to call him when you got to the hospital."

"It's almost two-thirty, Shack; do you think he wants me to call now?"

"I'm sure he does," Shack answered.

"Well, let's get out of here, or we're gonna wake Johnny. We can call him from the telephone booth downstairs."

Shack agreed, and they headed for the elevator. Clay told Shack about Harry and he got a real kick out of it. They got to the bank of pay phones in the lobby and realized that neither one of them had any change.

Clay went to the front desk to speak to Chamberlain. Chamberlain was his old self once more.

"Oh, it's you again," he said nastily. "I was hoping you'd come back this way."

He started around the desk and nearly ran into Sergeant Shackelford.

"Do you have a problem Sailor?" Shack inquired.

Chamberlain glared at him. "Yeah, I got a problem, I'm gonna kick some butt."

Shack put his hand in the middle of the man's chest. "I am SFC Glenn Shackelford, and if you don't want to be a raw seaman again, you better start adjusting your attitude, right now."

Chamberlain's eyes widened. "Yes, Sergeant, anything you say, Sergeant."

"That's better. Now, Son, we need some change for the pay phones."

Chamberlain backed around the desk and gave them change for a dollar.

Shack took the change and patted him on the hand.

"I saved your life and your stripes tonight, Sailor. Don't forget that." Shack smiled. "This man would have destroyed you."

"Thank you, Sergeant," he replied. "I'm sorry I got angry, it won't happen again."

"I know it won't," Shack responded. "Goodnight, Sailor."

"Goodnight, Sergeant."

Clay had been standing there, quietly observing, and trying not to laugh.

As they walked away, Clay commented. "Oh, you're good, Shack, you're really good."

"Yeah, I know. Anyway, I didn't want the kid embarrassed. He was way out of his league; he just didn't know it."

Clay poked him on the shoulder. "You sure of that, are you?"

Shack reached for the telephone. "Yeah, I'm sure."

They called the senator, and Clay explained everything as best he could. It seems that Shack had not told him very much. Apologizing for waking him, Clay told the senator that they were coming home, and that he would drop Shack off at the house. The senator asked Clay to stop and have a nightcap. Clay agreed, and he and Shack headed to the senator's house.

It was three minutes after three when they got there. The senator was up and waiting for them. When Clay and Shack got inside, the senator was almost giddy. It was more than apparent that he was relieved and happy to see them.

"I'll mix the drinks," the senator began. "Shack, go help yourself to a beer."

Shack said. "I think I might like some Bourbon and water, Sir, if you don't mind."

"Mind, no I don't mind. As far as I'm concerned, Sergeant, you've earned the whole damn bar."

That pleased the sergeant, and he smiled broadly.

Cutting the Fringe

The senator mixed drinks for each of them, then he handed them out. Clay went for the cigars.

Offering Clay a light the senator spoke. "I understand that three more bad guys bit the proverbial dust this evening. I am also excited to know that the good doctor is well and back in the hospital. How is the young lady?" he asked.

"Susan is doing remarkably well. She was; however, a little miffed at me for not coming to see her today. I told her I would explain everything to her tomorrow."

The senator's head dropped. "All things went smoothly here this evening. More than three hundred people came by to pay their respects. I'm sorry that the two of you missed it. We are going to have the graveside service at noon today. I sincerely hope the two of you will be there."

"You know we wouldn't miss it, Sir," Clay said solemnly.

Shack chimed in, "I'll be right by your side, Senator."

The senator was making every effort to control his emotions. "I am grateful to the both of you, and I could talk to you all night, but I guess we had better get some sleep."

"Yes, Sir, I think we probably should," Clay concurred.

"Clay, Jolene is in the kitchen. She has been sitting up with Talbot, and she won't go to bed till she sees and talks to you. You best go speak to her."

"I'll take her with me, Sir; she's probably driving Talbot crazy. I'll see that she gets back here by ten AM, so that she can fix food before the funeral. Is that okay, Senator?"

"That'll be fine, Clay. I leave her in your capable hands. Goodnight, Gentlemen."

Shack headed for the guest bedroom, and Clay headed for the kitchen. Jolene was waiting for him. It took him only seconds to take her by the hand and get her to the car for the trip around the block to his place. When they got into the car the questions began.

"Is Johnny alright?" she asked.

"Yes, believe it or not, he's doing okay. I'll tell him you asked; he'll be pleased, I'm sure."

"Are you alright, Mr. Clay?"

"Except for being dog tired, I'm great. My friends are all safe and sound, and the bad guys lost once more. How could I be otherwise?"

"Are you angry with me for waiting up?"

"No, I'm not angry with you, but I don't want you to get too attached to me, for if you do, something bad will surely happen to you, as well."

"I don't believe that for a minute."

As they pulled into the garage, he looked at her, sitting there shivering. "You better believe it, I'm cursed, and I don't want you hurt."

She didn't speak until they got in the house. "I've been thinking," she admitted. "You are the most amazing man I have ever known," Jolene paused. "Do you know what is better than all that? You have an amazing heart for other people, and the softest touch I have ever felt."

"Thank you, Jolene. I don't care for most people; but those I love, I love with every fiber of my being."

"I know you do. That is why I pray that nothing bad will ever happen to you. I want to know all about you, but it can wait until tomorrow. You need some sleep, and so do I."

Jolene was already getting in the bed. She had been going in that direction from the moment they entered the house. Undressing under the covers, her clothes came flying out and landed in a pile beside the bed, on the floor. Clay watched her with great interest.

"We've seen each other naked," he said. "Why did you choose to get undressed that way?"

She smiled, and this little gleam appeared in her eyes. "I didn't want to tempt you. You told me I was beautiful, and you need some sleep. Am I doing the okay thing?"

Clay jumped on the bed, penned her down with the covers, and kissed her as if there was no tomorrow. She tried to move, but he wouldn't let her.

"You are beautiful; a wild and wonderful kind of beauty, and I need a quick shower. Don't you go anywhere, I'll be right back." Kissing her on the forehead, Clay slid off the bed and disappeared into the bathroom.

As he re-entered the bedroom he noticed a freshly made drink sitting on the table beside the bed.

"I made you a drink," she said. "I thought it would make you sleep better."

Clay said, "Thanks, but weren't you afraid?"

Jolene threw back the covers on his side of the bed. "I'm not afraid anymore; you make me unafraid. I am only afraid for you; because, you don't have enough sense to be afraid for yourself."

Carl R. Smith

Clay watched her speak, as he sipped his drink. When she finished speaking, he set the glass down on the table, turned out the light, and slid under the covers. She surrounded him with her long incredible body, and they slept.

Chapter 19

Five hours of sleep was not nearly enough. They were restful; however, and that did make a difference. Jolene was already up. He could smell the coffee, and it smelled wonderful. Clay shaved, showered, and brushed his teeth. It was five minutes after nine when he entered the kitchen. Jolene had made some Banana Buns; she called them Banana Sticky Buns. They might, very well, be the most delicious thing Clay had ever tasted. My gosh, they were marvelous, and he told her so at least a dozen times.

He heard the shower running when he exited the kitchen. Heading for the bedroom, his intention was to finish dressing. Jolene stepped out of the bathroom, wearing only a towel.

"Will you dry my back, please?" she purred.

He gulped. "Sure, I'd be glad too."

She walked to him, removed the towel and turned, offering him her backside. He rubbed her back briskly, and then, as in one motion, he swept her in his arms and threw her on the bed.

They kissed and cuddled for only a minute or two. That was all there was time for. A quick roll in the hay was not his style. Making love was like eating a gourmet meal; it should take a long while. Each course should be savored, and the palette cleansed. Then, and only then, should one move to the next course. If one eats slow enough and gives the body a chance to digest, there is usually room for dessert. Getting to the main course is fun, if done properly. However, leaving the main course once in a while and moving on to the dessert can be equally important. Although, when time is of the essence, a little bite of each can really hit the spot.

They left the house on time, and when they pulled into the senator's driveway, Jolene was staring at him. "What are you thinking about, Clay?"

"Now, I'm thinking about how glad I am that you finally called me by my name. Before, I was thanking God for bringing you into my life. I hope that's okay."

They got out of the car and walked toward the front door, arm in arm. As they stepped up on the small porch she turned to him.

"I thanked him yesterday, and I'll thank him again today," she said proudly.

When the sergeant opened the door it was close to ten AM. Jolene went straight to work and in no time she had set a table to be envied by almost anyone.

"Jolene," the senator began, "Without a doubt, you set the most beautiful table in the world. Patricia would have been proud."

"Thank you, Sir. I wish Ms. Lazar could be here to see it. She had such exquisite taste. I hope she's looking down at this very moment, and somehow, I think she is."

The senator's hand began to shake. "I can feel her presence, too. God, how I miss that woman, she meant so much to me and the children."

Feeling that the mood needed to be broken, Clay said. "Are the children coming for the funeral, Senator?"

"No, Son, I changed my mind. Their aunt and I thought it would be best to keep them away, they are so very young."

"I understand," Clay replied.

Tim stepped up. "I need a drink, and people are starting to arrive. Can I fix drinks for anyone else?"

"I'll take a quick one," the senator replied. "Then I guess we had better get to the funeral home, we'll have plenty of time for visiting afterwards."

"You are absolutely correct, Sir," Tim answered, as he went toward the den.

Everyone joined him, and moments later they left for the funeral home. The service was indescribable. Clay was relating it to the funeral for his Aunt Ella, and the one for Pamela and her sister. Those were quite ordinary, by comparison. There must have been senators and congressmen from every state, and dignitaries from around the world and the nation. The President did not attend, but the Vice President was present, along with most of the cabinet. They returned to the house. The people came by the droves, and they just kept on coming.

Clay stayed for more than two hours. Then when the time seemed right, and he was able to get the senator alone for half a second, he asked to be excused.

"Go on, Son," the senator urged. "You have been wonderful, and I know you need to see your friends."

"Are you sure it's alright, Sir?" Clay repeated.

"The senator hugged him, closely. "I think the world of you, My Boy. Go to your friends, and give them my best, but please drop by when you return home. The time doesn't matter."

"I will, Sir, you can count on it."

Clay took a couple of minutes to explain to Jolene what he was going to do. He told her he would be back for her before it got too late.

"Do what you have to do," she replied. "I'll most probably be up until after midnight cleaning up the mess anyway, but I'll miss you."

"I'll miss you too," he said, squeezing her hand, and kissing her on the cheek.

He said good-bye to Shack and Tim, and he was gone.

Back at the hospital, things were reasonably normal. Nurse Ford was in an unusually good mood. The rangers were on the job, and Susan was understanding as usual. When Clay gave some thought to how much time he had actually spent with her he felt guiltier than ever. Thank goodness she was truly doing well.

"Clay," she said. "I have had the strangest dreams. I guess it must be the medication."

He held her hand. "I'll bet that's the answer. Do you want to talk about the dreams? I have the rest of the day to spend with you, and you know I'm a good listener."

"No, I don't," she answered. "Cause you'll think I'm nuts, and if I talk about it, it might become even more real."

Rising from his seat on the edge of Susan's bed, he stopped her. "Babe, let me take a quick trip to the nurse's station and I'll be back in less than fifteen minutes. I have to ask Nurse Ford a question about Johnny, before I forget."

"Sure, Clay, will you bring me a little coke to drink. I sure am thirsty."

"Will do, Doll Face," he answered.

Clay was able to corner the nurse, without difficulty.

"Ms. Ford, is Susan strong enough to hear about the death of the senator's wife?"

"I can't think of any reason why not," she replied. "She is making remarkable strides."

Clay smiled, "That's great, I've been afraid to tell her anything. You know? She doesn't even know about Dr. Murphy."

"Well, Mr. Smith, I think you should start telling her what's been happening. She may shed a few tears, but I think she has the right to know why you have been gone so much of the time." She paused. "By golly, if I was her I'd want to know, and I'll bet you'll feel a lot better."

Clay was so excited that he hugged Nurse Ford. She didn't try to back away, but she came darn close to blushing.

Carl R. Smith

"Go on," she stammered. "Get back to your girl and whether you tell her or not, she needs to have you with her for awhile."

"Yes Ma'am, I'm on my way."

When he got back to the room Johnny was there. Clay's heart jumped for joy. "Wow, the 'Three Musketeers' are back together again. Don't it feel great, Guys?"

Susan smiled, that infectious smile, and Johnny hugged his neck.

"I'll bet you're getting tired of rescuing my sorry butt," Johnny blurted out.

"What does that mean?" Susan asked.

Clay and Johnny spent the next few minutes trying to explain. Susan listened carefully. She didn't get upset, in fact, she seemed rather stoic.

"When were you going to tell me about all this, Clay?"

Clay was a little flustered. "Actually, Babe, I just asked the nurse if it would be alright to tell you. She said you were strong enough to handle it, and I was coming to break the news, I swear."

Susan said. "Well, is there anything else you need to tell me?"

"Yes," he answered. "The night after you got hurt, the senator's wife was killed. Her funeral was this afternoon."

Susan's eyes flooded with tears. "Oh Lord, when is this going to end?"

Clay was sitting on the edge of Susan's bed holding her left hand. Johnny reached up from his chair and placed his hand on theirs.

He said, "Tell her everything."

She gasped, "You mean there's more?"

"I'm afraid there is," Clay began.

Cutting the Fringe

Over the next couple of hours he laid everything on the line, holding nothing back from her. They talked, like old times. They cried, they hugged, but mostly, as was the norm, they were there for each other.

Susan's dinner tray arrived. Clay decided to go to Johnny's room and get his tray. When he returned, he sat with them as they ate. Susan kept trying to talk Johnny into giving her some of his food. She had more than Jell-O, but not much more.

"You two finish your meal," Clay said. "I'm going down to the cafeteria and get milkshakes for everyone. I know two chocolates, and one strawberry, right Johnny?"

"Yep, that'd be great, Old Buddy."

In a few minutes Clay was back and happy as he could be to have his friends together again. *If only they could be whole once again,* he thought.

Susan had a question. "Guys, if the general is dead, who's doing this?"

"I hope it was orchestrated by General Matthews before he died," Clay replied. "If not, I haven't a clue."

"Well," Johnny said. "If that is the case, it's over, right?"

"God, I hope so," Clay replied.

"Oh, I forgot something," Clay said excitedly. "The President has asked to see me."

"The President, the big guy?" Johnny chimed in, seemingly even more excited. "Can I go too?"

"I'd like to go too," Susan injected. "But, alas, I have nothing to wear."

Clay's eyes widened, and Johnny's head spun around. "I'll get you for that, Missy."

The laughter was warm and wonderful. They talked and laughed until Johnny's pain got the better of him. It was time to return to his own room, but Tim Siler walked in at that moment.

He had a quirky grin, but; nonetheless, it was a grin. "Together again, I see. There's not much that can hold you guys back, is there?"

Clay grabbed his hand. "Hell, there's not much that can hold any of us back. How's the senator?"

"He's okay," Tim replied. "Did you tell them about the President?"

"He sure did," Johnny answered, reaching to shake his hand also. "How did you swing that?"

"I think the senator had a great deal to do with it, but he would have never said anything. Heck, I'm just the messenger boy."

"Sure you are," Clay replied.

Tim shrugged his shoulders. "I am, but enough about the President. How's the most beautiful woman on the east coast?" he said, shyly.

Susan looked surprised. "Ah, c'mon Mr. Siler, look at my hair it's turned completely white. I can't do a thing with it."

"When you get those bandages off," Tim replied, "You'll be as beautiful as ever. Hell, I think you'd be beautiful even if you were bald."

Johnny said, "Would you two like for Clay and I to leave? Anyway, in Susan's own words she thinks you're as cute as a bug's ear."

"Johnny," Susan screamed.

Tim became as red as new flannel underwear. Johnny, on the other hand, was enjoying himself so much he almost forgot his pain. Then it reared its ugly head.

"Seriously, Tim," Johnny said. "I've got to get back to my room. Will you visit with Susan while Clay gives me a hand?"

Tim grinned. "I'd be more than happy to keep this young lady company. Don't let the door hit you in the rear on the way out. And, Clay, don't hurry."

When Johnny and Clay were outside Susan's room, Johnny said. "That's the boldest I've ever seen Tim. He really is smitten."

Clay changed the subject completely. "Johnny, do you think it's over?"

"Lord, I hope so," Johnny responded. "I can't take anymore of this flying lead, and if you have to pull my sorry behind out of the fire one more time, I'll have to bear your children."

"Not a chance," Clay replied. "I'm not having any ugly kids."

Johnny tried to act insulted, but it was too funny. "Yeah, you're right. Could you imagine a child that looked like the both of us? On second thought, he could very well be a cross between, Sidney Portier and Paul Newman."

"What if it was a girl?" Clay asked.

"Well, in that case, she would be a cross between, Lena Horne, and your favorite, Natalie Wood."

Clay said, "I think I could live with a child like that."

They continued to laugh and talk, it was fun again, and they could both embrace the feeling.

They got to Johnny's room and his medication. In little or no time he was feeling better.

"You know," Johnny began, "I don't think I'll ever question another patient when they ask for something to ease their pain. When you hurt, you hurt, and it's no fun."

Clay made himself comfortable in the chair beside Johnny's bed. "And, before now, you thought it was just a bunch a malarkey, huh?"

"No! Well maybe. Hell, I don't know what I thought. I guess I thought they were over-reacting."

"Okay, I get it," Clay snickered. "Until you've walked in their shoes, don't be so judgmental."

"Actually," Johnny surmised, "That's probably good advice for anybody."

Clay's demeanor changed again. "Partner, there's something I've been waiting to talk to you about. It concerns Susan and Gidget."

"Shoot."

Clay smiled. "Another bad choice of words, huh, John?"

"Oh yeah, right."

For the next several minutes Clay tried to explain what had taken place in Susan's room; the eerie feeling and the unmistakable sound of Gidget's voice. As the picture began to unfold, the hairs on Clay's arms were standing tall.

"Did it really sound like Gidget talking?" Johnny asked.

"Sound like her? I could even smell her perfume. How weird is that?"

Johnny thought for a minute. "I've heard of such things, but I've never known anybody, personally, who said they had had the experience."

Clay stood and began pacing. "Well, I've experienced it, and I don't want to ever experience that again."

Johnny said, "Have you talked to Susan about this?"

"No! Are you crazy? She's been in no shape to discuss much of anything until tonight."

"Alright," Johnny replied. "Are you gonna talk to her?"

"I want to Johnny, but I'm still not sure she could handle it."

"Hey, Old Buddy. This is Susan we're talking about; she's a damn sight stronger than you give her credit for."

"You're right," Clay admitted. "Although, it might be nice if we had the conversation when the three of us are together, what do you think?"

Johnny grinned. "I think you need me to hold your hand. Its okay, I'll do it. I guess I owe you that much."

Clay moved uncomfortably in his seat. "I don't want to go there. You know darn good and well, you don't owe me a thing."

"Look, Old Buddy, we'll all be back at the house soon, and maybe you should save it til then. It won't be quite so hard to discuss when we're eating some of Susan's grilled cheese sandwiches."

Clay stopped pacing. "Thanks, Partner. That's exactly right, you always have the answer. I don't know what I'd do without you."

"Let's hope you never have to find out, at least not for the next hundred years or so."

Walking over to the bed, Clay laid his head on Johnny's chest and gave him a hug. "I love you, Partner."

"I know," Johnny replied. "Now go away, and stop slobbering on my pajamas. I think I'm about to fall asleep, but don't fret, I love you too."

Clay left Johnny to his dreams and headed to Susan's room. He was feeling much better. Talking to Johnny always made things more clear.

Tim was still there, and he and Susan were having a good time talking, about what, Clay hadn't a clue.

"May I come in?" Clay asked.

"Sure, Old Pal," Tim replied. "I was about to leave."

"Don't leave on my account, Tim; although, I do need to talk to you about the President. What time on are we gonna meet on Thursday, do you know?"

"I'll let you know tomorrow," he replied. "I think the senator wants to talk to the lot of us before then. I think he's a wee bit nervous, and I can understand why. He's afraid something may come out that he's not equipped to handle. I'm sure he feels as though his career's at risk."

Clay looked straight at him. "He has nothing to worry about. Damn, you'd think he could trust me by now."

"I don't think it has anything to do with you, Pal. He simply wants to be sure we're not stepping on the wrong toes."

"I can understand that part," Clay replied.

"Look, Clay, I'll give you a call late this evening or first thing tomorrow morning." He hesitated and turned his attention to Susan. "I'll see you later, Young Lady, and I'll remember what you said. I'm not much of a person for praying, but Clay's worth the effort."

Clay's head bounced from Tim to Susan and then back to Tim. "What's that all about?" he asked.

Tim grabbed Clay's hand. "Don't be so darn nosy. Anyway, I'm outta here."

Tim left, and Clay focused his attention on Susan. "You still trying to help me, aren't you? Well, I appreciate the thought."

"I can't help much from here," she responded, "But I know God can. Don't be angry."

"I'm not angry," he replied, laying his head on her breast. "I love hearing your heart beat; it beats so softly, for a big bruiser like you."

Clay jumped away, instinctively.

Susan was pleased and then shocked. "Henry Clay Smith, I've half a mind to kick that cute little butt of yours."

Clay ran two fingers across his forehead, as though he were wiping perspiration. "Whew, I guess I'm lucky you have all those wires holding you back, or I'd probably have to make a run for it."

She snickered. "You are totally incorrigible, but God how I adore you, you Big Jerk."

He went back to her bedside, putting his arms around her as much as it was possible. "How are you really feeling, Babe? Tell me what the doctors are saying."

"I'm doing pretty darn well, and Doctor Scarianno said I might be able to go home in a week or so. Isn't that great?"

Clay smiled broadly. "Yes, Susan, that might be the best news I've heard in years. I haven't had a good meal in days. I miss those grill cheese sandwiches."

"Yeah, I'll just bet you do. Now, will you help me up please?"

"Sure," he replied, a little stunned. "Are you supposed to do that?"

"I reckon so."

Clay began trying to help, not knowing exactly what to do. "Maybe you better not." he declared. "If you need something I'll get it for you."

Susan looked at him. "Well, Big Boy, I need to go to the little girls' room. That is, if you don't mind."

"Have you done that before?" he asked innocently.

"Clay . . . Just help me, will ya?"

He threw up his hands. "Okay, what do I do first?"

She was now on the side of the bed. "Get that pole; the one holding the bag. It's on wheels. You need to pull it around to this side of the bed. As you can see its holding the IV bag."

"Oh I see," he replied. "Do you take it with you to the bathroom?"

"That's the idea; otherwise, we'd have to disconnect all these tubes."

The feat was accomplished. Clay assisted her out of and back into the bed. It was quite an ordeal. Once she was re-settled, he said. "Boy, if you had to go in a hurry, you'd be in a lot of trouble, wouldn't you?"

This time she smiled. "You ought to see me take a shower. I got to do that for the first time this morning, it took me almost an hour."

Clay covered his face. "I've seen you taking a shower, and it's a beautiful thing, and I could watch that for hours."

Susan just waved him off. "Get me some water, Smart-aleck."

He did so, and they talked and laughed almost like old times. Susan had to take some medication a little before ten and Clay knew that that was his cue to leave. Kissing her good-bye he went to check on Johnny once more.

"Hey, Old Buddy, what are you doing back here? Did Susan run you off?"

Clay laughed. "Well she might have if I had stayed any longer. I just wanted to see how you were doing before I headed to the house."

"I'm doing darn good," Johnny replied. "I may get out of here tomorrow or the next day. Are you ready for me to come home?"

"Clay said, "Are you kidding? I can't wait."

"Me neither," Johnny answered.

"Oh Johnny, I did as you said, I didn't say anything to Susan about Gidget. We'll tackle that one together, I think."

"I think that's the best way," Johnny replied.

Clay rose up from the chair where he had been sitting. "Do you need me to get you anything before I go? I'll go to the nurse's station for you."

Johnny reached for his hand. "Clay, how can I ever thank you?"

"Hush, Partner. Don't say it. You are part of me, remember?"

"Yeah, I remember, Old Buddy."

"Seriously Johnny, when dad used to leave me tied to that tree all night, and you would come sit with me; do you remember what I'd say?"

Johnny's eyes suddenly filled with tears. "You know I remember."

Clay continued. "I told you every time that the day would come when I would repay you, and I've barely scratched the surface. You saved my life night after night. No one else even cared."

Johnny chimed in. "Your Aunt Ella cared. You know she did."

Clay held tightly to Johnny's hand, trying desperately to hold back the onslaught of tears that were sure to come. "Yes she did, thank God. Without the two of you I would never have made it to the John Tarleton Home." Clay paused. "Come to think of it, Partner, I've had some wonderful people in my life. The three years or so I spent at Tarleton were good years. One day I'm gonna do something nice for that place. I hope Coach is still around so I can tell him what he's meant to me."

Johnny squeezed his hand. "I would really like to meet him sometime. He must have been a God-send for you."

Clay said, "He was, he really was."

Johnny stirred in the bed. "When this is over, let's go back there. I would like to meet him."

"You got a deal," Clay replied.

Johnny said, "Okay, go home and get a good night's sleep. Dream about the good times we've had, and there have been a few."

"You better believe it," Clay responded. "I'll see you tomorrow."

"Good night, Old Buddy."

Clay walked out of the room, a myriad of thoughts running through his brain. For some strange reason he was remembering high school. Some of those days were fun. He remembered a tall lanky kid named Calvin Browning. Calvin told him that he and Roberta Lewis had jumped the fence at one of those trampoline places the night before, and that it was scary, but boy did they have fun. It's funny how something like that will stay in one's mind, and then, for no apparent reason, out it pops.

It was nearly eleven PM when he finally got to the senator's place. Everyone was up, and Clay really needed a drink. Sergeant Shackelford opened the front door before he could ring the bell.

"Come in, Clay. How are Johnny and Susan?"

"Everyone's doing well, Shack, thanks for asking."

Shack said, "The senator's in the den, he'll be glad to see you."

"Where's Jolene?" Clay asked.

"She's in the kitchen baking some chocolate chip cookies, can't you smell them?"

Clay sniffed, "Yeah, I can, and they smell great. I wonder if the senator's got any milk. I'd love to have some milk and cookies."

Shack smiled. "You go on into the den and I'll see if I can't talk Jolene into bringing you some."

"Thanks, My Friend," Clay said, heading toward the den.

When he got to the den, he stopped abruptly. The senator was sound asleep on the couch. Not wanting to wake him, Clay made tracks for the kitchen. He got there just in time to stop Shack from coming into the den with the cookies and milk.

Shack said, "What's up, Clay?"

"The senator's sound asleep on the couch. I guess I'll take the cookies and milk in here. Is that okay, Jolene?"

Jolene looked at him and winked. "You know, Mr. Clay, you can have whatever you want. I'll make some more coffee if you like?"

"I'd rather have milk, but Shack may want some coffee."

"No, Miss Jolene, I'm fine," the sergeant replied. "I'll have some milk too, if you don't mind."

"Not at all, Sergeant, you two have a seat. I'll get the milk. The first two batches of cookies are on the table, help yourself."

They ate some great cookies, drank milk, and chit-chatted. Neither one of them wanted to discuss the senator's situation.

"Oh, by the way, Johnny may get to come home in a day or so," Clay declared. "Isn't that good news?"

"Hell, yes," Shack replied. "I'll bet he can't wait to get out of that hospital. I hate hospitals."

Jolene jumped in joyfully. "I'll help take care of him, if you like, Mr. Clay."

"Thanks, Jolene, I appreciate the offer." Clay continued, "Shack, I'm gonna call it a night. Tell the senator that I'll talk to him tomorrow. Jolene, are you coming with me, or are you staying here?"

"You know I'm coming with you, Mr. Clay."

"Then get your coat, let's go."

She looked befuddled. "I can't leave for four minutes. The last batch of cookies is still in the oven."

Clay grinned. "I'll wait. Maybe I'll have another cookie."

Chapter 20

The night with Jolene was grand, but the morning came much too quickly. They arrived at the senator's before seven-thirty. Jolene went to work fixing breakfast. She was incredibly efficient, and in what seemed like only minutes she was calling everyone to the table.

Senator Lazar walked in ready for the office. "Clay, I'm so glad you're here. Do you think it would be possible to have a small meeting in Doctor Murphy's room this evening, say, around six-thirty?"

"Certainly, Sir, should I ask Tim to be there?"

"Yes, of course," the senator answered.

Clay took a sip of his coffee. "Tim said that he would call me last night or this morning. When he calls I'll tell him. I know he's expecting to meet with us sometime today anyway."

The senator patted Clay's hand. "Thank you, Son, I'll consider it done."

Clay nodded, "Yes, Sir."

There were a dozen things leapfrogging their way through Clay's mind. He knew; however, that this was not the time to expose the senator to a barrage of questions. Tonight would be soon enough, at least he hoped it would be.

No time wasted, the senator and the sergeant were off to the Senate Office Building. Clay continued sipping his coffee, trying relentlessly to forget the days plan. Jolene was clearing the table, and he found himself watching her intently. She was humming a tune, and that cute little butt was keeping time with the beat.

She must have felt him watching her. She turned abruptly. "Are you enjoying the view?"

Clay flushed at getting caught. "Yeah, I am. Do you mind?"

"Heck no," she replied, quickly. "I watch you sometimes; you just haven't caught me."

Clay laughed. "I hope it's as much fun for you as this is for me. You are so slim, yet so well put together."

She picked up a hand full of dishes and started for the kitchen. As she passed him she bent down and kissed him gently. "I'm honestly glad that you approve."

He took the dishes from her and stood. "I'll get these, you get the others. That way we'll have more time for each other."

"Set them on the sink," she instructed. "I'll put them in the dishwasher shortly."

"Okay, Boss, will do," he replied.

They worked together, bumping into each other at every opportunity. The radio was playing, "Daddy's Home". Clay took her in his arms and they danced. He placed his right hand on the back of her neck, and his left hand on the small of her back, forcing her body against his.

She looked into his eyes. "Could we have a house like this, and would you love me forever?"

"That would be so easy to do," he replied, kissing her on the tip of the nose.

They swayed to the music, every muscle in their respective bodies, straining to meet with their counterpart. As the music came to an end, he bent slightly at the knees. Sliding both hands around her middle, Clay raised her to his level and they kissed, long and hard, then, soft and searching.

When they paused for a moment, she whispered, "You are the softest, and yet the strongest man on the face of this earth. I don't ever want to be without you."

"Thanks, Love," he replied. "I like you too."

Their morning together was a thing of beauty. Hours of mounting passion, and quiet gentle times of sheer love, a time poets write about, and a time for which songs are composed.

The telephone, as it often does, brought them back to reality.

Clay answered, "Senator Lazar's residence."

"Hey, Pal, it's Tim. Sorry to be so late calling, but I have had one of those mornings. Do we have a meeting time?"

"We are meeting tonight at six-thirty in Johnny's room at the hospital. Can you make it, Tim?"

"Wouldn't miss it, I'll see you then Clay."

"I'll be there," Clay replied, hanging up the receiver.

"Do you need to go?" Jolene asked.

Clay held her close. "I do need to go to the hospital, do you want to go with me, or will you be okay here?"

She thought for a moment. "I'll be alright, the guards are still out front, and if I hear anything unusual I have a great place to hide. Anyhow, I don't want you to think I'm a coward."

He stared deep into her soul. "I want you alive; that's all that matters to me, and don't you forget that."

"Will you come back and get me before you men have that meeting you've been talking about. I don't want to be here alone after dark. Is that alright?"

Clay grinned. "You betcha, I'll be back before six o'clock. You can visit with Susan while we are having our meeting. Is that alright with you, Love?"

"Positively," she replied. "If she can put up with me, I'll enjoy the visit. Do you think it would be okay if I took her some of my cookies?"

Clay said, "I think so. I believe she's on a regular diet now. Either way, she'll be glad to see you."

"You love her a lot, don't you?"

"Yes I do," he answered. "Fortunately, there's plenty of room left in my heart for you, Love."

Jolene's smile was illuminating. "I'm so very thankful. You have my heart filled to overflowing, but I will try to make room for those you love as well."

Clay didn't want to leave, but it was after lunchtime and he needed to get moving. The hot shower felt especially good, and even shaving wasn't a chore. Life was suddenly good again.

He couldn't believe how fast he had gotten to the hospital; it was just short of one-thirty when he arrived. Johnny was up and pacing like a caged animal.

"What's the matter?" Clay asked.

Johnny turned, irritation showing on his face. "I thought they were going to release me, but I can't go home until tomorrow."

"With that scowl on your face, I'm relieved. I don't need a 'Grumpy Gus' at my place."

Johnny said, "Thanks a lot, Old Buddy. I thought you would be on my side."

"I am on your side, but we have a meeting planned for six-thirty in this very room, and if you went home we would have to change all that. See how much easier it is this way?"

Johnny sat on the bed. "Sure, it's much easier this way. I'm just so darn selfish sometimes."

Clay plopped down in the chair beside the bed. "Its okay, Partner, you had no way of knowing. Now relax, and I'll have Jolene bring you some great cookies."

Johnny finally smiled. "A bribe, I'm up for that. What kind of cookies?"

"Chocolate Chip with huge pecans, and they're almost as soft as cake. If you're nice I'll even go and get you some cold milk."

"That settles it, no more complaints."

"Good," Clay responded. "That's 'The Lone Ranger' I know and love."

Johnny said, "There's only two more things I need, and if I had those two things I'd be a happy man."

"I know," Clay replied. "A beautiful woman and what's the other thing?"

Johnny looked at him, he's eyes had that old sparkle. "Make that three things; a stiff drink, a good cigar, and you know."

Clay adjusted himself. "I believe, a really good woman, could bring you back from the grave."

"That's terrific," Johnny retorted. "If I get killed, bring a couple of incredibly beautiful women to my funeral."

Laughing heartily, Clay said, "I've missed having you around, Partner. You light up my world, and that's a fact."

"Yeah?" Johnny responded. "Well, being around you is hazardous to my health, but it sure is fun."

"I'm glad you feel that way, Partner. Do you feel like taking a little trip?"

Johnny perked up even more. "You bet I do. Let's go see Susan, I never did show her my scars."

Clay rose from his chair. "I'll bet she's been waiting with bated breath, I know I have."

He watched, as Johnny slid off the bed and planted his feet on the floor. There was no sign of pain.

"Let's go," Johnny said. "And stop picking on me, some women like that sort of thing. In spite of that crooked nose, the girls seem to love you. Why do you think that is, Old Buddy?"

Clay opened the door for him. "I always thought it was my incredibly charming personality."

They spoke to the rangers who followed them to Susan's room. They were not about to lose the good doctor again. Anyway, it gave the two rangers a chance to talk to their buddies who were sitting in front of Susan's door.

Susan was delighted to see them both; however, when Johnny showed her his wounds she grimaced and shrank away. "That's gross," she cried.

Clay grinned. "I tried to tell him, Babe, but he wouldn't listen."

Johnny got this hurt look on his face. "Alright, but when you want to show me yours, Young Lady, I'm not gonna look."

"Darn right you're not," Susan replied. "Until my hair grows back, I'm wearing hats."

Clay felt an uncomfortable pain in his heart. She wasn't kidding. That incredibly beautiful young woman had been scarred for life and it was his fault. He looked at both of them.

"I'll be back in a few minutes," he said, and out the door he went. He heard them saying something, but he never stopped.

He found the nearest empty bathroom, and he cried. *Why God, why do I cause so much pain for those I love? They've done nothing to deserve this. These people are my friends; is that the cost for being my friend? Tell me! C'mon, tell me! God I know you can hear me; please let this end. If you want me to take my own life, I will. I'm begging you; I can't live with the guilt any longer. They're all gonna die, and I know it. What do you want from me?*

He stood in front of the mirror sobbing, his right hand bleeding profusely. The glass from the broken right mirror was everywhere. *Is this what you want, God? Do you want me to cut my wrist, do you? Maybe I should just sit down and let it bleed. If that's what you want, you got it.*

Clay sat down in the corner of the bathroom, blood dripping all over his clothing. He laid his head between his knees, and sat there, not wanting, or willing to move.

"Sir, are you alright?" a voice said. "My God, you're bleeding like a sieve. Stay put, I'll get you some help."

In only seconds, people were all around him. He recognized Nurse Ford. "What happened?" she asked.

Clay looked up, "Just a little test between me and God."

"From the looks of this place," she said, "I think you flunked."

Clay tried to smile. "You can't fight with God, you'll lose every time."

On the way to the nurse's station a doctor met them. The doctor and the nurse spent the next several minutes trying to repair the damage. It wasn't nearly as bad as it had looked.

"What happened?" the doctor asked.

"I slammed my fist into one of the mirrors in the men's bathroom, I think."

The doctor was steadily working. "Why didn't you go for help afterwards? You've lost a lot of blood."

Clay said, "I don't know, Doc. I don't really know; it just didn't seem all that important at the time."

Then the doctor said something that Clay would always remember. "Well, Son, it just wasn't your time. If you had sat there for another ten minutes, you might have been too weak to have gotten any help."

Those words kept ringing in Clay's ears. *Okay God, I think you've made your point,* he acknowledged.

"Did you say something?" the nurse asked.

"No Ma'am, I was just mumbling to myself, sorry."

It took awhile for the doctor to finish, and by the time Clay returned to Susan's room it had been close to an hour.

She and Johnny were frantic.

"Where the hell have you been?" Johnny asked. "You had us scared to death. Is something wrong?"

Susan chimed in. "Why are you so pale, are you ill?"

Clay had his hand behind his back, not wanting them to see. When he brought his hand to the front of his body, Susan yelled. "Johnny, look! Clay, what happened to your hand?"

Still a little woozy, Clay tried to explain. "I punched a mirror. It's no big deal. The nurse cleaned it up, and the doctor sewed it up."

Johnny reached and grabbed him. "Here, Old Buddy, sit down, you don't look so good."

"I'm okay," Clay declared. "I just lost a little too much blood."

Clay could see the worry on Susan's face, and the stern look on Johnny's.

Johnny spoke first. "How much sewing did he have to do? How many stitches, Clay?"

"Five, five, and four," Clay replied reluctantly.

Johnny's eyes widen. "Fourteen stitches? My God, you must have hit that mirror awfully hard."

"I guess," Clay replied. "I don't even remember hitting the damn thing. I was angry, and I hit the mirror. That's all there is to it."

Susan raised the head of her bed a few more inches. "Damn, Johnny, this is all your fault. You and your darn scars."

"But, Susan," Johnny whined. "I was just kidding around."

Clay tried to stand. "C'mon guys, we all three know who's fault it is. I'm so damn tired of everyone getting hurt. I love you two."

Johnny steadied Clay with his hand, and then he began hugging him. "We love you too, Dummy. Anyway, hurting yourself is not the answer."

Susan stuck out her one free arm. "Come here you Goofballs. I need a bit of a hug."

They hugged each other gingerly, kinda like three Porcupines making love. Ouch, oh, aw, ugh. Actually, they were determined to make this work, in spite of the groans and moans.

Clay was the first to pull away. "We better stop before we hurt each other any more."

Johnny said, "I think you're right. Then he started laughing heartily. "Look at us; we look like the walking wounded."

"We are, Partner," Clay agreed.

Susan got this sheepish grin on her face. "Clay, sweetheart, would you go and get me another milk shake?"

"Sure, but you know it's almost dinner time," he replied.

"I don't care," she screeched. "I need some chocolate, and I need it now."

Johnny said, "I think you better do as she asked, and I guess you could bring me one too."

Clay started for the door. "You two are just a couple of big babies. Hell, I'm the one that's just been injured, and I don't see anybody waiting on me."

Johnny gave him a stare. "Go, get out, and stop your whining."

"I'm going already."

Clay returned with two large milk shakes, one chocolate, and one strawberry. Thank God the bag didn't break, considering he only had one good hand with which to carry them.

It was less than two minutes before Susan's dinner tray arrived. "I guess I'll finish this with my supper."

Johnny said, "Let's go, Clay. My tray should be in my room, I'll let you watch me eat."

As they were leaving Clay turned, "Susan, I have to go and get Jolene. She's gonna stay here with you while we have our meeting, is that alright?"

"Yeah, that'll be super. I was wrong about her; she's a really nice person. You tell her I'm looking forward to her visit."

"I will," he replied. "See ya later."

He walked Johnny back to his room, along with the two rangers. When Johnny was settled, Clay took off. The ride back to the senator's place took less time than he'd expected. Jolene was in the den dusting.

When she saw him she panicked. "What happened, are you alright? Talk to me, please. Did someone hurt you?"

He put his hand to her mouth. "It's okay, I punched a mirror. Can we talk about this later? I need to go home and take a shower."

"Okay, Clay, I'm just worried about you."

"I know. Are you coming with me now, or do I come back after I've cleaned up?"

"I'm coming with you. Let me get my coat. I've already told the senator where I'll be, and he said that would be fine."

They hurried to the car and were back at Clay's place in minutes. When they got in the house, Clay had trouble getting his coat off, and then his shirt. Jolene wrapped his hand in a plastic bag so he could shower.

"I could not have done this without your help, Jolene. Thank you, Love, you're a prize."

"Does it hurt?" she asked. "I'd take the pain away too, if I could."

He looked at her, with gratitude. "I believe you would. You become more special everyday. When we were first together, it was just instinct. Now, I'm learning to care, and that scares the hell out of me."

She put her arms around his waist and laid her head on his chest. "Don't be afraid for me. I would not pass up this time we've had, for fifty more years with anyone else. You are my champion."

Clay put his left hand in her hair and gently pulled her head back. They kissed. "Be patient with me, Love. I'll try to be worth the wait."

She kissed him a second time. "I will wait as long as it takes. When you are in my mind nothing else can intrude, and when you touch me, I have difficulty breathing. Apart, I think of you constantly, together, I can't keep my hands off you."

He took his left hand and ran his fingers across her forehead, down the tip of her nose, and cradled her beautiful face in his hand. He kissed each eyelid, the tip of her nose, and her mouth, one lip at a time. She was trembling.

"Oh God, Clay, I love you so."

"Do you love me enough to make me a drink while I shave?"

"Of course I do, Meany. Go on, I'll bring it to you."

He shaved while she watched, then ran her into the bedroom while he showered. However, when he had finished, she had to help him dry off. They both enjoyed that. Clay considered it dumb luck that he hadn't cut his own throat while shaving. He had never shaved left handed before. It was even difficult brushing his teeth, and flossing was out altogether.

Carl R. Smith

They talked and laughed, as it took a while to get him dressed. Jolene had an incredible touch. Even her buttoning his shirt sleeve turned him on. That was a first, and it gave him goose bumps, but he liked it.

Once he was fully clothed, they went into the den. He sat her on the sofa. "Don't move, I'll be right back."

He went into the kitchen and got her a beer, a glass, and a napkin. "Here you are, Love, enjoy. I'm gonna fix me one more drink, and we'll be on our way."

She started to get up.

"No, no, you relax. I'll make the drink this time. I can do it with one hand, you watch me."

She laughed, as he spilled ice from the little fridge, all over the carpet. "I'll get it," he declared.

"Clay," she said. "You look so cute when you're helpless."

"I may be a wee bit handicapped, but I'm not helpless, see?"

He held the freshly made drink high, as though it were a trophy. He found and lit a cigar. Then he sat on the hearth across from her, smoking his cigar, and blowing the smoke up the chimney.

"I'm sorry, Jolene, I've been remiss in not telling you how beautiful you look, but then you always look terrific."

"Thanks and ditto."

"What did you say?"

"Ditto, it means you look terrific too."

"I know what it means. Where did you hear that word?"

"Gosh, I don't know, I've always used that word. Is there something wrong with the way in which I used it?"

"No, Love. It's just that the first girl I ever loved taught me that word. It was kind of our secret word."

"I'll not use it again if you don't want me to."

"No, please, it's okay. Use it, I love it."

Clay spent the next few minutes telling her all about Taylor, and how they used the word. He told her how Taylor died, and she cried.

"I'm so sorry, Clay. She must have been very special."

Clay's eyes became glassy. "She was special, and so are you."

"I'm glad you had someone that special in your life. I hope I can become that special to you. Oh, I know I can't replace her, but I can still love you as much as she did, and that is happening more everyday."

Clay put out his cigar, sat the glass on the bar and walked over to her. He got down on his knees in front of her. "I hope I don't ever disappoint you, Love."

She leaned forward. "You could never disappoint me; I told you that you are my champion."

"It is time to go," he said. "The senator will be waiting."

Chapter 21

With Jolene safely in Susan's room the meeting could begin. The senator was the first to speak.

"Gentlemen, I'm grateful for each and every person in this room, and, God knows, I'm especially happy to have Captain Murphy here with us. Clay, I know you are going to meet with the President tomorrow, and I will be there to support you. I worked that out today, and I hope it pleases you. Does it?"

"Are you kidding, Sir?" Clay responded. "I get ill just thinking about the meeting, but with you there, Sir, maybe, just maybe, I won't throw up on his shoes. Seriously, Senator, nothing could please me more."

"Good. The meeting is set for four o'clock; I would suggest you wear a tie, and your most fetching smile." The senator paused. "Meet me at my office around three and we'll talk before going to the Oval Office."

Clay took a huge breath of air. "The Oval Office, my God, I still can't believe it. You don't think he's gonna have me shot or something, do you, Senator?"

"The President doesn't usually invite people to his office to announce their execution. I think he simply wants to meet you, Son."

Clay began pacing. "I wish we were meeting at your place Senator, I could sure use a drink. In fact, I could use two or three."

Johnny interrupted. "I'm going home tomorrow. Clay you come and get me sometime around ten, and by the time you meet with the President you'll be as mellow as can be. Don't worry, Senator, I won't get him drunk. It's just that I know how to handle him better than anybody else."

"Yeah," Clay laughed. "Well, you can't drug me either."

"Actually," Johnny replied. "I thought we'd find the closest Waffle House and have some breakfast."

Clay couldn't hide his pleasure at the thought. "That should do it," he replied.

The senator looked curious. "I don't get it," he said. "Is that some private joke or something?"

"You see, Senator," Johnny continued. "When everything was going crazy with General Essex, and before he was arrested, we spent many hours at the Waffle House next to Clay's apartment. It's kinda sacred, if you know what I mean."

The senator motioned to Tim. "Okay, Siler, you know everything; where's the nearest Waffle House?"

Tim was caught totally off guard. "I hate to be a disappointment to you Senator, but I don't know. However, I will find out post-haste."

Sergeant Shackelford who had been standing quietly all this time chimed in with, "I like the Waffle House, they have great hash browns."

Realizing Shack was a little embarrassed by his outburst, Clay said, "I reckon it'll have to be you and me, Shack, the doctor's still a might puny."

"I'm not puny," Johnny declared. "You get me out of here tomorrow and I'm there for you, Old Buddy, but, Sergeant, you're welcome to come along."

Nobody said anything for a few seconds, and it seemed like minutes. Each person was fidgeting in their own subtle way. The senator had lost control, and no one else was willing to take it. Tim finally broke the silence.

"Senator, do you know what the President wants to talk about?"

"I don't have the foggiest. Of course, I've been bragging about Clay for months, and he may simply want to meet him."

Tim became stoic. "This President always has an agenda. He may want someone's legs broken, or he may want some dictator deposed."

The senator's face showed immediate disapproval. "I think that's enough, Tim. After all, the man is the President of this country, and we owe respect to the office, if not the man."

"I'm sorry, Senator," Tim replied.

Senator Lazar forced a smile. "It's okay, Tim. You and I both know that we Republicans must support our President, even if he is a Democrat. Anyway, he's not running again, and the next President will most certainly be from the Republican Party."

"Why doesn't he end the war in Vietnam?" Clay asked. "All we're doing is sacrificing young Americans on a daily basis, and we're getting nowhere."

Senator Lazar looked at him sternly. "What would you do Clay? I mean, if it were your choice."

Clay thought for a moment. "Well, I can only speak from my own experiences, and what I think I know. I would either bring the Americans home, or I would drop a few well placed bombs and end this thing."

"What do you think the rest of the world would think if we did something like that?" The senator paused, "Do you think they would support us, or hate us?"

"Actually, Sir, if I were the President, I wouldn't care what they thought," Clay replied. "One thing I know for sure is that they would respect us, and I'll choose respect every time."

Tim jumped in. "This war is about the economy. It's the only way the Democrats can solve the jobless problem. They make the government bigger, and do it by telling the poor they deserve an equal share of the pie, even if they never work a day to earn it."

Sergeant Shackelford was getting antsy, and Johnny had had enough. "Stop it," he yelled. "This is getting us nowhere fast."

"Right you are," the senator concurred. "The Republicans will put a stop to it, and then we'll get blamed for a weak economy."

"I would have to agree with you, Senator," Tim interjected.

The senator looked directly at Johnny. "Doctor Murphy, you've been itching to say something for awhile now. What is it?"

"I just want to know if it's over. Now that the general is dead, can we go back to living our normal lives? Although, with all that's happened lately, someone else must have taken the reins, or I would never have been kidnapped; is that correct, Senator?"

The senator replied. "I think the order to kidnap you came before he died, but I am not absolutely sure of that. I would advise all of the people in this room to be cautious, and that includes you, Mr. Siler."

Tim was startled. "Me, Sir, I don't follow, why would they want to harm me?"

Clay poked him on the arm. "Like it or not, Tim, old pal, you are one of us."

Johnny grinned. "Tim, you are known by the company you keep. You've got to stop hanging around with us troublemakers. Being in our company will destroy your fine reputation, and I know you don't want that."

Tim folded his arms across his chest in an act of defiance. "Okay, Guys, if my reputation is to be sullied at least let me in on some of the fun."

At least three voices resounded. "Fun?"

Now embarrassed, Tim continued. "Even in the bad times, you guys seem to be inseparable, and I love that."

Clay said, "You have to take a blood oath, and you have to eat at a Waffle House every day for one week, and it must be breakfast food."

Even the senator laughed at that one. The group had taken more than half an hour to settle down, but they had finally gotten to that point. Whew!

Johnny just had one more, off the wall, question. "Can I meet the President too? After all, I am a veteran."

Clay smiled. "Tomorrow is not Veteran's Day."

"I knew you were gonna say that," Johnny replied. "I don't think it's funny, not one little bit."

"Doctor Murphy," the senator injected. "When you are well, I will take you to meet the President. I promise."

"Okay," Johnny said, pouting a smidge. "I can live with that."

They continued to talk for some time. Unfortunately, very little was settled, and they still didn't know the present situation concerning the "Ten Little Indians". The senator and the sergeant left for home, knowing that Clay would be along soon with Jolene.

Tim said his good-byes as well. It became unusually quiet in the doctor's room.

"Say something, Old Buddy," Johnny implored. "Have you talked to Susan yet, about Gidget?"

"No," Clay replied. "The time hasn't seemed right. Anyway, you said we'd do it together, and I was counting on that."

Johnny lay back on the bed. "How does it really feel?"

"What? How does what feel?"

"Ah c'mon, you know, getting to meet the President. You're not really scared are you?"

Clay began pacing. "I'm not scared, but I am pretty nervous. The first time I hugged Senator Lazar, I thought I was gonna faint."

Johnny laughed. "Well, Stupid, you're not gonna hug him are you?"

Clay stopped pacing. "Not right off. I do think he's cute though, don't you?"

Johnny threw the plastic water pitcher at him. There was enough water in it to make a splash.

"What was that for?" Clay screamed.

Johnny was holding his stomach. Laughing so hard was causing him some discomfort.

"Clay, I swear I didn't know there was any water left in that thing. Boy, if you could have seen the look on your face."

Cleaning up the mess, Clay started chuckling. "I hope you popped a stitch, laughing so hard, you jerk."

"I really am sorry, Old Buddy. I'd help you clean up, but if I got down there you'd have to help me back up."

Clay glanced at him out of the corner of his right eye. "John Wayne Murphy, when you least expect it, I'm gonna baptize you. And you know the best part? You'll never know when it's coming."

"Don't do that," Johnny pleaded, "You know I can't stand that."

Clay laughed. "I know. Boy, do I know."

Johnny suddenly became very pensive. "I love you, Clay, and I am truly sorry."

Clay walked over to the bed. "I love you too, and I forgive you."

He laid his head on Johnny's chest and hugged him gently. "I couldn't make it in this world without you, Partner."

Johnny held him close. "It sure wouldn't be any fun without you."

Clay stood up. "I had better go and get Jolene, she'll be wondering what's happening. I will be back in the morning to take you home."

Johnny gave him a thumbs-up. "I can hardly wait. Boy could I use a drink and a cigar about now."

"Tomorrow, Partner," Clay replied, "You get a good night's sleep."

As Clay started out the door, Johnny said, "Would you do me a favor?"

Clay turned. "What?"

"Would you refill my water pitcher?"

There was silence as the door closed. If a bomb had gone off in Johnny's room Clay would not have looked back, but he was grinning.

The girls were having a good time together. When Clay apologized for being late, they were completely oblivious of the time.

Susan asked. "How's my favorite doctor doing? Are they gonna let him go home tomorrow?"

Clay responded in the affirmative, but he could see a twinge of abandonment looming in her baby blues.

He smiled broadly. "You'll be coming home next, and I bet it won't be long. I can almost taste those grilled cheese sandwiches. Anyway, did you like the chocolate chip cookies? I thought they were delicious."

"I ate three, and I saved the other three for later." She replied. "They were the best I've ever had."

Clay laughed. "They may just be on par with those grilled cheese sandwiches."

Jolene caught on quickly. "I've heard about those. I'm told they are the best ever. Would you make me one sometime?"

"Damn right I will," Susan replied, "You're welcome anytime, as long as you bring some more cookies."

Jolene grinned. "You know I will. When you come home we'll throw a regular party."

Clay touched Jolene's arm. "Would you stay here for another minute or so, I've got an errand to run. I promise I won't be gone more than fifteen minutes."

Knowing he had very little time, he almost ran to the cafeteria. He obtained a large chocolate milkshake and hurried back to Susan's room.

When he entered the room she lit-up. Looking at Jolene she said, "See why I adore this man? He is always thinking of someone else's comfort. Thanks, Clay."

"You're welcome," he replied. "We need to put some meat on those bones." He paused, scratching his chin. "In this room we have the most beautiful women from both sides of the Atlantic."

Susan tried to act embarrassed, and Jolene glowed with pride. Clay stood silent, taking it all in.

"We had better be going, Jolene. I need to speak to the senator once more before he retires."

"You guys spent the last two hours or more together," Susan declared. "Did you forget something?"

"Yeah, I need to get his opinion on a matter of some importance, and, I only now realized what a big deal it is."

Susan stuck out her bottom lip. "In other words, you're not gonna tell us. Are you, Spook-key?"

"Not right now, no," he replied.

Jolene's head had been going back and forth. Clay, Susan, Susan, Clay. "What's this Spook-key? I don't understand. Is it a private thing?"

Susan looked at her, as Clay threw up his hands. "It's merely a nickname," Susan answered. "You see, Jolene, he's afraid of cats."

"Susan," Clay said, raising his voice. "Tell the truth. I'm not afraid of cats; I simply, don't like, or trust them. They're sneaky."

Susan sat quietly, smiling.

Jolene, or the other hand, was intrigued. "Do you like dogs?" she inquired.

"I love dogs," he replied. "They are very loyal and trustworthy."

Susan couldn't hold back any longer. "What he's trying to say is, dogs are like men, dumb and slow. Cats, however, are smart and quick, like us women."

Clay went, playfully, for her throat. "Give me back my milkshake," he teased.

Susan moved away as far as she could. "Save me Jolene. See what a brute he is?"

Jolene stood there, transfixed. "But, Susan, you just got through saying how sweet and thoughtful he is."

They stopped; mid grab-ass. Clay laid his head on Susan's chest, and she hugged him, kissing the top of his head. Then the two of them stared at Jolene. "Gotcha!"

They could see the relief on Jolene's face.

"As they say in America," Jolene began. "You'll pay for that one. The both of ya."

Clay ignored Jolene briefly, while kissing Susan good-bye. "I'll come by tomorrow, Babe, when I come to pick up Johnny."

"Okay, Spook-key," she replied. Then she whispered. "I love you. You be good to Jolene, she's really fond of you. Don't blow it."

Clay squeezed her hand. "See you later. C'mon Jolene."

"Just a moment," she replied, walking over to Susan and giving her a mock hug.

Susan took her hand. "You be good to My Boy, he needs someone to love. If you want to be that person treat him right."

Jolene smiled, eyes shining. "Oh, I will. He is the most. Really!"

The drive to Senator Lazar's was pleasant. They held hands like school kids. They sang to the radio, and Jolene was quite good. Clay loved doing that, and he was pretty good.

When they arrived at the senator's, Clay went straight to the den. The senator was talking on the phone and motioned for Clay to be seated. He cupped the receiver in one hand and instructed Clay to make them a drink. Clay obliged, and before he was finished the senator's conversation ended.

"Make mine a double," the senator requested.

"Yes, Sir," Clay replied.

When the drinks were in hand the senator asked. "What's on your mind, Son."

"Does the President know what I've done?" Clay asked. "That's a bit frightening. He could have me put away for the rest of my life."

The senator took a long drag on his cigar. "Clay, trust me, you have nothing to worry about. The man holds you in high regard, I promise."

Cutting the Fringe

Clay breathed a sign of relief. "I'm sure glad you're on my side, Sir."

"Likewise," the senator replied. "We make a good team, don't you think?"

Clay took a drag from his own cigar. "Absolutely. We even think alike. Well, sometimes we do."

"More times than not, Son. However, I can't let it show as easily as you can. My position requires me to be slightly less direct in my approach."

Clay grinned. "That's the position you have to maintain, Sir. I understand. Otherwise, you might never be re-elected, and I would personally hate that. Someday, I hope you're President. That would be a great day for our country."

The senator became, noticeably, thoughtful. "Do you mean that, Clay?"

"Of course I do. You, Sir, are a man I would trust with the running of this country. I believe your heart is strong, and you are a man of great principles."

The senator was moved. He stood and walked around the huge desk. Placing his arm around Clay's shoulder he said. "I appreciate that, My Boy, more than I can tell you. There are those who would like to see that happen."

"Anything I can do to help, Sir. You tell me what needs to be done and I'll see to it. Surely there is something I can do to help."

The senator's smile was illuminating. "I would not run without you there to protect my backside. I mean that, Clay."

"Thank you, Sir. I don't know what to say."

Giving Clay a nudge, the senator said. "We're going to have fun tomorrow. Don't be nervous, I'll take care of setting the stage for you, be your charming self, and we'll make out quite well. You have my word on that."

Clay excused himself and headed to the kitchen, hoping to locate Jolene. There she was. She had organized everything for the next morning, and she was patiently waiting for him to come for her.

She looked at him. "I put some stuff in a bag. You are gonna let me stay with you tonight, aren't you."

"I wouldn't want it any other way," he replied. "C'mon, Doll Face, let's go home."

She took his arm and they went for the car.

Chapter 22

The next morning they showered together. By seven-thirty they were at the senator's home having breakfast. It was a meal consisting of Scotch-eggs, crisp bacon, link sausages, and the best little biscuits ever to caress a man's taste buds. There was also homemade strawberry freezer jam and the finest coffee this side of the Pecos.

It was nearly eight-thirty when the senator and the sergeant finally left for the Senate Office Building. The senator assured Clay once more that the day would go well, and that meeting the President was indeed a big deal, but worrying about it would only destroy the joy of the occasion. Believe it or not, that seemed to help.

Clay helped Jolene around the house a little and then made his way to the Bethesda Naval Hospital to see Susan and to pick up Johnny. Susan was in good spirits, all things considered, and Johnny was in her room giving her a pep-talk.

Seeing the two of them together, alive and getting well, brought a much needed smile to Clay's face.

"What's up?" he asked.

Johnny slapped the bed. "I ask you, is this not the most beautiful woman ever? Even with that turban on her noggin, she is umph."

Clay stood close to the door, taking in the sight. He was enjoying the view, and he wanted to snap a mental picture.

Susan adjusted herself in the bed. "Clay, are you okay? You look like your mind is somewhere else?"

Clay gathered his thoughts. "I'm okay, I'm glad we're together again, and I was trying to appreciate the view. And, yes, Johnny, she is the most beautiful thing I've maybe ever had the pleasure of being near. But then, Johnny, at this moment, even you're beautiful."

The three of them talked and reminisced for more than thirty minutes. Although Gidget's name never came to the forefront, Clay knew they were all merely, once again, skirting the issue. The time would come, and he secretly hoped it would be sooner rather than later. In his head, he could still hear the sound of Gidget's voice, it was as clear as a bell, even though it had come from Susan's body.

He and Johnny said their good-byes to Susan. They gathered Johnny's belongings, what few there were, and made their way to the parking lot, giggling and laughing all the while. One would have thought they were two kids skipping out of school on a "fake-note" from their parents.

When they reached the car Johnny went bonkers. "Holy Cow, Old Buddy! Where'd you get the new wheels? It's even prettier than the GTX. Of course, blue is my favorite color. Well, say something!"

Clay smiled. "Give me a minute and I will." He unlocked the doors. "I think it's a rental; the senator got it for me to use. Boy it's nice though, it'll run like a deer, and you could sit still and burn the rubber off the back tires."

"Wow," Johnny replied, sliding into the passenger's seat.

Placing himself behind the wheel Clay turned the key. "Listen to that purr. I think it has a glass-pack; anyway, it sounds great." Clay paused to get his breath. "The radio has five speakers, three in the front, and two in the rear."

"And an '8 track'," Johnny screeched. "I see it has an AM band, and an FM band. Why do they put FM in a car? Those FM stations never play the kind of music we want to hear."

"I don't know," Clay answered, "But some people like that high-brow stuff. Maybe we're just a couple of dummies."

Johnny stared at him. "Hell, I don't care, maybe we are. Put in a tape, I wanna hear some music."

"I can't," Clay replied, "I haven't had time to get any."

Johnny sat back in his seat. "Then turn on something and take me home."

"You got it," Clay replied.

"One, two, three," by Len Barry, was playing. By the time they hit the highway, Johnny was singing at the top of his lungs. A hot car, great music, and two incredible friends together once more; suddenly, everything was wonderful.

At five past eleven they entered the garage at the house where they had been staying. Everything seemed alright as they walked into the den. Crash, bang! Clay almost threw Johnny on the sofa.

"Don't you move, Partner," Clay whispered. "I mean it! I'll be right back."

Clay positioned himself beside the staircase. The sounds had come from the upstairs and there was only one way down. He waited.

A shadow on the wall; footsteps, faint footsteps, but Clay stayed quiet. *C'mon, do something, you scumbag. Show yourself; let's end this thing here and now.*

Clay couldn't hear anything moving around upstairs; however, there was a distinct odor. Perfume, it was perfume, and he recognized the scent. He quietly made his way back to where Johnny was waiting.

"What is it?" Johnny whispered.

Clay just stared at him. "If I told you what I thought, you wouldn't believe me."

Johnny sat up to face him. "You look like you've seen a ghost."

"Exactly," Clay replied.

Johnny grabbed him by the shoulders. "What? What the hell are you talking about?"

"Do you have your gun?" Clay asked.

"Yeah, it's in my bag. Why?"

"I'm going up those stairs; you cover me." Clay stood. "I've got to see if I'm as crazy as I think I am."

Clay proceeded very cautiously to the bottom of the steps, Johnny at his heels.

"Wait here," Clay instructed. "I'll wave you up when I get to the top and can see down the hallway."

"Okay, but I don't like this."

Clay ascended the stairs two at a time, throwing caution to the wind. When he had successfully reached the top, he gasped. "C'mon, Johnny, there is nothing to fear, we are among friends."

"What?" Johnny exclaimed, mounting the stairs, somewhat gingerly.

By this time Clay was halfway down the hallway, and the smell of perfume was almost overwhelming.

"Oh, My God, Johnny come see this."

Clay disappeared into the bathroom as Johnny hurried toward him. When Johnny looked into the bathroom he couldn't believe his eyes. Clay stood motionless in front of the huge mirror, pale as ash.

Reaching Clay's side, Johnny saw the writing on the mirror.

Because I loved you so unselfishly, God has allowed me to become your "Guardian Angel". The danger is over for now, but I will continue to protect you.

Love, Gig

Both men stood in silence for a long time; Johnny, holding on to Clay's arm for support. The noise they had heard earlier had obviously come from the soap and shampoo bottle hitting the bottom of the tub.

The writing was made with something that looked a bit like white paint. Nothing they could see, nor find later, could have been used to do the job.

The two of them searched the upstairs thoroughly, finding nothing amiss, and God knows they tried. Then they went back downstairs and did the same thing, again, everything was as it should have been.

Clay went to the bar and began making drinks. Johnny found two cigars, clipped and lit them both, and handed one to Clay. Drinks in hand, they collapsed on the sofa. Finally, Johnny broke the silence.

"I've heard of these things happening to other people, but I don't think I ever really believed it until now. You did see what I saw, didn't you, Old Buddy?"

"Yeah," Clay answered. "Now, do you believe me?"

Johnny looked up from his drink. "You mean what you told me about hearing Gidget talking from Susan's body?"

"That's what I mean. Do you believe me?"

"Well, I did believe you when you told me, or at least I tried to."

"I know," Clay replied, "It's a little weird. I've wanted to talk to Susan about it but I can't seem to. The time is never right, but when she gets home we'll do it together, right?"

Johnny finished his drink in one final swallow. "I told you before, when she gets out of the hospital, and we are all together again; that's the time to bring it up."

"I know that's what I was trying to say."

Johnny walked across the room to the bar. "I've seen a lot, Old Buddy; although, this is without a doubt the spookiest thing that I have ever witnessed."

Clay jumped, throwing his cigar at the fireplace. "Spookiest!??! Couldn't you have chosen a different word? Anything but spookiest." It took both men a minute or so to clean up the mess. They were trying to be sure they'd put out the bits of fire, before the carpet burned.

"That's unreal," Clay stammered. "Susan keeps calling me that, and, neither she nor I know where it came from."

Johnny was getting a little irritated. "Calling you what? What the heck are you talking about?"

"Spook-key, she calls me Spook-key. Haven't you noticed?"

Johnny thought for a moment. "I don't think so. Well, maybe. Shit, I don't know. What difference does it make?"

"Damned if I know," Clay replied. "It's just that when you used that word, spookiest, it came to me. She gave me some cock-eyed reason once, but it made little or no sense."

"Don't you like the name?" Johnny asked.

"Partner, you're killing me here." Clay began pacing. "It's the two things together, it seems a bit eerie. I think you're taking too much pain medicine."

Johnny stopped him in mid-pace. Placing one hand on each of Clay's shoulders, and looking him straight in the eye, he said, "I get it. I understand, but let's not dwell on it, its spoo - - -"

"See, you did it again," Clay pointed out.

"No I didn't, I caught myself." Now, Johnny was pacing.

In order to return some sanity to the moment, Clay changed the subject. "I've got to be at the senator's office in about an hour, and I don't want to meet the President looking like this."

Johnny smiled. "Then go. I'm gonna sit here and get drunk."

Clay said. "No you're not. You're gonna entertain Jolene while I'm gone."

Johnny sat up straight. "Is she coming here, or am I going there?"

Sticking his head around the bedroom door, Clay answered, "You told me you needed to walk, well why don't you walk over there and bring her back here. This place needs some cleaning, but don't you dare tell her that I said that."

Johnny stood, slowly. "I'll do that, but first I have to use the facilities."

"Use my bathroom," Clay yelled. "While you're doing that, I'll try to figure out what I'm gonna wear."

"That was my intention," Johnny responded. "I wasn't about to go back upstairs. I can fight anything head-on, but I don't like dealing with the unseen, it gives me the willies."

Clay grabbed him as he started to pass. "Don't let Jolene see that mirror, it will scare the crap out of her."

"Right, you can count on me, Old Buddy. I won't even let her go upstairs."

Clay had his suit laid out on the bed, and was waiting for Johnny to exit the bathroom. He could hear Johnny washing his hands for the longest. Finally he returned to the bedroom.

"Partner," Clay began. "I really like Jolene, so please, make her feel as special as she truly is. Will you do that for me?"

Johnny looked surprised. "That's super. Okay, I'll be on my best behavior. Stop worrying, will ya?"

They embraced.

Clay said. "Thanks, I knew you would understand. Now, take it easy walking over there, you don't have to hurry."

Johnny poked him in the ribs. "Yes, Daddy, I'll be careful. Go take a shower and get all pretty for the President."

"Will do."

Clay went toward the bathroom and Johnny went for the door, each smiling, and their admiration for one another even stronger.

The water felt especially good, and Clay stood for some time allowing the water to sooth his aching muscles. The warm water caressed each area of his torso. Finally he reached for the shampoo, always using too much.

"You really are beautiful."

Clay froze, even in the hot water. "What?" he yelled, trying to get the shampoo out of his eyes so he could focus.

"Is someone here? Damn you, say something."

"Watch your language, Young Man, or I'll be forced to wash your mouth out with soap."

"Gidget, is that you? Where are you?"

"I'm right here in the shower with you. I know, you can't feel me, can you?"

"No I can't," he gasped. "I wish I could though. I'm sorry about what happened; if I'd only gotten there a little sooner, I'd - - -"

"Don't fret its okay. I came back to tell you that I didn't betray you or any of the others. I didn't know that my stepfather was involved until weeks later. You must believe me."

"I do believe you, Gidget."

"And I didn't tell them anything about Susan or Sydney, I swear. Oops, I'm not supposed to say that."

"Say what," he inquired.

"We're not supposed to swear."

"Gidget, am I going crazy? Is this really happening?"

"Yes, this is happening, and it is really me; well sort of."

Clay stuttered. "How'd they find Pamela and Janice?"

"I don't know, but it wasn't me. I didn't know where they were, remember?"

"Right, I didn't think you knew."

"Clay, I must go. One thing though. Don't trust anybody but Johnny and Susan, and Jolene is for real. Treat her nice."

"Gidget, wait, say something that only you and I know. Please, I want to know for sure it's you, and can we talk again sometime?"

"I doubt it; this is not part of the norm. Good-bye, Clay, I will love you forever."

"Gidget, Gidget, don't go."

"Clay, you'll be happy to know that there are no pussycats here. Bye, My Love."

There was silence, except for the sound of the running water, and the rapid beating of Clay's heart. As he stepped out of the shower he heard the opening of the front door and the sound of Johnny's voice, then Jolene's.

He peeked around the edge of the bedroom door as they came toward the den. "Jolene, would you fix me a sandwich of some kind? I just realized that I haven't eaten lunch, and I don't want my stomach growling in front of the President."

"Sure, Clay," she answered. "What do you want to drink?"

"Milk, if we have any."

"I haven't eaten either," Johnny declared.

Jolene smiled. "I'll fix you one too, Doc. Do you also want milk?"

"Yeah, why not, I guess I need it."

Jolene toddled off to the kitchen.

Clay yelled from the bedroom. "Come here, Johnny, I need to tell you something,"

"Coming, Master!"

"Two things," Clay began. "I talked to Gidget, while I was in the shower. I know its crazy but it's true."

Johnny never said anything; he just stood there shaking his head. "What's the second thing?" he asked.

Clay continued. "Can you remove these stitches from my hand? I think it's about time, and it looks so tacky."

Johnny gave him that 'I knew you needed me look'. "Let me get my bag, it's in the other room. I'll be right back."

He returned in a minute and got straight to the matter. When he was through, it looked and felt better. Clay was a quick healer, but it was still very noticeable.

"Do you think I can shake the President's hand?" he asked.

"I wouldn't," Johnny replied. "He'll understand. He's a big man, with hands like ham hocks, and he could set the healing process back for days, or worse."

"Damn, I get to meet the most important man in the world and I can't even shake hands with him."

"Stop whining, you big baby, at least you're getting to meet him."

"You're right, Partner," Clay replied. "Don't worry; you'll get your chance."

Johnny's expression changed completely. "Tell me about Gidget."

Clay spent the next few minutes explaining in as much detail as he could muster. When he got to the part about cats, Johnny had to take a seat on the bed.

"Holy cow," he exclaimed. "Were you scared?"

Clay looked up. "Yeah, at first, but then it was pleasant, in a strange sort a way. Mind you, I couldn't see her."

"Oh yeah, right," Johnny said, shaking his head. "Did you feel her presence, or could you feel her touching you?"

Clay finished putting on his shoes. "Not literally, but I could sense her."

Jolene stepped into the doorway. "Lunch is ready, Gentlemen."

Clay smiled at her. "Will you come here?" he asked. Then turning to Johnny, he said. "Would you excuse us for a couple of minutes?"

Johnny became a little flustered. "Sure, no problem, I'll be in the kitchen eating everything in sight."

Clay put his arms around Jolene's waist. "I've missed you."

She snuggled close. "Me too. You know, I'm all empty inside when we're not together, it's the strangest feeling."

"I know how that feels," he answered, kissing her softly. "Thanks for being here, Love."

Her eyes were sparkling. "I wouldn't want to be any other place."

Clay ran the back of his hand down the side of her beautiful face. "I sure would like to go to Scotland and meet your family. Do you think we could do that?"

She stepped back. "Don't kid me."

"I'm not kidding," he replied.

"Oh my lord, do you really mean - - -"

He stopped her. "Yes, I really mean it. Do you think they would like me?"

"What's not to like?" she replied, smiling from every part of her anatomy.

"We'll do it then; you can count on that."

"Clay, you have made me very happy," she said, hugging and kissing him repeatedly.

Clay smiled widely. "Let's go eat. I've got to go meet the President of the United States. Do you think he'll like me?"

Jolene took his hand and pulled him toward the kitchen. "He had better, or we'll move to Scotland."

Jolene was so happy that even Johnny could see the elation on her face; although, he hadn't a clue why she was glowing.

"Boy, you two look great," Johnny submitted. "How long have I been in here by myself?" He paused, looking at the two of them. "No way," he chuckled, "I haven't been in here that long."

Clay gave him a stern look. "Hush, Johnny, we're just glad to see each other, that's all."

Jolene squeezed Clay's good hand. "That's right, by golly. Eat your sandwich, Doctor."

They sat together, eating and talking. Johnny was as polite as Clay had ever seen him. He knew that Johnny was aware that something major was taking place. Jolene said almost nothing, but her eyes were fixed on Clay.

"Will you do me a favor, Johnny?" Clay asked.

"Sure, Old Buddy, what can I do for you?"

Clay reached into his pocket and fished out his wallet. "Send some flowers to Susan, will ya? She loves yellow roses."

He handed Johnny fifty dollars.

"Keep your money," Johnny insisted, "This is my treat. I'll send her two dozen long stemmed yellow roses from the both of us."

"I've got a little money," Jolene declared. "Can I chip in? Then they can be from all three of us. I like her too, you know."

Johnny looked at Clay who was nodding his head. "Yeah, she'll like that. But keep your money, Little Lady, I'm loaded you know."

Jolene's eyes brightened. "Thanks, Doctor, I knew you were one of the good guys, and I'm pleased you two would include me. That means a lot to me."

Johnny smiled. "Not another word. Anyone who can make a sandwich this tasty is okay by me. By the way, what is this we're eating?"

She laughed. "It's fried bologna, cheese, and plenty of mayonnaise, just the way Clay likes it. I thought you liked it too."

"Like it?" Johnny exclaimed. "I love it, and the milk was delicious."

"Are you making fun with me, Doctor?"

"Nope, I just love to hear you speak."

She patted his hand. "Then I'm happy."

Clay came to his feet. "I gotta get going. Don't forget to order the flowers. I'd like for her to get them today. With you coming home, Partner, she's probably a little down right now."

"I'll take care of it post-haste," Johnny replied. "Good luck with the President."

Clay kissed Jolene on the cheek and departed.

Chapter 23

The drive to the senator's office took less time than Clay had allowed for; consequently, he was almost twenty-five minutes early. Fortunately Senator Lazar had had a shortened meeting and was waiting for him.

Clarisse was always happy to see Clay, and when he walked into the office she was all smiles.

"You look very handsome today, Mr. Smith, but then you always look great to me." She arose from her chair. "Would you care for something to drink?"

"Nothing for me," he replied. "Actually, I could use some tranquilizers."

She grinned. "I could calm you down, but I don't think we have the time, and this certainly isn't the place."

Clay looked her up and down. She was an attractive woman in her late thirties, or early forties. She stood about five-three with long brown hair, and she was a little on the plump side. Clarisse had striking features; however, she used too much make-up, and way too much perfume. Although, it was probably expensive; too much, is still too much. She was classy though, and that was one thing that had always appealed to him. He liked her from the first time they had met, but not the way she obviously liked him.

"I'll just bet you could," he replied, offering her his most gracious smile.

Clarisse became rather serious. "Mr. Smith, is that Sergeant Shackelford married? I sure could learn to like him, you know. He always looks at me in the most peculiar way. Has he ever mentioned me?"

"No, he's not married, and yes, he has mentioned you many times."

Clay was lying, but the sergeant had mentioned her on one occasion, and he did think she was pretty. Truthfully, the sergeant was bluegrass, and Clarisse was more classical.

"Well," she said, touching his arm, "Tell him I asked about him. Would you do that for me?"

"I will do that very thing, today," Clay replied. "And, never fear, I will be discreet."

She ran her hand down his arm. "Thank you, Mr. Smith, I'll tell the senator you're here. Have a seat, if you like."

She moved back behind the desk and picked up the telephone. "Sir, Mr. Smith has arrived. Shall I send him in?"

There was a momentary silence.

"Yes, Sir, I have taken care of that. I will show him in, Senator."

Clarisse looked up in Clay's direction as she returned the receiver to its cradle. "You may go in now, Mr. Smith."

"Thanks," Clay said. Then leaning forward, he winked. "I'll take care of everything; you're as good as on your first date."

She flushed a little. "Do it carefully," she whispered. "I don't want the senator to get angry."

Clay stopped. "I will be careful," he assured. "Just call me Cupid."

The senator was all smiles. "Nice to see you, My Boy, you look ready to meet the man."

Clay carefully extended his left hand.. "I'm a wreck, but I'm here."

The senator handed him a cigar. "Here, this will calm you down. How about a drink? Maybe a little scotch will slow the old heart rate."

"If you think it's alright, Sir."

Sergeant Shackelford walked into the room. "Hey, Clay, you look fit to bury. Are you still nervous?"

"Thanks, Shack," Clay replied. "That comment should bring me around; fit to bury, huh?"

"Where I'm from, that's a compliment. It simply means you look good."

The senator interrupted. "I think he got it, Sergeant."

Shack flushed. "Well, you do look good."

The senator became serious. "Clay, when you are addressing the President you always address him as Mr. President, and you never sit in his presence unless he is seated first."

"I understand, Sir," Clay answered. "In other words, I treat him as though he were a lady, correct?"

The senator stared, not knowing what to say. "Clay!"

"Sorry Senator; humor relaxes me." Clay paused. "Anyway, he's a democrat, isn't he?"

Sergeant Shackelford was trying desperately not to laugh out loud.

The senator looked from Clay to Shack, and then back to Clay. "Yes he is a democrat. But, truth be known, he is probably the most powerful man ever to hold the office. Did you know he has forced the passing of more legislation than any other two Presidents combined?"

Clay said, "Is that true?"

"Absolutely true," the senator replied. "This President will go down in history as the most powerful man to ever hold the office."

"Now, I'm even more nervous," Clay screeched. "Will he be re-elected?"

"I don't think he's going to run," the senator answered. "He's plagued by the ghost of the past, and it's killing him."

"What does that mean?" Clay asked.

The senator's face showed signs of uncertainty. "There are two many questions concerning the death of his predecessor; questions, that will probably never be answered."

"Do you know the truth, Senator Lazar?" Clay asked. "Please, you know I can be trusted."

"Not really, My Boy, but I believe - - -"

Clay actually interrupted. "What do you believe, Senator?"

The senator moved uncomfortably in his chair. "I'm not sure what I do believe. However, I think he hoped the war would camouflage everything, and that is not happening."

"If you were President, would you bring the boys home?" Clay asked.

The senator's face lit up. "Yes I would, and I've said that very thing in public many times. We should not be expected to police the entire world; we have too many problems here at home."

Clay took a long drag from his cigar. "I'd blow the bastards away. A few well placed bombs and there'd be no more war. Hell, those people hate us anyway; I'd put the fear of the 'God Almighty' right on their doorstep."

"Right you are Clay!" Shack could no longer be silent. "I'm sorry, Senator Lazar, but I think he's right."

"Its okay, Sergeant," the senator acknowledged. "You have a right to your opinion, and you may be correct. I just don't want to have anymore killing."

Clay felt that it was time to be silent, and to get on with the business at hand.

The senator finished his drink and set the glass on the desk. "Let's go see the President. This is one meeting, for which, I don't want to be late."

Clay said, "Me either. And, thanks for the conversation, I'm not nervous anymore. Of course, I will be, when we walk into the Oval Office."

The sergeant laughed, and the senator patted Clay on the back and took the lead.

He said, "Let's go, Gentlemen, the President awaits."

When the three of them arrived outside the Oval Office, once again, knees were shaking. Everyone spoke to the senator as they entered the outer office. Clay was almost positive his fear was evident, but he tried desperately to act otherwise.

A very attractive and immaculately groomed young lady walked toward them, smiling.

"Senator Lazar, it is so nice to see you," she greeted. "The President will be ready for you in about ten minutes, can I get you something?"

Senator Lazar took her hand. "Nothing for me Miss Abernathy; however, I would like to introduce you to Clay Smith."

She removed her hand from the senator's and extended it to Clay. "It is indeed a pleasure to make your acquaintance, Mr. Smith."

She looked at him as though she was taking a long cool drink of water on a hot summer's evening, and she didn't spill a drop. Her hand was as soft as a baby's breath, but her grip was firm.

"Ouch," Clay grimaced.

She was startled. "Oh I see it's your hand, what happened?"

"Just a small accident," Clay replied. "It's nothing really; just a little sore yet."

"I'm sorry if I hurt you," she cooed. "It was purely unintentional, I assure you."

There was that look again.

This time Clay returned her look, staring deep into her pastel blue gaze. "It is indeed a pleasure to make your acquaintance," he replied. "I thought meeting the President would be the height of my day, but this will be hard to match."

She fought a blush with every ounce of strength she could muster. "Oh my, I am completely lost for a response. How sweet you are, Mr. Smith."

"Call me, Clay. Please!"

"And you may call me, June," she responded, sliding her hand from his, slowly, carefully, and reluctantly.

"Miss Abernathy," came a voice from the other end of the room. "The President will see them now."

She came back to awareness in a hurry. "Follow me, Gentlemen. The President is waiting for you."

Clay took a deep breath and walked forward. *What an office!* The president walked from behind his desk and extended his hand to the senator.

"How are you, Bob?" he said in a voice that resounded throughout the room. "This must be Mr. Clay Smith, from Tennessee?"

"Yes, Mr. President," the senator replied. "This is the young man I spoke to you about. Please excuse the injured hand, he had a slight accident."

"It is a pleasure to meet you, Clay. I'm sorry about the hand, but I hope it's alright to call you Clay?"

"Yes Sir, Mr. President, it most certainly is. I am honored that you would take time from your incredibly busy schedule to meet me."

"Don't give that another thought, Clay. Texans and Tennesseans have always had a kinship, dating back to the Alamo."

"Yes Sir, Mr. President," Clay said proudly. "I hope it will always be that way."

The President smiled. "Me too, Clay, me too." He paused. "Be seated gentlemen; may I offer you something to drink? I'm gonna have some coffee."

"A cup of coffee would be nice," the senator replied.

"How about you, Clay?"

"Coffee would be just fine, Mr. President."

With the coffee ordered the President got right to the heart of the matter.

"I think the group you have been battling, Clay, has finally realized the error of their ways. I don't expect they will be bothering you any longer." He grinned at Clay. "To be honest, Son, I think you put the fear of God in them, and I love it."

"Thank you, Mr. President."

A young man came into the room with coffee on a silver tray, china cups, and linen napkins.

"May I serve you, Mr. President?" he asked.

The President gave him a look. "No Bruce that will be all. We can get our own coffee. But, Bruce, bring us some of those little divinity cookies I like so much."

"Right away, Mr. President," Bruce answered, as he backed out of the office.

In seconds he returned with the cookies.

"I'm sorry, Mr. President, I should have brought them the first time."

The President glared at him. "That will be all."

Clay noticed that as soon as Bruce was out of the room the President's demeanor changed completely.

The President looked at the senator. "Would you do the honors, Bob?"

"Certainly, Mr. President," Senator Lazar replied.

Clay was beginning to feel uncomfortable.

When the President had been served he looked in Clay's direction. "Try some of those cookies, Clay, they are truly sinful."

"I shall. Thank you, Mr. President."

The President seemed pleased with Clay's response.

"By the way, Clay, what happened to the hand?"

"A minor accident, Mr. President, I inadvertently punched a mirror." Clay replied. "It's almost healed, but I was told, Mr. President, that you are a powerful man with a powerful handshake."

The President smiled. "All the men in my family had large hands; a sign of virility you know?"

"I've heard that said many times, Mr. President, and in your case, Mr. President, no one would question the validity of that statement. You are, in point of fact, the most powerful man in the world."

"Right you are, Clay. Let me come directly to the point, Gentlemen." He paused, gathering his thoughts. "As the President of this great country of ours I am forced to make many decisions. Sometimes they are good, and sometimes even the President makes a mistake. What I am trying to say is this. Clay, I would like for you to work for me. You would have 'Carte Blanc' and be free to use your own judgment in matters of national security and the like. You would answer to no one other than the President."

"What would I be doing, Mr. President?"

"I would like to send you to the FBI Training Academy; however, you will not be a student. I would like for you to observe the class and let, me alone, know what you think of our training methods."

"I can do that, Mr. President."

"Good, I knew, and so did Bob, that you were the man for this job. Bob says you are honest, and totally loyal to those you love, and to your country. I know everything there is to know about you, and I like what you stand for, and you are decisive."

"I simply want to do the right thing, Mr. President."

The President's mood brightened. "Now, you can do it legally. You will answer to no one but God, your own conscience, and me. That can be a great burden, Clay. Can you handle that?"

"I believe I can, Mr. President."

The President stood abruptly. "Then I best get back to work. You will report to Miss Abernathy on the seventh of next month. She will give you all the details, pay and such."

"Thank you, Mr. President."

The President took Clay's hand carefully. "You are the President's Man, don't let me down."

"I won't, Mr. President."

"I will have a letter for you by this time tomorrow. The letter will give you the authority to do as you see fit. In other words, if you need one last shot at those pesky Indians, take it, with my blessing."

"Thank you, again, Mr. President."

The President looked at Senator Lazar. "You did a good thing today Bob. I'll get that letter to your office before the end of the day tomorrow."

"I'll deliver it to Mr. Smith tomorrow evening, Mr. President."

"Of course you will," the President replied. "Now, if you Gentlemen will excuse me, I am late for another meeting."

The meeting was over, and in seconds they were, once again, in the outer office. Clay's head was still spinning. He wanted desperately to talk to the senator, but that would have to wait until they had some privacy.

Miss Abernathy was delighted to be Clay's coordinator, or whatever her job title was in this particular instance.

"I will see you here at seven-thirty AM on March the seventh," she declared. "If you have a need for anything in the meantime, call me."

Clay smiled. "I'll need a number, Miss Abernathy."

She became a bit flustered. "I meant to give you a card." She fumbled in a drawer. "Here, take this card. Call the top number during the day and the bottom number after six PM in the evening, and on weekends."

Clay was enjoying this. "What about holidays?"

"And holidays as well," she replied. "Oh, you're playing with me aren't you, Mr. Smith."

"Yeah, I guess I am. Please, don't be offended. I only pick on people I like."

She looked at the senator. "Is he telling the truth, Senator Lazar?"

"Yes, Miss Abernathy," the senator replied. "I believe he is."

"Well then, Mr. Smith, at what numbers can you be reached?"

Clay said, "Okay, you got me."

The senator interrupted. "He can be reached at any of my numbers; or at the home of the Ambassador to Britain. I'm sure you already have that number, don't you?"

"I do indeed," she replied. "Thank you both."

Clay could hardly wait until he and the senator were alone. There were so many questions running around in his brain, he was sure his head would explode at any given moment.

Chapter 24

As they walked briskly into the Senate Office Building, it was difficult to tell which one of the two of them was the most anxious to speak. The door to the senator's outer office opened, and Sergeant Shackelford was waiting patiently.

Clarisse spoke first. "How'd it go, Sir? Did you do well, Mr. Smith?"

"Of course he did," the senator replied. "He always does."

Shack grinned. "I'm proud of you, Clay."

"Thanks, My Friend, I wish you had been there."

The sergeant said, "Me too."

Senator Lazar looked at the sergeant. "Sergeant Shackelford, will you pull the car around please? I'll be down in a few minutes. If they give you any trouble for parking on the street, tell them you are following my orders."

"Yes Sir, right away, Sir." The sergeant reacted immediately. Then he looked back, "See you at the house, Clay."

Clay raised his hand as if to wave. "You can count on it. And, thanks again for the kind words."

The sergeant answered shyly, "That's what friends are for," and he was gone.

As soon as the door shut, the senator spoke. "Well, My Boy, you have over three weeks to relax before reporting to the President. How do you feel?"

"Pretty good, I think," Clay paused, and this strange look came to his face. "I have the utmost respect for the leader of our country, but, Senator, that man scares me."

"Maybe, but we got what we were after, the letter. Once you have that in your hand, My Boy, you are home free. Nothing and no one can touch either one of us, period."

The light went on in Clay's head. "That's what this is all about isn't it, Sir."

The senator put his arm around Clay's shoulder. "Damn tootin, I wanted you in the clear so that nothing could ever come back to haunt you, or me."

"Senator, you are amazing. You had this all worked out for me. I don't know what to say. May I give you a hug, Sir?"

The senator grabbed him. "Damn Tootin. Now, let's go home and have a great meal. The doctor and Jolene are at the house and she is preparing a brisket. Do you like corned beef?"

Clay helped the senator with his coat, sore hand and all. "Yes Sir, I surely do."

"Well," the senator said, "Let's get your topcoat from Clarisse and head to the house."

"Do I have time to go by and see Susan for a few minutes?" Clay asked.

The senator smiled. "Sure, I'll see you at the house, for dinner, at seven. Will that be okay?"

"Yes indeed, Senator, I'll be there."

Clay could hardly wait to get to Susan and give her the good news. When he pulled into the hospital parking lot it was five-forty; he had plenty of time.

Susan was looking great, and of course she was delighted to see him. "What's the big grin for Spook-key?"

"Why do you call me that?" he asked.

"I don't know, it just came out one day. Does it bother you?"

"Yeah, a little, and I don't know why," he replied. "Well, actually, it makes me feel a bit odd."

"Okay, Handsome, no more. Now, why the big grin?"

Clay went on to explain everything that had taken place. He talked about the letter and how it would absolve him of any wrongdoing. Susan was ecstatic.

"Come here, Big Boy, and give me a kiss," she ordered. "I owe you for the beautiful flowers anyway. Look at them, aren't they magnificent?"

Clay was quick to respond. Their love for each other was so real, and it had nothing to do with sex. It was simply adoring respect. These two were friends, and what made the other happy was their major concern.

Clay said, "Look, Babe, I'm gonna have you transferred to the University of Virginia Medical Center, in Richmond, as soon as the doctors will allow. When you are ready to come home, I will take you to Sydney's."

She looked up from her water glass. "Have you talked to Sydney about this plan of yours?"

Clay sat down on the bed beside her. "Not yet, but I will, maybe tonight. He will be delighted."

"Are you gonna stay with me?"

"Yes, some, and Johnny too."

"I have some time before the President needs me, and I'm gonna see that the two of you are completely healed and better than ever. I do have a couple of errands to run, but it will only take a couple of days."

"What about Jolene?"

Clay blushed a little. "I thought I might take her to Scotland to visit her family, if I can work it out with Senator Lazar." He paused, "What do you think?"

"I think she's a very lucky girl, and if she does you wrong I'll rip her heart out."

"Shall I tell her that?" he joked. "Maybe that will make all the difference; fortunately, she knows how mean you are."

Susan punched him hard on the arm. "You'll pay for that one, Spooo— Buddy Boy. Oops!"

Clay laid his head on her breast. "It's okay. When you are totally healed we'll talk about that nickname."

Carl R. Smith

She put her free arm around him; she did have one IV yet in the other arm. "I love you, Clay, and whatever makes you happy is okay by me."

He looked up into her incredible blue eyes. "I know, Babe. Would you like for me to get you a milkshake before I go? I'm having dinner at seven with the rest of the gang, I hope you don't mind."

"Will you be back in the morning?"

"I'll be here by ten-thirty, and I'll bring you one of your favorite things for lunch. We'll have a blast. Hell, maybe I'll bring Johnny too."

She kissed his forehead. "Just you alone will be fine, okay?"

"Sure, Cutie. Now, how about that milkshake?"

"Nah, I think I'll just go to sleep. Tomorrow will come sooner that way."

He smiled. "You're the boss."

As he started for the door, Susan said, "Clay, I'm glad you're my friend, I love you. You know that don't you?"

He turned and threw her a kiss. "I know! Sleep well Susan."

He arrived at the house at six thirty-five. He had to use the facilities and brush his teeth; not necessarily in that order. He stood there, his heart racing. *Are you here Gidget? If you are, please speak to me, this is making me a nervous wreck.*

Nothing!

C'mon, Little One, you know I love you.

Still nothing!

Clay was shaking so hard in anticipation; he could barely hold the toothbrush.

Turning on the water, he bent down over the sink to rinse the toothpaste from his mouth. Then he grabbed the towel in order to dry his face.

Oh, My God, he screamed. *You gotta stop doing this, I'm gonna have a heart attack.*

There, scrolled on the mirror. "I have to be leaving. We're all the same size here. I'm not *little* anymore. Love ya."

It was five minutes until seven, he had to hurry. He ran out the front door, down the steps, and took off up the alley toward the senator's. Looking up into the almost totally dark sky he said aloud, *God, if you're trying to give me a stroke or something, just keep it up, Sir, its working. No disrespect, Sir. But hey, could you lighten up, or at least give me a little notice, next time?* At that very instant a beautiful star fell from the sky, and somehow he felt better. He didn't know why, but he did.

Everyone was waiting for him, even Tim Siler, a pleasant surprise. The entire area smelled delicious, and having Johnny there made the occasion much more festive.

"Go to the dining room, Gentlemen," Jolene suggested. "I'll be serving the soup shortly. Doctor Murphy, will you please serve the wine?"

"I sure will," he replied. "C'mon everybody, soup's on. Well, almost, anyway."

Everyone filed into the dining room behind the senator, of course. Senator Lazar took his usual seat at the far end, which was the head of the table. Clay was seated to his right. Johnny was across from Clay and to the senator's left. Sergeant Shackelford was seated to the right of Clay, and Tim Siler to the left of Johnny. Jolene did not join them at the table; however, she served the entire repast. At this point in their relationship Clay was not too happy about that, but said nothing.

Jolene was unnerved, but continued to do her job with calm and precision. Every time she served Clay she would brush against him in some fashion. He was grateful, and he made every possible attempt to return the attention, carefully.

Tim Siler was incredibly excited about the Presidential Letter, and so was Johnny. Shack was too, but he was not very demonstrative.

"This is a real coup on our part, Fellas," the senator insisted. "Everyone starts out with a clean slate; and I couldn't be happier."

"Do you think we'll have any more trouble with the Ten Little Indians, Senator?" Clay asked.

"I don't think so," the senator replied. "Although, I wouldn't suggest letting our guard down completely."

"I'll buy that," Johnny injected.

Tim and Shack nodded in agreement.

"Well anyway," the senator began. "May I purpose a toast? Here's to the greatest group of friends on the planet."

There was a resounding, "Here, here," from everyone present.

Clay was squirming in his seat. "Wait a minute, Guys. Senator, what about Johnny and Shack, and even Tim for that matter, will they be absolved too?"

The senator raised his glass a second time. "Yessiree! Anyone accompanying you will be cleared as well," he declared. "To be honest, it will be as though it never happened at all. How's that?"

"That's great," Clay replied. "On behalf of all my cohorts in crime, and crime fighting, I thank you, Sir."

This time every glass in the room went toward the ceiling. Johnny was orchestrating with both hands. "Okay, Men, on three. One, two, three. Thank you Senator Lazar."

Glasses clanged.

Johnny looked directly at Clay. "And, thank you, Old Buddy, for looking out for the rest of us."

Things calmed considerably, and after a wonderful and marvelous meal the men retired to the den for cigars and something a little stronger to drink. Clay excused himself and made his way to the kitchen. He walked up behind Jolene who was standing at the sink, slid his arms around her middle and began kissing her on the back of the neck. It was Clay who was trembling. She turned her head slightly and their lips met.

"I have a wonderful surprise for you," Clay whispered. "Do you want to hear it now or later?"

"Now," she insisted, turning to face him.

"We're going to Scotland to visit your people and your country."

"What?" she screamed. "Please don't kid me, Clay."

He took her face in his hands. "I'm not kidding."

She kissed him all over the face. "Oh, Clay, I am so happy, I think I'm going to cry. I love you, I love you, I love you."

He pushed her back with one hand on each side of her angelic face. He looked her straight in the eye. "I don't ever want you serving anyone else again, except me, and we'll do that part together. Okay?"

Carl R. Smith

She began to cry. "I have never before, in me life, been this happy."

He handed her a tissue. "Here, Love, blow your nose, and dry those green eyes. I have to go back to the guys. When we're through we'll walk home together; I'll try to hurry."

"Take your time," she responded. "I have a lot of cleaning to do, and I want to get everything ready for breakfast tomorrow before we leave. I do still have a job to do, you know?"

"Yeah, but not for long," he replied. Then he kissed her on the end of the nose and hurried from the kitchen.

When he entered the den everyone was chatting. They became quiet, all four men looking straight at him.

"Everything alright in the kitchen, Old Buddy?" Johnny asked.

Clay flushed. "Yeah, you big jerk, everything is fine in the kitchen."

The senator held up his left hand to hush everyone. "Son, you have some well deserved time off coming, and I am going to see my children for a little while. Why don't you take that young lady home to Scotland for a week or so? I'll bet you two would have a glorious time together."

Four glasses went into the air. "Here, here."

Clay looked directly at Johnny. "Would you be okay, Partner, if I were gone for a few days?"

"Hell, Old Buddy, I'll be fine, you go have a good time."

Clay looked at the four of them. "Well, I told Susan that I was going to send her to Sydney's as soon as she was able to travel. She could check in with the Medical College of Virginia, and be treated as an out-patient, for as long as was necessary. Maybe you could go with her for a short time, Partner."

Johnny's smile widened. "Sydney's, I love that place, and I'll take care of everything."

Tim jumped in. "I'll help."

"Me too," Shack replied.

The senator walked toward him. "We all will, Clay. Let us do this for you. How about it, Son?"

Clay was so overwhelmed he was without words.

"He's speechless," Johnny yelled. "Somebody get the man a drink."

Fighting with his emotions, Clay finally spoke. "Boy, do I love you people. I have so much to be thankful for."

"Because of each other," the senator said, "We all four have much to be grateful for."

Tim brought Clay a drink. "Here you go, Sport. Drink up, you've earned it."

The senator walked to his desk and retrieved an envelope from his top drawer. "Speaking of things to be thankful for, Clay, we all have one more little surprise for you."

Clay took the envelope from the senator's hand. "What is this?" he asked.

"Open it," the senator urged.

"Holy cow," Clay screamed. "Did you do this Senator?"

"We all did it," he answered. "Everybody in this room chipped in. We all four knew how much you loved that car of yours. This is simply our way of making the loss a little more bearable."

The warmth and love present in that room was amazing. It was all Clay could do to hold back the tears of joy.

The senator said, "We tried to find a car just like the one you had, but we decided something different might even be better. We didn't want you to have any bad memories, and; therefore, a new beginning."

Clay smiled. "You know, you guys could be in the movies. Tim never let on, and he was the first one to see the car. Shack never said a word. And you, Johnny, I thought you were genuinely surprised when you saw the car."

"Well, in a way I was," he chuckled. "I knew about the car, but I had never seen it before you brought me home from the hospital."

A group hug was in order, and they were all willing participants, even the senator got right in the middle.

They drank, they smoked, and all was peaceful in their little corner of the world. The sheer dignity portrayed by these five men was serendipitous. Like a small platoon in the middle of a war zone, they relied on, and trusted each other for survival. They fought against incredible odds, and because of their values and remarkable spirit, they overcame. These are the friendships that transcend all things.

Chapter 25

In the next few days plans were made and executed. Everyone did their part to make it a joyous occasion, for both Jolene and Clay. On February 13th the two boarded a plane for Scotland. The entourage at the Washington National Airport numbered many, even the FBI, the army rangers, and a bunch of hospital personnel showed up, including Nurse Ford.

The tearful farewell at the hospital with Susan had been difficult for Clay, but this was wonderful. Clay hugged darn near everybody. He had never been to Scotland, but he had the prettiest tour guide a man could hope for.

Everything went off without a hitch. Clay and Jolene waved from the airplane, and they were off, and ready for a super adventure.

On the home front, Johnny was just about packed, and he was anxious to be picking up Susan from the hospital. The doctor had said it would be alright for her to travel by car to Richmond. Johnny was trying desperately to leave the house in as good a shape as was possible. He had set his last article by the door when the telephone rang.

"Hello."

"It's me," the senator replied. "Is it okay with you if I meet you at the hospital? I would like to say good-bye to Susan?"

"Absolutely," Johnny replied. "I'll meet you there in forty-five minutes. Will that work for you?"

"That's perfect," he replied. "See you then. By the way, is Tim picking you up?"

"He sure is, Senator; in fact, I think he just pulled in."

"Good, Doctor, I'll see you two at the hospital."

Johnny rushed to the door to open it for Tim. They got there at the very same instant.

"Ready to go, Doc?" Tim inquired.

Johnny grabbed a couple of bags, his and Susan's. "You bet I am, let's go."

"Is that all the stuff you have?" Tim asked, looking around. "Where's Susan's things? I can at least carry them."

Johnny reached for the door handle. "This is everything."

Tim backed down the steps and they made their way to the car. The trip to the hospital was relatively quick; although, Johnny did explain to Tim that the senator was going to meet them there.

They wheeled into the parking lot and parked in a fifteen minute zone. Then they headed for the elevators. Susan was waiting for them impatiently.

"Get me out of here, Doc," Susan urged. "I need to smell some fresh air."

"Relax, Susan. The senator is coming by to see you off. He should be here any minute." Johnny paused to get his breath. "Anyway, I know Shack wants to say good-bye as well."

Susan got a dejected look on her face. "Oh well, I guess a few more minutes won't kill me."

Tim smiled. "I wish you wouldn't use that particular terminology."

Nurse Ford walked in with a wheelchair. "Get in, Susan; I'll give you a ride."

"No thanks, I'd rather walk."

"Regulations, Girl. This is the way we have to do this. I don't make the rules, I simply enforce them. Now, get that behind in this seat."

Susan grinned. "Okay, Miss Bossy."

Nurse Ford patted her on the arm. "Now, that's my favorite patient. I'm gonna miss you, Young Lady."

Susan laid her hand on top of Nurse Ford's. "I'm actually gonna miss you too, but I'm still glad to be getting out of here."

The senator and the sergeant walked into the room. All eyes went immediately to the senator.

"Is something wrong," Tim asked.

It looked like both men had been crying.

The senator pulled out his handkerchief and wiped his eyes. "There's no easy way to say this. Two hours ago, Pan Am flight 562, the plane on which

Jolene and Clay were flying, left the radar screen. They haven't been seen or heard from since."

Susan passed out. Johnny and Tim began to sob, unashamedly. The devastation was paramount. And, for many minutes, the only sounds that could be heard coming from Susan's room were that of sobbing and muted prayer.

The End

Epilog

"Doctor Murphy," the senator screamed. "They found the plane. It made a belly landing in the Atlantic just short of the English Channel. There are a few survivors, but we have no names yet."

Johnny almost dropped the phone. "Oh lord Senator, Clay is a terrible swimmer."

"Maybe," the senator replied, "But he's a fighter, and a survivor, isn't he?"

Johnny perked up. "Damn right he is, Sir. Look, Senator, I've got to get to Susan, she's at the UVA Medical Center. She really needs to hear this."

"Listen, Doctor," the senator began. "If you can be here by five PM I'll take you to England with us. We're going over to the crash site, and we'll stand vigil there with the other hopefuls. That gives you three and a half hours, Doctor Murphy. Get to Susan, tell her the news and meet me at Andrews Air Force Base, south hanger, you know the drill. I'll leave a pass for you at gate one."

"I'll be there, Senator," Johnny replied, gasping for air, one gulp at a time. "He's alive, Senator! I just know it. I think I've known it all the time."

"Me too, Doc, and thank God."

About The Author

Having spent part of his early life in a children's home, Mr. Smith enlisted in the army at the age of sixteen in order to finish his education. He is a veteran of the Berlin Wall crisis, the Cuban missile crisis and the Vietnam War. The decade of the sixties was spent in service to his country—in one way or another. After putting government service behind him, Mr. Smith became a hotelier and has been president of three corporations, and CEO and founder of another.

Mr. Smith has signed copies of his books at more than fifty military bases, including Walter Reed Army Medical Center, Bethesda Naval Hospital, and the Pentagon.

Mr. Smith's educational background is in mathematics and journalism, disproving the popular theory that men are unable to use both sides of the brain.

In December of 2003, Mr. Smith officially became the Tennessee Ambassador of Goodwill, an honor bestowed on him by the Honorable Phil Bredesen, governor of the state of Tennessee.

Printed in the United States
18833LVS00002BA/4-12

7-16-04

To:
Dora

Carl E. Stern